SAVING
RUTH

Also by Zoe Fishman

Balancing Acts

SAVING RUTH

ZOE FISHMAN

WM

WILLIAM MORROW

An Imprint of HarperCollinsPublishers

SAVING RUTH. Copyright © 2012 by Zoe Fishman. All rights reserved. Printed in the United States of America. No part of this book may be used or reproduced in any manner whatsoever without written permission except in the case of brief quotations embodied in critical articles and reviews. For information address Harper-Collins Publishers, 10 East 53rd Street, New York, NY 10022.

HarperCollins books may be purchased for educational, business, or sales promotional use. For information please write: Special Markets Department, Harper-Collins Publishers, 10 East 53rd Street, New York, NY 10022.

FIRST EDITION

Designed by Diahann Sturge

Library of Congress Cataloging-in-Publication Data has been applied for.

ISBN 978-0-06-205984-0

12 13 14 15 16   OV/RRD   10 9 8 7 6 5 4 3 2 1

We'll talk of sunshine and of song,
And summer days, when we were young;
Sweet childish days, that were as long
As twenty days are now.

—"To a Butterfly" by William Wordsworth (1801)

SAVING
RUTH

1

P lease turn your iPod off," the flight attendant barked as she made a counterclockwise motion with her finger. I nodded in response and pretended to press the Stop button as I inched down in my seat and gazed out the window. Red dirt, pine trees, swimming pools, giant churches, and car dealerships—all encased in a wall of shimmering heat. Summer in Alabama.

Reflexively, I smoothed my hair. As soon as I stepped off the plane, it would take on a monstrous, frizzy life of its own. And then there was my outfit. If I had deliberately planned to look this way, I could see how my parents might take it as a giant "fuck you." My ratty, navy blue Michigan sweatshirt hadn't seen the inside of a washing machine in an easy six months. I could smell the pot and cigarettes emanating from its fabric from just sitting on the air-conditioned plane. Once I stepped into the humid heat, the stench was going to envelop me and everyone in my path. Innocent bystanders were going to tumble to the ground, covering their mouths with their hands and gasping for air.

My jeans were just as abused—the same jeans that I had begged my mother for right before school had started.

"Mom, everyone has skinny jeans. If I show up for college without at least one pair, I'm doomed, I'm telling you."

"A social outcast. Ruth, really?"

She fingered the price tag in disgust, but I could tell I almost had her.

"Mommmmmmmm, please? I mean, c'mon, they look good, right? You can tell I lost some weight."

"Don't tell your father about this," she whispered, surrendering to me.

I had never owned fancy jeans before, mostly because I'd never really been able to fit into them. I could get them buttoned and zipped, but my flesh would bulge over the waistband like raw dough. Last summer had been the beginning for me. Ten pounds came off before I left for college. My mom told me that I was a *late bloomer* and lit up like a Christmas tree every time I entered the room. I hated that phrase, "late bloomer." It conjured up Georgia O'Keefe paintings and kumbaya circles. Blooming? Please. I had just laid off the McDonald's.

Looking down at those same jeans now, I cringed. Thirty-five pounds later, the term "skinny jeans" was a joke. They hung on me, with ripped knees and frayed hems that trailed behind me like seaweed. I hadn't showered in days. Well, two days.

I had planned to wake up early that morning, pack the rest of my belongings that hadn't already been shipped home or stored elsewhere, and make myself presentable. Up early and on to the airport. All it took was one phone call, however, and good-bye plan. I had been out all night. What I had envisioned as a civilized taxi ride to the airport (some indie crap on the radio; me looking out the window as we drove through campus, smiling slyly as a rousing pictorial montage of my freshman year flashed through my mind) had turned into my roommate Meg yanking me out of bed and us both running around our dorm room like maniacs, trying to stuff everything into my too-small suitcase. I had made my flight, but just barely.

The plane's wheels hit the runway, and I was officially home for three months. It seemed like an interminable amount of time. What the hell was I going to do? I made a mental list: lifeguard, coach, and not gain weight. Hang out with Jill and M.K. Be nice to my parents. Really. And David, of course. My brother. This year I'd spoken to him less than I had spoken to even my most random acquaintance. You know, the girl that you sat next to in your humanities class but never saw elsewhere on campus? Yeah, that girl and I had a deeper bond than the one that I had with my flesh and blood.

The seat belt light went off, and everyone immediately jumped up as though we were actually going to move in the next ten minutes. In front of me, a family of blond and permed mullets—mom, dad, and two sons—struggled with their suit- cases in the overhead bins.

"Dangit, Bobby, I done told you to help me!"

"Mama, can we git corndogs on the way home?"

"Not now, Bobby."

"Mammmmmmmmmmaaaaa!" The littlest one's mouth was ringed in red. Kool-Aid mouth—a hallmark of the Deep South. I was home.

I filed out of the plane and walked toward baggage claim. The airport was quiet—a ghost town almost. Black-and-white photos of football teams and debutantes in frilly cupcake dresses holding parasols lined the walls.

My phone rang.

"Hello?"

"Yeah, Ruth?"

"Yeah?"

"It's David. Can you speed it up? I'm circling the pickup point because they won't let me park."

I picked up my pace. "They won't let you park? No one is even here. Who are you blocking?"

"I know, I know. So speed it up, okay? I'm getting dizzy."

"Okay, okay."

I reached the baggage carousel, and there she was—my destroyed suitcase. Misshapen and split, with electrical tape encasing it in its entirety. My mom was going to kill me. I grabbed the handle, which poked out of the silver cocoon apologetically, and rolled/carried it out the door. The air hit me like a bucket of melted peanut butter. In the distance, I could see David's car chugging toward me. He honked a hello, and I waved, feeling strangely shy.

He pulled up beside me and got out.

"Hey hey, stranger," he said, stopping for a moment to take me in before reaching in for an awkward hug. He looked good, but then, he always did. Brown hair, blue eyes, and lean muscles. Beyond having the same face shape—square, but easily turned round thanks to ample cheeks—we didn't look anything alike. My girlfriends had always swooned for him—something that annoyed the hell out of me when I first realized it but then became amusing as I got older. Watching them strut and giggle in his presence had become a sort of sociological study for me. The line between intriguing coquette and desperate clown was a thin one, and I had seen many girls teeter on its precipice in his presence.

"You look good?"

His appraisal was more of a question than a statement. This happened a lot. People who knew me as my former, larger self were uncomfortable when they saw me now. It was hard to tell whether they were jealous or concerned. Most likely it was a little bit of both. My reaction to their reaction was mixed as well—what I knew was probably a perverse sense of pride along with immediate defensiveness.

"Thanks," I answered.

"Skinny," he added.

"You look good too," I offered.

"Jesus, what the hell happened to your bag?" He took the handle from me, and it rolled on its side like a seventeen-year-old basset hound.

"Long story."

"Mom's gonna kill you," he said, surveying the damage. He looked up at me and laughed.

"I know," I sighed. "Let's go already. This heat is brutal."

He tossed my bag in the back, and we got in. The interior smelled like Febreeze, French fries, and cigarettes.

"You smoke?" I asked.

"Sometimes."

"Since when?"

"Since whenever, I guess."

"But what about soccer?"

"What about it?"

"Your lungs? Athletes don't smoke. It's weird."

"Okay, then, I'm weird."

I examined him. This close, he looked tired. Gray circles ringed his eyes, and his fingernails were gnawed to the quick. Strange. Or maybe it had just been a while since I'd sat this close to him.

"Take a picture, it will last longer," he mumbled. I fiddled with the radio.

"How long have you been home?" I asked.

"Since yesterday. I got in around dinnertime, I guess."

"How was the drive?"

"Fine. Long. A lot of traffic."

"How's Mercer?"

"Same."

I sighed. It was going to be a long summer. We passed a Super Wal-Mart, and I thought of the mulleted plane family.

Did Bobby ever get that corndog? And how did Kool-Aid come off human skin? Soap and water seemed impossibly mild. I grimaced, thinking of poor Bobby's teeth.

"You seen Jason yet?" I asked.

"No, not yet. Gonna go down to the pool and meet him later, actually." Jason was the head lifeguard and pool manager—the year-round keeper of all things pool-related. You'd get an email from him about Fourth of July relay ideas in February. He lived for summer.

"Cool. And do you know when swim practice starts?"

"We have a kickoff meeting on Friday—kids and parents. School ends next week, so we'll start right up, I guess."

I was already tired, thinking of the kids. I was in charge of the six- to ten-year-olds. The first few weeks were always the toughest—getting them used to me and the routine was hard enough, never mind teaching them to swim the entire length of the pool. Seeing them hold up their ribbons when swim meets were over—their excitement oozing out of every tiny, water-pruned pore—always made it worth it, though.

David was in charge of the older kids, which was its own mess of hormone-fueled distraction. There was nothing like seeing a fifteen-year-old boy in a Speedo to remind you why being a teenager sucked. The combination of skinny limbs, errant pubic hair, and giant Adam's apple was almost blinding in its awkwardness.

He made a left into our neighborhood. There was the Smith house in all of its manicured lawn glory. Felicia Smith and I had played Barbies together as kids. She always wanted Ken and Barbie to go to church. I was more from the Ken and Barbie having lots of sex school, and thus our friendship was pretty much over before it began.

"Do the Smiths still live there?" I asked.

"Naw, they moved out a couple of years ago. I think to Tampa or something?"

"Oh. Who lives there now?"

"Not sure. I think a black family. I saw a kid playing in the yard on my way out to pick you up."

A few houses down was the Crawford place. Its front yard was carpeted in orange pine straw, and no fewer than five cars were parked on the front lawn at any time. The eyesore drove the whole neighborhood crazy, but the rumor was that the dad was in prison, so they were left alone. I'd never seen anyone go in or out of there. I imagined the inside to be straight out of *Hoarders*. They were probably all buried alive under an avalanche of Jimmy Dean breakfast sandwich boxes and velvet paintings of wildlife.

And suddenly, we were making a right into our driveway. I was home. It looked so much smaller to me now, as if college had turned me into a giant. My dad had mowed the yard for our arrival, and the earthy smell of grass clippings hung in the humid air.

"Here we are," said David. "Home sweet home." We looked at each other then, and in everything we did not say passed a history that only the two of us would ever understand. I guess that's what family is. Awkward car rides and stilted conversation aside, you would always have that.

2

The screen door opened and my mom peeked her head out.

"Helloooooo," she sang.

"Hi, Mom!" I yelled back. She looked like Mom—roundish, medium height, with the same dark hair and eyes as me. Her hair was shorter than I had ever seen it—a kind of Mia Farrow meets Blanche Devereaux mom-do—and curled softly around her face. Pretty.

As she got closer, I watched her features freeze in a mask of worry, and my hands balled themselves into fists reflexively.

"Ruthie." Her voice trembled a bit.

"Mama," I whispered back as I hugged her. "What are you crying for?" I pulled back and looked into her eyes, which were welling up behind her glasses.

"Oh Ruth, I'm just glad to see you." She paused. "Are you sick? I mean, what is this?" She gestured toward my body, her hand flipping up and down its length.

"I'm not sick!" I flew into defensive mode. "Can we please not talk about this for the thousandth time? I went on a diet and I lost weight. Funny how that happens."

For as long as I could remember, my mom—and my dad,

actually—had been trying to get me to go on a diet. Not in a passive-aggressive way either. Aggressive-aggressive was a Wasserman trademark. Now that I had gone too far in their eyes, they both took turns giving me shit for it. Christmas break had been one melodramatic confrontation after another. I had found my mother up to her elbows in a box of Oreos late one night, only to have her blame me for her demise. *I'm eating for you!* she had cried, with chocolate lodged in the corners of her mouth and capping one of her front teeth.

"Okay, I'm sorry. There's no need to be a smart-ass. You know me, I can't help it. I say what I think. Forget it." She sighed. David dragged my suitcase around to us. I braced myself.

She bit her lip, and I imagined her anger brewing like a pot of coffee. Few things enraged my parents more than our abuse of things they had bought us. She hadn't gotten a good look at my jeans yet. Between that and the suitcase, it was going to be a tense welcome-home lunch.

"Ruth, why?" she asked.

I dug my hands into my pockets and imagined lighting a cigarette. "I'm sorry, Mom. I overslept and packed like a jerk."

"You know you're going to have to buy yourself a new one, right?"

"Yes."

"Okay, as long as we're clear on that one."

I nodded.

"And the next time you beg me for million-dollar jeans, I am going to ignore you. Are we good on that too?" Wow, she had already noticed. She was quick. Quick-Draw Marjorie.

"Roger that, Mom. I'm sorr—"

Her hands flew up in front of her chest, palms out. "Not going to talk about it anymore. I'm glad you're home, Ruthie." She hugged me again, and I relaxed into her softness. "Even if you're ungrateful."

"I'm really not, Mom. Just careless. I'll try to be better." She sighed again and gave me a final squeeze.

"Where's David?" she asked.

"He went inside."

"Well, pull that sad thing in the house, will you? And where's your father? He's probably passed out from the excitement of you coming home. He's been up since daybreak, I am telling you. Running around the house like a maniac and driving me crazy."

I followed her inside, lugging the suitcase up the two concrete stairs by the back door and into the kitchen. *Home.*

"Close the door, for goodness' sake, we don't want to let out all of the air conditioning!" yelled my father as he shuffled around the corner. "Ruthie girl!" He held out his arms and walked toward me.

"Hello, Dad," I whispered as I melted into his hug. He was wearing what I liked to call his dad weekend uniform—a knit Polo and tennis shorts. He released me, and we looked at one another in silence. Same dad—blue eyes, salt-and-pepper hair, big smile.

"You're too skinny," he offered.

"Bet you never thought you'd say that," I replied.

"It's not a joke, Ruthie." His smile faded as he switched gears into stern mode. "Every time I see you this year, you're smaller. Enough already. You looked great ten pounds ago." He smoothed my hair. "Enough already," he repeated.

I nodded. How could I tell him that the mere thought of gaining weight gave me a panic attack?

"Hey, where's Maddie?" I asked, changing the subject. Maddie was our Shih Tzu. We'd gotten her on my eighth birthday when a client of my dad's couldn't take care of her any longer. Tiny even for a Shih Tzu, with a caramel and white coat that badly needed brushing, at first she had strangely terrified me.

"Ruth, what's your problem?" David had asked in all of his nine-and-a-half-year-old wisdom. "It's a little dog. Look! Look at how cute she is." My stiffness didn't break until we got home and let her run through the house. She had careened into every room, sniffing around their perimeters and nodding to us in approval, until she got to mine. She trotted around the Barbies and the baby dolls, looked up at me, and proceeded to pee right in the middle of my floor. *You're mine*, she was telling me. And from that point on, I was.

"Here she comes," said my dad. Tiny nails tapped tentatively around the corner. She was getting old—eleven years now—and it showed.

"Maddie!" She looked up and swung her hips in greeting as her tail swished from side to side. I picked her up. She was as light as a bag of pretzels.

"Old girl," I cooed, nuzzling my face into her fur. She licked my nose.

"I need a shower," I announced as I put her down.

"Okay, but make it quick," said my mom. "We're going to have lunch in a half-hour or so." Lunch. The word made me nervous on principle. A meal with carbs and protein and chips and who knew what else, not to mention the three pairs of eyes that would study everything that went into my mouth. I chewed on the inside of my cheek.

"What the hell did she do to that suitcase, Marjorie?" my dad asked as I dragged it out of the room behind me.

I made a left into my bedroom and dumped it on the blue carpet. My room. My mom and I had redecorated it a few years ago—the summer David had left for college. It had been her way of coping with the fact that he was gone, and although it had started out under the guise of a bonding project for the two of us, it had quickly evolved into The Marjorie Show. I had wanted an *Us Weekly* bedroom—a canopy bed with mosquito

netting was the height of chic to me at that point—and my mom
had wanted Laura Ashley. Laura had won in the end, but I had
at least scored mirrored closet doors after hours of begging. The
walls were papered in blue stripes with tiny flowers weaving in
and out of them, and a vanity table sat in the corner, freshly
dusted. A wooden bookcase that had been painted white leaned
against the wall, filled with *Anne of Green Gables* books and
trophies from my various soccer, swimming, and softball teams.
My twin bed was covered in a mauve, pink, and blue quilt. I
collapsed onto it.

I glanced to my right, smirking at my reflection. How many
hours had I spent in front of those mirrors with my door locked,
trying to gather my stomach with my hands in an attempt to see
it flat—mottling my pale flesh with red welts in the process? The
three of us had spent a lot of time alone in our respective rooms
the year David had gone to college. Without him around, our
family dynamic was strange, forced even.

"You taking a shower?" David asked from my doorway. "I
need to get in there." Already it was starting.

"Jesus! Yes, I'm taking a shower. I'll be quick."

I got up and walked across the hall, slamming the door
behind me. I turned on the water and peeled myself out of my
sweaty, smelly clothes. The mirror revealed someone I only sort
of knew. Who was that girl with the protruding rib cage and
the tiny breasts? Oh right, me. I turned to the side. To see a
back with no back fat was a sight to behold. That was when
I first knew that I had lost weight—when I had noticed in my
dorm mirror that my back was as smooth as a car's hood. Meg
had walked in once while I was admiring myself fully naked—
standing on my desk chair with my hand mirror angled up to
get the view from behind.

"So, this is what you do when I'm not around," she had
mumbled, blushing and making a beeline for her bed. I was

mortified. But not as mortified as I might have been had she walked in and seen me trying on her clothes, which was my other activity of choice when I had the room to myself. Meg was a girl who could eat Whoppers and pizza and never gain an ounce. The day that I could fit into her jeans without suffocating was going to be a good day. That day had come and gone around February.

As I washed my hair, the smell of smoke billowed around me. And Tony. His smell was unmistakable—pungent and rich, lingering as I scrubbed him away. Tony was the real reason I had overslept. I soaped up my legs and dragged the razor carefully around my bony knees. I thought it would be a good way to go out—to blue-ball him into submission and then leave, the way all of the cool girls did in the movies. Instead, because I wasn't a cool girl in a movie, I had slept with him and fought back tears as he had rolled off of me and returned to the party beyond his bedroom door.

"Ruth, you minx," he had said as he stepped back into his jeans and winked at me. "Let's get back to the party, babe. This is it for me. Graduation is tomorrow, dude, I can't believe it."

"Yeah, *dude*, me either."

He had left me there, twisted in his dirty sheets. The same sheets I had lost my virginity on, a few months prior. I wondered if they had been washed. I wondered if he had slept with anyone else since we had broken up two weeks ago. Instead of asking those questions, I had just gotten up, pulled on my jeans, and slipped out the back door.

I let the water pour over me one more time before turning it off. I toweled off and opened the door, sending a cloud of steam into the hallway. In my room, I attacked my suitcase with some scissors—puncturing its layers of electrical tape until my clothes spilled out. I thought about the rest of my stuff at Meg's house in Milwaukee. She was holding on to it for the summer—

storing it in her basement with the rest of her college life. I imagined our winter coats sitting in the corner and reading Psych 101 textbooks together. *When clothes come alive!*

There was a knock at the door.

"Ruthie, lunch is in five minutes," my dad bellowed through the wood.

My face grew hot as I began to formulate a game plan in my mind. *I'll eat a few bites of whatever vegetables are available, push the rest around on my plate, and then go for a long walk later.* I pulled my cutoffs up my freshly shaved legs and a clean tank top over my head. *Wash it down with a couple of glasses of Diet Coke to fill up the empty space in my stomach.* I dragged a comb through my hair, scooped a glob of gel from its container, and slicked the whole mess back into a wet bun. *Keep talking throughout the meal to distract everyone from my plate.*

"Ruuuuuuuuuuuuuuuth!" my mom yelled from the kitchen. "Let's go!"

I can do this.

"Comingggggggg!" I yelled back. God, how I hated being bellowed at. A lot of that went on in my house. What was so hard about walking your lazy ass down the hall to someone's door? Sometimes I wondered if my parents ever had conversations at close range. They were constantly summoning each other from remote parts of the house:

Marjorieeeeeeeeeeeeeeeeeeee!!!!

Sammmmmmmmmmmmmmm!!!!!!

"Could we make a rule this summer not to yell for each other?" I asked as I slid into my place at the table. David and my parents looked up from passing bowls of potato and chicken salad. Great, a mayonnaise fantasia.

"No," answered my dad.

"But it's so annoying."

"Tough."

"Who wants to be yelled at before they've even engaged in conversation? It sets a tone, can't you see that?"

"Ruth, you're wasting your breath," said my mom.

I sighed and surveyed the table. Calorie counts hovered over each dish in my mind like Pac Man bubbles. Mayonnaise fantasia, no way. Baked beans I could do. And corn on the cob. Tomatoes. Pickles. Okay, I could work with this. I began to assemble my lunch.

"Ruth, have some chicken salad," my mom said.

"I can't, I'm a vegetarian."

"Since when?" asked my dad.

"Since vegetarian became code for anorexic," mumbled David. I shot him a dirty look.

"Since this year," I answered.

"Then you'll eat the potato salad."

I locked eyes with my dad, who was giving me his best *I mean it, Ruth* face.

"Mayonnaise makes me want to puke," I retorted. "I'm not eating it." I looked away and reached for the jar of pickles. What was he going to do, shove a forkful down my throat?

"Do you have a workout plan for the summer, David?" asked my dad. David played soccer for Mercer University. The star player on our high school team, he had been recruited aggressively and was there on scholarship. This was a huge source of pride for my dad, who still hadn't given up on my own potential for some sort of sports stardom, despite the fact that I had been an award-winning bench rider all of my sporting life. Well, except for swimming. I had been decent until my breasts arrived. Unfortunately, that had been around age nine.

"Yeah."

"Well, this is an enlightening conversation."

"Sorry, Dad, I just don't want to talk about the work I have to do right now," explained David in a measured tone. "I just got home yesterday, okay? Can I have a little bit of summer?"

"You're right, David," said my mom, glancing sharply at my dad.

He looked at me. Great, my turn. I cut my tomato in half and speared it with my fork, pulling it toward my mouth in the hopes that chewing would delay the inevitable.

"And what about you? Do you have a lot of reading to do this summer?"

"Dad, it's called summer for a reason."

"Really, no assignments?"

"Nope."

"Okay. I just have a hard time thinking that an English major doesn't have any reading—"

"Sam, please?" pleaded my mom. "They just got home. Can we eat lunch?"

He put his fork down and held up his hands in defeat.

"Mom, everything is really good," said David as he spooned another gelatinous glob of chicken salad onto his plate.

"Thanks, Davey. I never cook anymore, with you two gone. This morning may have been the first time I've stepped into the kitchen since December."

My dad nodded. "It's true." I wondered what he had been eating all of this time if that was the case. The man didn't even know how to boil water. My mom's jaw clenched. A sore subject apparently.

"Want me to do the dishes?" I asked as I pushed my chair back.

"Did you eat anything?" David asked.

"Yeah, your face."

"Very mature, Ruth. Wow."

"Wow," I replied, switching my voice to a lower decibel to mock him. I walked into the kitchen and surveyed the damage.

My mom was an excellent cook, but she made messes of tornado-like proportions. Crumbs on the floor, sauces splattered across the stove, and dishes teetering in gloppy, precarious piles were always left in her wake.

It had been my job to clean the kitchen post-meal since before I could remember. Ten bucks a week to do so, when David received the same to feed the dog. The blatant inequality of our tasks had always annoyed me, but the actual act of cleaning was soothing for me. I liked erasing messes.

"What's on tap for the afternoon?" asked my mom as she brought more lunch dishes in.

"I'm going to call M.K. and see if she wants to go for a walk." *And smoke a damn cigarette before my head explodes.* Her silence forced me to look up from my suds castle.

"Mom?" I turned off the water. "I'm here all summer." I put my wet hand on hers. "We'll do a lot of stuff together, I promise."

"Okay." Her smile made me sad. I wasn't sure if it was her own loneliness or her worries about me that made her look so lost. Both possibilities overwhelmed me. I turned the faucet back on.

"I'll see you later," she said. "I think I'll take a nap." She walked away, and I continued to scrub.

3

ey, girl!" yelled M.K. She was a block away—all smile and
blond hair, wearing her standard summer uniform of athletic shorts and tank top. Her legs were already tan from a
spring in Tuscaloosa and possibly a few trips to the tanning bed.
I waved back with broad sweeping motions and turned myself
around in an impromptu jig of happiness.

M.K. (short for Mary Kate, which was a name that fit
her as much as "Tiffany" or "Jessica" would have fit me) and
I had been friends since the third grade. Sometimes best, and
sometimes not, depending on the extenuating circumstances of
middle and high school. We had been through it all—Barbies,
periods, boys, drugs, booze, sex—the whole gamut of the girl
experience thus far. We met finally, and I hugged her fiercely.

"Reeeeeed!" I squealed, inhaling a giant whiff of her sig-
nature raspberry lotion.

"Wassss!" she yelled back. "Watch out for my tea." We had
been calling each other by our last names since our peewee softball days.

"Are you seriously carrying around a glass of sweet tea?"
I asked, laughing. This was a southern phenomenon that fas-
cinated me. At dusk, women would emerge from their homes

clutching open tumblers of sweet tea, their ice tinkling in time with their pace. They paired off one by one, not to power-walk or jog, but to gossip and stroll.

"Yeah, what about it? I'm thirsty." She took a long swig and looked me up and down. "Damn, do you eat?"

"Reed, shuddup. You saw me over Christmas break."

"Yeah, but you didn't look quite so Skeletorish then. Maybe it's because you were wearing more clothes or something." She paused. "You're not into those horse diet pills from Tijuana or anything, are you?" We started walking.

"Horse diet pills? What are you talking about?"

"This sorority sister of mine got into them and lost like, a thousand pounds. Sorry. I just—I mean, I just don't want you to be doin' anything dumb, is all. You know I love you," she cooed with a drawl. "But I guess you look good, if you like that sort of thing."

"I love how you're givin' me the third degree, when you're skinny your own self." My southern accent was returning. It had disappeared in Michigan about two months in. Now, breathing in the humid air of my hometown and absorbing the rhythm of M.K.'s voice, it was swimming back to the surface.

"You're smoking crack! I have ten pounds of Busch Light around my middle, and you know it. I swear, I drank more this year than the entire starting line. This summer is Operation Fat-Ass. I'm gonna run every day."

"You're nuts. You look exactly the same. Where's Jill today?" We picked up our pace. Jill was the third member of our squadron.

"Oh, she's at work. But she's coming out tomorrow night for Bootsie Compton's party."

"We're going to Bootsie Compton's party?" I sighed.

"Oh God, don't be such a snot, Wass. It'll be fun. Besides, you have to debut your new bod."

"*Bod?* Really?"

"Really. So, any boys to tell me about?"

I laughed. "They're all a bunch of pussies."

"Wass! You know I hate that word. It's ugly."

"Oh, okay, this from the girl who pees her pants every time she gets drunk."

She punched me in the bicep. "I'll have you know that I don't do that anymore. I went to a hypnotist."

"For real? In Tuscaloosa?"

"Yep. All better. And let me tell you, that cure did not come a moment too soon. My bladder was not doin' me any favors in the bedroom."

"How's Dwight?" I asked. Dwight was M.K.'s high school sweetheart. They had gone to college as a couple, but had since broken up and gotten back together more times than I could count.

"He's sweet. For the moment, anyway."

"You're together?"

"Yeah. He messed up real bad in the spring with this Chi O slut, but he apologized with some diamond stud earrings, so it's all good." Dwight was rich. Well, his family was. They owned a giant shoe store chain—The Shoe Corral. Their empire stretched all over the South. Personally, I thought Dwight was an asshole, but trying to talk M.K. out of him was a fruitless endeavor. I had wasted enough breath on the subject already. Enough to inflate a baby pool twelve times over.

"You seein' anybody, Wass?"

"I was. Tony."

"I remember him. Y'all started datin' last winter, right? Weren't you tellin' me about him over Christmas?"

"Yeah, we had started talking right before break."

"He's the real hot one, right? Looks like Johnny Depp?"

I laughed. "How do you know?"

"That's what you told me, genius."

"Well, I think Johnny Depp may have been a little generous."

"Did you sleep with him?"

"I did."

"Get out of here!" She stopped walking and grabbed my shoulders. "You lost the big V?" Her blue eyes danced. We had been talking about this moment since she and Dwight had done it sophomore year of high school.

"Gone forever."

"Aw, Wass! Congratulations! I can't believe you didn't call me."

"Yeah, well, it's official. I'm no longer a virgin." We began to walk again.

"So, do you like it?"

"What? Sex?"

"No, my highlights. Of course, sex!"

"Oh yeah, for sure." This was a lie. I didn't see what the big deal was. Tony always pumped away at me like a jackhammer, came, and then collapsed on top of me in exhaustion. I would have rather been doing almost anything else, to be honest. My lack of interest in the whole endeavor embarrassed me almost as much as my virginity had.

"Oh my God, isn't it the best? When Dwight goes down on me, I am telling you!" She raised her fist toward the sky. "Thank you, Jesus!"

I smiled feebly. Tony had done that for me once, and I had been less than impressed. All of that wetness and then the worst part—seeing his expectant eyes watching me, his nose and mouth obscured by my vagina. It was like a horrible surrealist painting, or a really offensive muppet.

"Hey, you want to swing by the pool?" I asked, wanting to change the subject.

"Yeah, let's." We made a right. The pool was at the bottom of a big hill, and we began to descend down its slope.

"How's David?" she asked.

"I guess he's okay. We barely talk these days." I swatted at a mosquito that had landed on my thigh. "I don't think we spoke once last semester."

"The whole semester? Dang. That's like, months."

"Yeah." Despite myself, my eyes filled up with tears. "I mean, it's not like we were super close before I left, you know? I dunno why I'm all dramatic about it now."

" 'Cuz it sucks." She put her arm around my shoulders. "Did you try to call him?"

"Just once or twice. Okay, six times." I wondered why I hadn't given him hell about it today. Too awkward, I supposed. What was I, a psycho ex-girlfriend stalker or his sister?

"Did you tell your parents?"

"No. I ain't a rat." I smiled weakly at her.

"Okay, okay. This isn't *The Sopranos*."

The mosquito was back. I swatted at it again, and this time crushed it underneath my palm. I pulled it back to find a giant red smear on my upper arm.

"Speaking of the Gulf, we have to go to the beach a lot this summer, Reed. Whenever we have days off." I licked my fingers and rubbed the blood away, hoping that it was mine.

"Definitely. I guess I'll need to drive your ass, huh?" She smirked at me.

I smiled back. "Yes, please. I'm your Miss Daisy for the summer."

"Bitch, you've been my Miss Daisy since we were sixteen." I'd never had a car, and borrowing my parent's or David's had always proved to be more trouble than it was worth. My friends had begrudgingly accepted my passenger status, and as a result, I now drove like a ninety-year-old.

At the bottom of the hill, the pool came into view. It sat at the bottom of another small hill, on the left of this one's base.

It was protected on all sides by a tall barbed-wire fence, which some asshole climbed at least once every summer to get in and push the giant, electric blue lifeguard stand into the pool. Cars could park at the top of the hill in a sea of white gravel—the kind that always found a way to lodge itself in your sandal or flip-flop. They could also park around back, which was basically an unused field of red dirt and bramble. Beyond that were the railroad tracks.

David and Jason stood inside the empty pool, surrounded by the bleached whiteness of its sides. They were examining the bottom drain and hadn't noticed our approach. Shirtless and pale, their muscled torsos gleamed. Jason looked up as the gate creaked and we made our way toward the pool.

"Who the hell is that?" Jason asked. "We're closed, dumb-ass!" he yelled from the bottom of the pool as we rounded the corner and entered the snack bar area. The concrete floor had just been washed, and the smell of ammonia was amplified by the heat. M.K. and I shielded our noses with our hands.

Jason leaped over the shallow end's wall, ready for a fight.

"Who's the dumb-ass now, dumb-ass?" I asked.

"Look who's here!" He grinned. Jason's blond hair would be white by the summer's end, and his torso mahogany, but for now he looked as sun-starved as the rest of us. "If it ain't the famous Yankee herself."

"Hey, Jason." I broke into a jog of excitement and hugged him. When I pulled back, his sweat had imprinted itself on my tank top like a fingerprint.

"David, you didn't tell me Ruthie was here!" He looked me up and down. "Or half of Ruthie. Girl, you are skinny as hell. They don't feed you up in Michigan?"

I wondered if everyone I saw that summer would have the same thing to say—behind my back rather than to my face most likely. It reminded me of going over to my rich friend Julia's house once when I was little. Her mother had been holding court in her giant kitchen with her friends, all of them poised daintily on bar stools and grasping glasses of amber-colored liquid with their manicured fingers. Their myriad wrist bangles clacked and jangled as they gestured dramatically about whatever it was women like that talked about. I couldn't imagine. They were the yin to my mother's yang.

Julia, y'all come in here and say hey to Miss Paula/Andie/ Sandra/Sue! We had trudged into the room with false smiles plastered to our faces. *Hey, Miss Paula/Andie/Sandra/Sue,* Julia said dutifully. As I took secret issue with the whole concept of "Miss" in front of a first name, I just emitted a general hello. We rambled on about nothing for a minute or two as the women ogled us, before being dismissed with a *Y'all be sweet, girls!*

I was old enough to expect that they would say something about my chubbiness after I left, like the ever-familiar *Such a pretty face, but. . . .* I was surprised to hear something else entirely once Julia's mom thought we were out of earshot.

"Isn't Ruth precious?" Pause. "Y'all know she's Jewish," she tried to whisper. My face had burned red, out of anger or embarrassment, I wasn't sure. It was the first time I had realized my Jewishness was something people could whisper about like a terminal illness. Weight comments stung, but at least I could change that. The Jewish thing, not so much.

"No, they don't feed us, Jason. I haven't had one meal since last August," I replied.

He cocked his head and scrunched up his nose as if he were smelling something bad. "Well, I guess ya look good. Gonna be nice to see you in a bathing suit."

"Hey, man, take it easy," said David as he pushed himself up and out of the empty pool.

"Yeah, you perv," chimed in M.K., her eyes glued to my brother's flexed arms.

"Hey, M.K.," said David.

"Hey, David," she replied, blushing slightly. Damn him and his good looks. Even M.K., who'd known him since he was in Underoos, was susceptible.

"So, how's she lookin'?" I asked.

"Who, M.K.?" asked Jason. "She looks pretty good to me."

"No, jackass, the pool," I answered as M.K. punched him softly in the arm.

"Oh! Not bad, actually. We just had her mildewed ass cleaned, and now we just have to fill 'er up and shock her." "Shocking" was pool-speak for chlorination.

"Just in time to have twenty kids take a leak in that same water," said David.

"You betcha," said Jason. "David and I are gonna fill 'er up now. Want to help?" I glanced over at David, who tensed at the mere mention of me invading their afternoon, and my heart hurt.

"Uh no, that's okay. Gonna head back to my house soon and take a nap."

"Cool, cool. I'll have your lifeguarding schedule tomorrow, at the swim team meeting."

"Okay, see y'all," I said, looking to David for some sort of fraternal nod of approval. Something. Anything.

"See ya," he said, mostly to M.K., and walked back to Jason—who was already jabbering about some sort of new pool-filling technique. M.K. and I climbed the hill back to the street.

"Want to have a cigarette?" she asked.

"Do I ever."

She smiled. "C'mon." We trudged up another hill in the back of the elementary school.

"How many hills can there be in one damn neighborhood?" she huffed. M.K. lived right across the street from the elementary school—the very one we had met at so many years before. We cut through its massive backyard.

"Is your mom home?" I asked.

"She is. She's watchin' *Judge Judy*." Sheila was the mom who let us drink and smoke in high school. With her acrylic nails, tanning-bed face, and affinity for all things bedazzled, she was a walking cliché. That said, she had always been really good to me, and I adored her for it. Once, when she found me in their bathroom lying in my own drunken vomit, she had patiently cleaned me up and put me to bed without a word until the next morning.

"I'm not gonna tell yer mama about last night, but you need to be careful, darlin'," she had said over Krispy Kremes. "You ain't cut out for that mess."

Before M.K. plopped herself down in her back porch swing, she pulled a pack of Marlboro Lights from her back pocket. We lit up in silence, the smoke hanging around us like a curtain.

"I can't believe it's really summer," I murmured. "This year flew by."

"It really did. Do you feel different, Wass, since you were so far away and all?"

"I can't tell yet. A lot is different, I guess." I exhaled. "But still the same, you know?"

"I know."

"Miss Ruth, you ain't gon' come in and say hello to me? Your mama raised you better than that, girl!"

"Sheila!" I squealed. I handed M.K. my cigarette and ran to hug her.

"Hey, Ruthie!" She patted my back. "How's the Midwest treatin' you?" She always looked so deeply into my eyes when she spoke to me that it felt like she was burrowing through my brain.

"Good, good. Happy to be home, though."

"I know it. M.K.'s been dyin' to see you and Jill. The Three Mouseketeers." She smiled, revealing newly whitened teeth.

"Sheila, your teeth are so white!" I exclaimed.

"I know, right? Isn't it somethin'? I went in for one o' those professional jobbies. I feel like Jessica Simpson!"

"Yeah, now Shelia's mouth looks bigger than her head," said M.K., swinging behind us.

"The only mouth I see that needs work is yours, honey. It could use a good smack." She stuck her tongue out at her daughter. "Well, gotta get back to *Judy*, but I jes' wanted to say hey and I'm glad you're home, Ruth." She turned around to go in and then abruptly stopped in her tracks. She leaned in close, her tangerine perfume singeing the hairs in my nostrils.

"Honey, you ain't throwin' your food up, are you? 'Cuz that's just nasty."

"No, ma'am," I answered.

"Okay, just checkin'. You let me know if you want to talk about anything."

I watched her go and then turned back to M.K. "I better get goin'."

"Aw, what happened, did she freak you out?"

I laughed. "No, not at all. I just should get home."

"All right, baby, I'll call you tomorrow." She got off the swing and gave me a hug.

" 'Kay," I answered. "Smell ya later."

"Nerd!" she yelled after me.

4

hould we at least talk about what we're going to say to the kids?" I asked David. I was eating a bowl of cereal at the kitchen table when he breezed past me without a hello. Cereal was one of my food groups. Some would have said that candy was my second, and raw vegetables my third and fourth food groups. They were pretty much right. Calorically, this didn't make much sense—I knew that—but I figured that sugar was easier to burn off than, say, protein. Also, the energy boost was immediate.

David's back was to me as he reached into the refrigerator.

"What's there to say? It's the same shit we say every year. Show up for practice, swim like hell, and don't get disqualified." He pulled out the cream cheese. "This we have to rehearse?"

"I mean, I dunno, I'm talking to kids who can barely read. I wonder if I shouldn't be a little softer in my welcome approach this year."

"That's your problem. You're the guppy master. If you want to pull them aside for some sort of private baby talk, be my guest. And by the way, all of the kids on this team can barely read. It's Alabama."

"Derrrrrr, very funny." I fished through the milk with my spoon, hoping for a drowned flake.

"Where the hell are the bagels?" David snarled at me. Whenever he was hungry he turned into The Incredible Hulk. I wondered how long he would last in my shoes before ripping someone's head off with his bare hands.

"You know where they are." I rolled my eyes. "A hundred bucks says they're in the freezer."

He opened it, and there they were—like an inflated roll of quarters. He grabbed them. "What is with her? Every piece of bread in this house has to be frozen?"

"No carbohydrate is safe."

"Well, I hate it. If you nuke one of these, it shrivels up into a weird little sponge. Shit." He pulled one out and tossed it into the microwave, where it landed with a thud.

"I'm out," I said, sliding my chair back from the table. "Are you going to the meeting straight from home, or no?"

"No."

"Oh, you'll be coming from Hillary's?"

"Hillary and I broke up."

"Really?" David and Hillary had been together on and off since their freshman year of high school. She was the kind of pretty that always put her in the running for Miss Teen Something.

"Yeah."

"Why?"

"Damn, Ruth, you are so nosy. Who cares why?" He took his bagel out of the microwave and pried it open before throwing it in the toaster. *Toss, throw, slam, shut.* All of his movements were so forcefully deliberate. *You're too rough,* my parents would say to us when we were toddlers—biting, kicking, and pinching at whim.

"And how would you understand, anyway? You've never even had a boyfriend." His insult stung. Technically, Tony had been my boyfriend. We had spent two months and seventeen days together. We had sex regularly, he told me I was pretty, and sometimes he bought me a drink when we were out. That had fulfilled my boyfriend requirements. I'd found out later (on day eighteen) that he'd been flirting and sometimes sleeping with various other girls the whole time, but still.

"Sorry, you're wrong. Maybe if you had called me once this year, you'd know that." I got up from the table, slammed my bowl in the sink, and headed toward my room. David said nothing. Of course.

My dad's frame filled my doorway. "You know, this is going to be a long summer if you two don't get along." I could feel the tears coming. My lip trembled like a five-year-old.

"Hey, whatsa matter?"

"David is an asshole."

"Language, Ruth," he warned. "And go easy on him. Can you imagine playing soccer in this heat? My nerves would be shot."

"Oh God, give me a break." I flung myself on my bed dramatically. "He gets a personality pass because he kicks a ball around?"

It had always been like this. Whenever David and I had gotten into fights growing up, my parents always figured that I was the one who had started it. *Moody Ruth*. Even the time when they had left us alone to go to the movies and returned to find me pinned underneath him with his knee in my throat and choking me, I had taken most of the blame.

"I'm heading to the office, but what are you doing tonight?"

"I'm going to hang out with the girls."

"I wish you would come to synagogue with me instead."

"Yeah, not so much," I replied. He pursed his lips in disapproval.

"I know, Dad. I'm sorry. Maybe later in the summer." He went to Friday night services every week—usually alone. My mom wasn't exactly a fan of synagogue either. It wasn't the Jewish part—that was okay with me on a cultural level—but the whole synagogue experience was just not my bag. If I wanted to leave the entire time I was there, how did that make me a better Jew? Because I endured it?

"Well, David's coming with me." Naturally. David: the golden Jew.

"Cool," I replied. "I promise I'll go another time, okay?" He nodded. I put my pillow over my face. Not even twenty-four hours in and the summer stretched ahead of me like I–95.

I closed the door behind me and crossed the garage to the workroom to find my bike. I dug the keys out of my backpack and unlocked it, immediately fighting the urge to lie down on the cool, concrete floor. Just for a little while.

When we were little, David had been obsessed with trains, and together he and my grandfather had built an elaborate, elevated train set atop a giant wooden table that filled more than half of the garage. Green felt-covered hills and valleys rose around an idyllic village complete with a post office and cars.

Now the table was piled with cardboard boxes of who knew what—clothes or baby crap, perhaps. I wondered if my old Barbies were hiding in there, with their botched haircuts and chewed-up feet. My appetite for those minuscule hunks of malleable plastic had been insatiable. By the time I had been done with a Barbie, she was hairless and crippled.

A bit wobbly at first, I peddled past Mrs. Mayfield's house, checking for the JESUS LOVES YOU flag waving from her front porch. Still there. I made a right at the corner. There was poor, tortured Nancy Fink's house—her yard was crisscrossed with scraps of missing grass, the skid mark scars left from the giant trucks of the jackass jocks who tormented her at school. I plunged down the hill that led to the pool and saw the lot filled with cars I recognized. *Here we go.*

"Coach Ruth, Coach Ruth!"

I pulled into the bike rack to a flurry of six- and seven-year-olds chanting my name. They burst from the picnic area like puppies—their mouths ringed in red, pink, and blue popsicle smear.

"Coach Ruth!" Tabitha exclaimed in a burst of sugar-fueled excitement. Oh Tabitha. Sweet, headed-for-teen-pregnancy Tabitha. Chubby, with an overbite that could shade a trailer, Tabitha always wore pink lipstick and jutted her hips just so when talking to any of the male lifeguards—especially David. She was six.

"Hi, sweetie," I said as she hugged my knees. I patted her blond head and uttered a silent prayer that her parents would allow birth control when the time came. Tyler brought up the rear of the pack of ankle-biters. Round and solid, he was like a baby manatee when he swam.

"Hi, Ty."

He blushed. "Hi, Coach Ruth."

"Hey, Coach Ruth!" screeched Crystal as she made a bee-line for me. All angles and sinuous muscle, she reminded me of a panther. Crystal may have been the first kid in her family to know how to swim in a body of water that did not come with the requisite rope swing. Her father Travis showed up at every swim meet in his cutoffs and T-shirts advertising his car shop with his long mullet pulled into a shoulder blade–skimming braid. He was her biggest fan, standing nervously by the side of the pool when she raced and cheering her on like she was part of the Indy 500.

"Hey, girly." I smiled at her. She smiled back at me and revealed pink gums. Three of her front teeth were missing.

"Look at those missing teeth!"

"I know, I lost 'em all this week," she explained.

"You must be rich!"

"I am," she whispered solemnly.

David was perched on top of one of the picnic tables talking to Julie. She was probably our best swimmer and had placed in the top ten for her age group in the city last year. That had been her last summer before high school, though, and I could tell just by looking at her that things had changed. Gone was the sweet, slightly nerdy eighth-grader who was obsessed with *Twilight*. In its place stood a daisy dukes–wearing temptress— her eyes ringed with black and a brand-new nose ring twinkling in the sun.

"Hey, Julie," I said as I arrived at the table. She looked at me sideways with a blank stare for a second or two. Then it registered.

"Holy sh——cow, Coach Ruth!" She stared, dumbfounded. "You lost like a million pounds!"

"Um, wow. Thanks. I didn't realize I had a million pounds to lose."

"Oh no, no. That's not what I meant. It's just that you're like, way skinny now."

"Yeah, sure that's what you meant," I teased.

"No, really! I swear—"

"Okay, let's get this show on the road," David interjected. "Ruth, you're late."

"Am not!" I looked at the clock atop the concession stand. "It's one minute past three." Julie took a seat with the rest of the parents and kids. Everyone stared at us expectantly.

"So, hi, everybody. Welcome back," David began.

"Hiiiiiii."

"There's really not a whole lot to say, except that I . . . ," he paused and looked at me, "I mean, we, hope you had a nice year. We're excited for a new swim team season and hope you're all serious about this commitment.

"As you all know, the pool opens this weekend." Everyone clapped and cheered in response. Derrick, perhaps the goofiest of the older bunch, let out a cat call. Stray mustache hairs marched haphazardly across his upper lip.

I decided it was my turn to say something. "We'll start practice on Monday. The guppies will be with me, at eight, and the big kids will be with David at nine. We're expecting the meet schedule this week, so we'll give it to you at our first practice."

"Meets are on Thursdays for you new guys joining us," said David. "They usually begin at five and last until around eight or nine." He paused and looked at me, as if to say, *Are we done?*

"I think we should break into two groups now," I said. "All of the six- to ten-year-olds come with me. The rest of you can talk to David."

I walked over to a picnic table in the back, and the little ones approached with their parents in tow. My favorite, Ali, hung back with her mom. Ali was like a miniature Audrey Hepburn, slight and sweet with a dark bob and bangs that marched across her forehead in a determined line.

"Ali!" I called as she ran shyly into my open arms. She smelled like bubble gum.

"Hi, Coach Ruth!" she replied excitedly.

"Did you have a nice year at school?" I asked. "How was kindergarten?"

"Fun. There was a boy who liked me, but I told him that I was too young to have a boyfriend."

"Very smart of you, Ali."

I continued greeting them until the last guppy/escort duo had flip-flopped away. David was holding court at his picnic table, speaking to his subjects in hushed tones about strategy. Somehow, he got them to take the season as seriously as he did, which was no small feat, especially considering our track record. We were lucky if we won one meet per summer.

"Hey there, sexy," Jason greeted me, sneaking up from behind.

"Hey there, yourself," I said. "You better have brought me a good schedule." David and I had lifeguarded every summer since we were sixteen. There were two shifts per day, and two guards on per shift.

"Only the best," he replied. "Is Kevin here yet?" Kevin was another member of our lifeguarding team. I liked him all right—he was cute in a kind of good ole boy, southern way with his shaggy brown hair and impossibly long eyelashes. He had gone to our rival high school and seemed to come from a relatively loaded family, as far as car and neighborhood went. The rumor was that his lifeguarding money was strictly for beer and weed purposes only. We never really spoke aside from the polite head-nod hello or heat commiseration. He seemed like the kind of guy who was into cheerleaders, deer hunting, and chewing tobacco.

"Haven't seen him," I replied. "Is Dana coming back this year?"

"She is indeed. That whole Vegas thing didn't work out, I guess." Dana had been the captain of the dance team at our high school back in the day. And by back in the day, I mean when I was a freshman. She was all hairspray, boobs, and French mani-cured nails. I had asked her once, on the stand, why she had taken the lifeguarding class, since it seemed so out of character for her, and she answered me like I was an idiot. "Um, hello, the tan?" She had moved out to Vegas last fall—visions of showgirl fame dancing in her head—but I guess that hadn't panned out like she had hoped.

As if on cue, she entered in a sea of perfume. "Hey, girl!" She hugged me. "You look good, Ruthie! Like a model!"

Kevin shuffled in behind her, offering Jason a complicated bro-handshake that involved a forearm bump and a hand clasp.

"So, losers, welcome back," said Jason. "A summer of bratty kids, poops in the pool, and absent parents awaits you. The good news is, we're all getting a twenty-five-cent raise on the hour. The bad news is . . . well, look around you. That's the bad news."

It was sort of a sad little spot, as far as neighborhood pools went. Weeds poked their heads through the cracks in the concrete deck, and half of the picnic tables in the snack bar area wobbled precariously. The blue carpeting on the starting blocks was worn thin, the white plastic deck chairs were all in various stages of disrepair, and the lifeguard stand's coat of electric blue paint was peeling off in ribbons. There was a basketball court behind the pool, but the blacktop was more like a graytop, and the hoops had no nets.

The pool wasn't completely devoid of charm, though. The surrounding yard was lush and green, and noble oak trees lined the fence. It was a very basic place, but it really belonged to its members in a sweet, kind of old-fashioned way. The no-frills element gave it character that a lot of the flashier pool clubs lacked. At least that's what I thought.

"C'mon, Jay, you love this place," I said.

"Yeah, yeah." He pulled some papers out of his backpack. "Okay, here's the schedule. I think I've worked it out pretty fairly." I quickly scanned the page. I wasn't working with David at all. Not a single shift. I wondered if he had asked Jason to draft it that way.

"All right?" We all nodded. "Tomorrow we open this puppy.

I've loaded up the concession stand, and the price list is in the back. No fireballs this year."

"Good," said Dana. A kid had almost choked on one the summer before.

"All right, see y'all," said Jason. I looked over at David, wondering if he would head out with me or stay behind. He made no moves to get up.

Dana and I walked out together. "You want a ride, babe?" she asked.

I pointed to my bike.

"You're still ridin' that thing? When are you gonna get a car?"

"Dana, I live down the street."

"Fine, fine. See ya later, hippie."

I wheeled it up the hill. The five o'clock summer twilight felt like honey on my shoulders. I hopped on and took off.

5

Hey, Mom."

She was lying on the hammock in the backyard, a book splayed open across her chest. She was wearing her favorite paint-splattered gray T-shirt and a pair of purple sweatpants that had been cut off into shorts.

"It's too hot to read, Ruthie," she whimpered.

"Scoot over."

She opened her eyes in surprise. "Okay."

She clutched the rope tightly and attempted to swing her ample bottom to the left. Although her body made no progress, the hammock flailed like a hooked fish. She began to laugh hysterically.

"Ruth!" she wailed. "This is not happening. You're going to have to ease on in."

I eyed her warily. "Never mind."

"Oh no, you're not backing out now! We're getting in this hammock together come hell or high water, missy. Let's go!"

I sighed deeply. "Fine." Sliding over the edge, I felt my mother roll toward me—her warm, soft stomach pressing against my back. She began to laugh again.

"Mom!" Her laughter was contagious, despite my best efforts to be too cool for the absurdity of our predicament, and I started laughing too. I pushed her away as best I could and eased myself onto my back. She pulled me with her as we both attempted to scoot toward the middle. Finally, we were there.

"That was exhausting," she said, wiping the tears from her cheeks. "Like a bear and a parakeet on a seesaw." She paused, then added:

"I don't know what's going on with me, Ruthie. I can't stop eating."

"That's not like you, Mom."

"I know it." She sighed. "You guys went to college and my waistline went to hell."

"How come?"

"Boredom, I guess." The hammock rocked us as it settled down. "It's almost as if I gained the weight that you lost."

"Mom, c'mon. You didn't gain that much weight."

"I'm serious. Post-umbilical weight gain. I'm going to look it up. I bet it's a real thing." She grabbed my hand. "Ruthie, I really missed you this year."

"I missed you too, Mom." All I had wanted with every molecule of my being was to get away from my parents, and away from the South. Imagine my surprise when I found myself hanging on to my mother's legs in the Detroit airport, begging her not to leave me there.

"Yeah, but just for a month or two. Then you moved on."

"What was it like for you when I made that crazy scene in the airport? You must have been so embarrassed."

"Ruth, I was not embarrassed! If I could look at you right now," she said as she attempted to prop herself up on an elbow to face me, "I would. Alas. Honey, my heart was completely broken. I didn't know what to do. I wanted to just bring you home with me, right then and there, but I also didn't want you to give up before you even began to try. Plus, I knew you'd grow into it."

"And you were right," I assured her.

"You met some friends and got used to a schedule—"

"Yeah, but I was a basket case for a while."

"Is that why you lost so much weight?" she asked. "Nerves?"

"Maybe." *That and a constant monitoring of every calorie and fat gram in a ten-mile radius.*

"I'm proud of you. You didn't give up."

"Thanks, Mom." We swayed in silence, looking up into the pine tree branches that reached far into the sky. The crickets hummed around us.

"Are you going out tonight?" she asked.

"Yeah, with Jill and M.K. to some party."

"Be careful. Nothing stupid." As my parents well knew from my high school partying career, stupid was very much a possibility.

"Okay," I agreed. "How are we going to get off this thing?"

"You roll first and then help me."

"Good idea."

I rolled off, took her hands, and pulled her to her feet. She adjusted her glasses and smiled up at me as she cupped my chin in her hand.

"I love you, Mom."

"I love you too, Ruth." Her eyes welled up. "I swear to God, this menopause is driving me crazy! One minute I'm laughing like a hyena, and the next I've collapsed in tears." She hugged me. "Oh, my skinny girl. Listen, you need to eat dinner before you go. I'll fix you a salad, okay?"

My breath returned. "Okay."

"And I have this delicious fat-free dressing that you'll like." My heart beat normally again. "Maybe having you here this summer will get me back on track. Salads and fruit twenty-four-seven." I followed her inside. A very small part of me wanted my mother to scream at me, to call me out on my issues, to force-feed me French fries. Instead, she was looking to me for diet tips.

I was just being careful about what I ate was all—it wasn't anything serious. Some people could eat whatever they wanted and not gain an ounce. I couldn't. Simple as that. This was the argument I used all the time when I was questioned about my eating. As the words came out of my mouth, they sounded perfectly rational, but I knew I was kayaking through a sea of denial every time I spoke them. I guess my mom was trying to help me keep the boat afloat.

"It's just us tonight," she said, walking ahead of me. "The boys are going to services." She turned back and rolled her eyes at me. I rolled mine back.

The doorbell rang as I zipped my purse closed. Perfect timing. I felt nervous to be going out. I'd be seeing most of these people for the first time since I had left for college, and I knew that there would be a ton of shit talking.

I heard Jill's voice first as I walked down the hall. She had the exact face of a doll I had when I was little—straight honey brown hair, a dusting of freckles across the smallest nose ever created, and giant brown eyes. No one would ever have guessed that she could smoke Snoop Dogg under the table. I turned the corner with a smile.

"Ruth!" Jill rushed toward me and scooped me into a warm hug that smelled of Big Red gum and beer.

"Hey, Jilly," I said, pulling back so we could size each other up. I waved to M.K., who hung back. We had already had our welcome home moment.

"Ruthie!" squealed Jill. "I heard you were skinny, but

damn." She turned to my mother, stricken. "I am so sorry, Mrs. Wasserman! I am cursing like a sailor. My mother would kill me." My mom gestured as if to say, *No biggie.*

"What size are those shorts? Triple zero?"

"Take it easy, Jill," I said. "You're making me feel weird."

"I'm sorry, Ruthie. You look great. Really. I'm just sort of shocked is all." I noticed that Jill's trademark cutoffs were straining at the seams. The curse of the freshman fifteen. *Shocked and maybe just a wee bit jealous.*

"Well," interrupted my mom. "Have a great night, girls, and please be careful."

"Nothing stupid," I promised as we all filed out of the back door in a chorus of good-byes. M.K. was driving. We piled into her silver Accord, and she backed out of the driveway.

"Ever think about maybe cleaning this thing out once in a while?" I struggled to find a space for my feet between the Diet Coke cans, Subway wrappers, and empty cigarette packs.

"Oh c'mon, neat freak, it's not so bad." I pulled out a cigarette.

"Are y'all ready?" asked Jill from the front. She passed a lit joint back to me. I took it with my free hand.

"What do you mean?" asked M.K.

"This party."

"How is old *Bootsie*?" I asked. Every time I said her name aloud was like the first time.

"Fine, I guess," answered Jill. "Still going out with Scott Shayers."

"Oh, the guy whose brother overdosed?"

"Yeah, that's the one. One speedball too many," she answered as I exhaled a giant cloud of smoke.

"Wow, Cheech, could you maybe aim out the window? I'm trying to drive here."

"My bad."

"This is supposed to be a huge party," Jill continued. "Her parents are in Guatemala on some church mission."

"Church mission?" I asked.

"Yeah, they're missionaries. They go to poor places to spread Jesus's love."

"I know what missionaries are, jackass," I answered.

"Sorry, geez. Do Jews have missionaries?"

"I don't think so." Did we? As far as I knew, Jews kept it close to the vest with summer camps and political fund-raisers. "David would know. I'll ask him."

"How is that fine-ass brother of yours?"

I rolled my eyes. "Gross, Jill."

"Well, how is he? Still dating Hillary?"

"Actually, no. He said they broke up in January."

"No shit? Wow. The Homecoming King and Queen break up? That's front-page news. Is he upset?"

"I don't really know." Was he? Maybe that was why he attacked me with the boyfriend comment. I wondered if I would see him at the party. Services were over, so maybe.

Jill passed me her Visine. "Oh man, thanks." I leaned my head back and dropped it into each eye, relishing the lubrication. Between the cigarettes and the weed, my eyeballs felt like two dimes covered in wool.

"Here we are," M.K. announced. Cars lined the street for blocks, and in the distance you could hear the faint throb of music.

"Is Dwight coming?" I asked.

"I think so. He was being a dick about it, but I'm sure he'll show up at some point. He can't deal with me being out alone."

"You're not alone, you're with us," said Jill.

"I am indeed." M.K. checked her makeup one last time in her visor mirror. "Let's roll." We all got out of the car and headed toward the music.

"You ready for up-downs?" asked M.K. That's what we called the classic southern girl greeting—a sugary *Hey, girl!* followed by a top-to-toe surveillance for shit-talking purposes the second you moved out of earshot.

"Bring it," I answered. My stomach growled. How fitting.

There we were, the three of us standing on a perfectly manicured lawn facing Bootsie Compton's huge house with its brick facade and navy blue shutters. Jill put her cigarette out in the monkey grass lining the walkway to the front door, and we walked in.

6

We opened the door into a mass of people holding red plastic cups. Boys with beat-up baseball caps, Polo shirts with the collars popped, khaki shorts and sneakers with athletic socks pulled up to midcalf, and girls with orange tans, straightened blond hair, perky summer dresses, and bright pink lips. I looked down at my cutoffs and tank top and felt second-rate. There was something about the uniform formality here that always made me feel clumsy.

"Hey, girls!" screeched Bootsie.

"Hey, Bootsie," we all screeched back, playing the game of *I'm so glad to see you!* even though we weren't. She up-downed us all before going in for hugs. Her beer sloshed out of her red cup and dripped down my back as she gave me mine.

"Ruth, it is so good to see you! I swear I wouldn't recognize you if it wasn't for your crazy hair!" *Zing.* "You look awesome!"

"Thanks, Bootsie," I mumbled. "So do you."

"Well, now I know you're full of shit. I am fatter than one of them Kobe beef cows. You're gonna have to share your diet secrets with me later." *Okay, here you go, Boots: don't eat.* I laughed nervously.

"Where's the beer?" asked Jill, saving me.

"Oh, the keg is in the back." She pointed us toward it.

We made our way through the crowd, tossing out the requisite heys and hugs. In the kitchen, I searched for a beer alternative amid Bootsie's mother's disturbing collection of ceramic cows. Everywhere you turned there was a cow—a cow cookie jar, cow pot holders, even a cow figurine inexplicably perched on a tiny toilet. *What's the message here?* I wondered. *Easy on the cookies, heifer?*

"Ruth?" I screwed the top back on a Jim Beam bottle and turned around.

"Chris!" I hugged him. Chris had been friends with David since they were in first grade, and I had had a crush on him exactly as long. He was always at our house—playing with GI Joes and then video games and then soccer and then who knows what. They would lock themselves in David's room for hours, emerging only to eat everything in the refrigerator.

Chris was tall, with broad shoulders, blue eyes, and dark hair that curled around his neck like ivy. His forearms were my favorite part of him—they were lean and sinuous like a pit bull's haunches. His whole body looked like that, actually. I had volunteered to chase enough rebound balls for their basketball games of 21 to know.

"Hey," he said sheepishly. "How are you?"

"Good, good," I answered. I nervously took a sip of my drink and almost gagged. *Holy Jim Beam, Batman.* As others crowded the makeshift bar, we moved to the other side of the kitchen.

"And how are you? How's Tech?" Chris had stayed in town for college, for reasons that weren't quite clear to me. I knew his family didn't have a lot of money, but he had been something of a basketball star in high school. I had asked David about it once, and he had called me a snob. *You're judging him because he decided to stay here*, he had said. He was right.

"It's fine." He took a sip of his beer. "You look all grown up, Ruthie." I smirked and blushed simultaneously.

"Thanks, I think. You don't look so bad yourself." *Had I really just said that?*

"No, really. You look great. Hey, is David home? I tried calling him, but no answer."

"Yeah, he's home. We're both lifeguarding and coaching again this summer." I took another sip. "Who knows, he may show up here tonight."

"Oh, cool." He put his hand through his hair. "How's he been? He's sort of avoiding me, I think. Trying to break up with me or something."

"Ah, the old, 'it's not you, it's me' bit?"

"No, more like an outright Heisman. The kid never calls me back."

"Join the club."

"Oh yeah?" he asked.

"Yeah." We stood there in awkward silence for a moment or two. My attraction to him had reduced my conversational skills to zero. "Well, I'm gonna go find M.K.," I mumbled finally. "I'll see you around, I guess."

"Yeah, of course. I'll see you," he offered, as I made a bee-line for the door.

"Um, he was flirting with you," M.K. informed me, appearing suddenly by my side.

"Give me a break, Reed." I took another sip. The sugary sweetness coated my teeth.

"Don't play cool with me, Wass."

"Is that what was happening? Really?"

"Really. This is your summer." She gave me a mock up-down. "By the way, everybody is whisperin' their heads off about you."

This was sort of thrilling, actually—to be the talk of the town. I don't think my name had crossed the lips of any of these people my entire life thus far, other than to say, *Oh, Ruth? David's sister? Yeah, she's all right.*

"Am I on my deathbed, dying of starvation?"

"No, but you do a lot of blow. And you may be a lesbian."

"No way."

"Way."

"Sweet Jesus." I lit a cigarette. "Gonna be a hell of a summer, Reed."

She slapped me on my bottom and went to use the bathroom. Alone, I retreated to the perimeter of the lawn to people-watch. Everyone here looked exactly the same. They acted the same, they dressed the same, they went to the same schools, dated the same people, and named their kids the same names. It wasn't as if Michigan was a giant melting pot. There wasn't a whole lot of room for individuality there either. I knew that. But at least there you could count on a couple of different shades of human at a party. I'd never been to a party here that hadn't been 100 percent white, except for Malik, Jill's boyfriend.

"Deep thoughts?" asked Jill, interrupting my inner rant. She handed me a joint. "You look mighty serious over here."

I took a hit. "Just thinkin'. Hey, where's Malik?"

"He's working tonight."

"How does he do it? Deal with all of these annoying white people all the time?"

Jill produced an exaggerated expression of surprise. "Oh, you're not white now?"

"No, of course I am." I stubbed my cigarette out. "I'm just lookin' around, you know? At this party. So I wondered."

"I mean, it bores the crap out of him most of the time, I guess. He goes to my parties when I drag him, but he never really takes me to his."

"Does that bother you?"

"Sure." She grabbed my drink out of my hand and took a

big gulp. "Ew, that tastes nasty, Ruth." She paused. "Listen, a white girl and a black guy together in this town is pretty rare, and people are ignorant. It is what it is. We deal with it."

"I can't imagine."

"No, you probably can't." She sighed. "Want to do some gravity bong hits in Mrs. Compton's tub?"

"You serious?"

"Do I look serious?" We walked toward the house.

"Oh look, it's your brother," Jill gushed. I looked up to see him leaning against the porch banister in his dress pants and a wrinkled soccer T-shirt. He was alone and smoking a cigarette—pinching the filter awkwardly and squinting through the cloud that hovered around him. "Go on in, Jill. I'm gonna say hey for a second."

"What's up with him? He looks pissed."

"I dunno. Go on, I'll meet ya inside." From behind, I tapped his left shoulder but lingered over his right. His head swiveled accordingly, and he greeted me with a smirk before turning around to face me.

"Hey," I said.

"Hey."

"How were services?"

"Fine."

"Chris was looking for you before."

"Oh yeah?" He put his cigarette out in his cup of beer.

"You should go find him. I think he's still out here somewh—"

"Nah, I'm gonna go. This party sucks. I shouldn't have come."

"You okay?" David loved a party. I'd never been to one with him where he wasn't the absolute center of it. Tonight he hovered around the edges judgmentally like—well, like me.

"Yeah, I'm fine. Look, I'll see ya."

He raised his hand in a half-wave as he walked away, but didn't turn around.

7

opened my eyes tentatively. I had set my alarm clock for 7:30, and it was 7:28. I switched it off before its shriek sounded. My head felt like rubber.

I had been dreaming of fountain soda and crushed ice—I was so dehydrated even my subconscious was thirsty. I sat up slowly. What a night. Nothing had happened really, but I had gotten pretty wasted. So much for "nothing stupid." I touched my growling stomach, checking for bloat. Later cereal, but first, I would hurl myself through a sweat-soaked run. I winced, thinking about it. *Too bad, Ruth,* I whispered. I hadn't exercised since I'd been home, and I could feel my thighs growing. I rolled out of bed and into the bathroom.

Minutes later I was in my running gear and guzzling a giant glass of water in preparation at the kitchen sink. Through the window, heat ribbons bounced off the driveway.

"You're going running in this?" I turned to find my dad behind me, his hair askew from sleep.

"Yeah." I sighed, still a little nauseous. "Gotta do it."

He nodded. "Be careful, please." The combination of just waking up and having to engage in conversation seemed to perplex him.

"When did you get home last night?"

"I think around one?"

"I thought I heard you come in. How was the party?"

"It was okay. Saw a lot of people I hadn't seen in a while."

"Any good gossip?" he asked, yawning.

"Dad!"

"So? I need some sort of news to jazz things up around here." He rubbed his eyes.

"Hey, how come you were sleeping in your office?" I had noticed him splayed out on the daybed in there when I got home.

"Oh, I just fell asleep there, I guess." He stood up suddenly, seeming uncomfortable.

"Okay, well, see you in a little," I said.

"See you." He opened the refrigerator and stared into it instead of making eye contact with me.

Outside, I switched on my iPod and slid it into the tiny interior pocket of my shorts. I took off slowly—testing my legs. They felt wobbly and unsure. I dug deep into myself with a giant inhale. My lungs creaked in response. My body was angry at me. Who could blame her? I pushed the old girl to the limit every day.

I made a right on Price Street, glancing down to acknowledge the drain that had taken my kindergarten lunch box after an unfortunate slip on the icy street. I pictured it floating down there still—101 Dalmations banished forever to the suburban underworld. I began a slow climb up what felt like Mount Everest and tried to distract myself from my burning lungs.

As I ran I thought about David. I'd never seen him alone at a party. Ever. He was the person who was constantly surrounded by groupies hanging on his every word—guys and girls alike. Last night he'd been a ghost.

At the edge of our neighborhood was a giant church, and I crossed its front yard at a decent clip. The South loved it some churches. And banks. Giant structures of money and Jesus worship were a dime a dozen.

David had taken me, Jill, and M.K. to our first high school party. Oh, the weeks, the hours, the minutes we had spent laboring over the most minute details of what we would wear and how we would talk and who we would emulate. Walking in with David, though, it was clear that our time had been wasted. Because I was David's sister, we were okay. I'd lingered in every corner of that house, too self-conscious to make conversation, sipping Schnapps and observing him. He was the King, and I was in awe. It seemed so effortless for him. *Your brother is the shit*, M.K. had whispered, her beer breath hot in my ear.

In the driveway of Heather Garby's old house, a little black boy and girl diligently tossed a tennis ball back and forth. The ball went over the girl's head and rolled to a stop at my feet. I stopped to toss it back to her before running on. Where had Heather Garby gone? One day we had been painting eye shadow on each other and the next day she was gone. To Arkansas maybe? That rang a bell.

It seemed like a lot of people had left the neighborhood in the past five years or so, and in their place, black families had moved in. The pool had been slow to reflect the change—we had only two black families as of last summer—but already you could feel the tension brewing. Most of the parents exchanged nervous glances anytime they showed up.

I was at the end of my run, headed downhill. I could see my house on the corner, the yard already sprouting weeds. Finally finished, I walked it off gratefully.

Good work, Ruth, I whispered to myself. This skinny thing wasn't easy.

An hour later, slathered in sunscreen and my stomach at long last filled with cereal, I coasted down the hill to the pool. Kevin was already there, opening up the snack bar.

"Hey, Ruth."

"Hey, Kevin." I joined him inside and took off my backpack.

"Here we go, right?" I pulled out my towel and hung it on the back of a plastic chair.

"Whaddya mean?" he asked.

"You know, the official start of summer and all." I slipped my whistle over my neck as he looked at me blankly.

"I guess so. How was Boston this year?"

"Michigan. I was in Michigan."

"Oh yeah, shit. Sorry. What's it like up there?"

"It's cool. I had a good time. Just different from the South, you know? Are you at Tech? I can't remember." He took off his T-shirt, revealing a taut stomach and those little hip divots that only the genetically blessed could claim.

"Naw, college ain't for me."

"Oh."

"I was workin' for my dad, doin' some real estate stuff, but then summer rolled around. This job is easy as shit, you know?"

"Yeah, it is a pretty sweet deal." This was the longest conversation we had ever had. "Hey, have you heard from Jason?"

"He just called me. He'll be here in a few."

"Okay. I guess I'll check the chlorine."

"Already did that. Gonna burn the shit out of some eyeballs since it's the first day, but you know—just the way it is."

"Yikes. I'll check the bathrooms then. Make sure no one is living in a stall or anything." He looked at me blankly. "Right, well—be right back."

The bathroom looked just as it had the summer before, and the summer before that—dark and dingy with the faint smell of

Lysol and mold. There were two showers and two stalls. I had spent a good thirty minutes trying to insert my first tampon in one of those stalls, at a swim meet long ago. I checked it for toilet paper now. All set.

"Y'all ready?" asked Jason, who had arrived to shepherd us into the new summer season.

"Ready as we'll ever be," I replied. "I guess I'll go up on the stand first, Kevin, if that's cool with you."

The pitter-patter of flip-flopped and Croc-ed feet came storming down the hill. They had arrived. In no time at all, the entire snack bar area was filled with children, as though they were multiplying like rabbits.

The sun began to broil my translucent, Michigan-winterized skin as I made my way to the stand. I climbed the wooden rungs slowly. All eyes were on me, waiting for the inaugural whistle that meant the pool was open for business. That meant I had to take off my shirt and shorts in front of what was essentially a live studio audience. *Jesus, Ruth, don't make such a big deal about it. Just do it.* One, two, three, and they were both off. I looked down at my red midriff with a sigh of disgust. No matter how many crunches I did, my stomach still refused to be flat. When I sat, my belly button disappeared beneath a generous swell of flesh. I adjusted my suit in an attempt to disguise it.

I blew the whistle and on cue the pool was filled in an instant. I watched nervously as kids splashed around and screamed, dove for tossed rings, shot baskets at the water hoop, and threw themselves off the diving board. For the thirty-minute intervals during which I was on the stand, it was up to me to make sure no one was running, peeing, roughhousing, or drowning. The stimulation had my brain firing on all cylinders. Parents waved to me as they set up shop on their lawn chairs and lubed themselves up with tanning oil. As the minutes passed and I found my surveillance rhythm—shallow end, deep end, diving board, basketball hoop, and back—I began to relax. It was all so familiar, after all. I'd either been part of the mayhem myself as a pool member or watching it from above as a lifeguard for my entire life.

Jason canvassed the deck, hugging hello with various moms and parents. Kids attached themselves to his legs, and he carried them around until they were giggled out and ready to go back into the pool. Kevin manned the snack bar—handing out corndogs and popsicles begrudgingly.

As the day wore on I watched my skin turn pink and the fingers and toes of everyone around me turn into prunes. Kevin and I exchanged places on the stand every thirty minutes, and the shade of the snack bar provided welcome refuge from the blazing sun. I wrote the kids' names on their hot dogs with squirtable mustard, much to their delight. I might as well have been Van Gogh the way they watched their names emerge from the depths of that yellow bottle. Meanwhile, I kept my own hunger at bay with Lemonheads and Skittles.

"Well, hey there, Miss Skinny Minnie!" I turned around to find Mrs. Moorehouse standing at the counter, her fuschia manicured hands on her flat brown hips. She was a fixture at the pool, with the kind of commitment to tanning that you had to admire, even if facing her head-on made you grimace.

"Hey, Miss Laney," I replied, adhering to the southern code of Miss First-Name-No-Last-Name. It drove me nuts.

"Honey, just call me Laney. You're makin' me feel old, and Lord knows I don't need any more of that."

"Okay, sure. Sorry. How've you been?"

"Well, fine, I guess. Another year down the tubes."

"How's Khaki?" I asked. "I haven't seen her yet today. Is she here?"

"Oh, Khaki's doin' just fiiine." She fidgeted with her swimsuit top. "She didn't feel like comin' down today. She . . . well, she wasn't feelin' well."

"Ugh, summer colds are the worst. I hope she feels better soon." Khaki was Laney's only daughter. She seemed like a sweet girl—quiet and reserved despite (or more likely because of) her mother's over-the-toppish-ness. I didn't know her that well; she was probably around eight or nine, but had never swum on the team or taken swim lessons. I had a soft spot for her nevertheless. She was plump, and I could see a lot of me in the apologetic way she carried herself.

"Listen, Ruth, can I be frank with you?" Laney beckoned to me to lean in closer. Up close her wrinkled chest folded like an accordion.

"Sure."

"Let me get right to it. You look wonderful. The whole pool has noticed. I'd like you to help my Khaki this summer. She just will not listen to me about anything diet- or exercise-related, and I know she's miserable. Bless her heart, she just keeps gettin' pudgier and pudgier."

"I'm not sure I'm following you, Laney. How can I help her?"

"I was thankin' y'all could exercise together a few times a week or so. You know, you could come over and y'all could ride bikes or go for a walk, or maybe jog or somethin'. I'd pay you well, and we could work around your work schedule." She gazed at me expectantly.

"Well, I . . . I guess that could work. Khaki's a sweet girl, and I could use the money, but. . . ."

"Oh, wonderful! That is the best news ever, sweetie. I am so thrilled. And Khaki will be too—eventually. Oh, I just love it! So, we'll start next week or somethin'? I'll give you a call to set it all up."

"But I don't have to help her with her diet or anything, right? Just exercise?"

"Well, no, not outright. But maybe you could mention the healthy foods that you love or somethin'. You know, just get her thinkin'." I nodded warily. Employing me as a diet guru could be classified as child abuse. I would stay mum on that topic.

"All right, I'll talk to you soon, darlin'. I am just over the moon about this! Toodles!" She waved daintily, as though she were playing air piano, and walked away. I took a gulp of water from my bottle. This qualified as the strangest job opportunity I'd ever been offered.

Finally, the sun began to make its slow descent. At 2:30, the shift changed, meaning that Kevin and I could leave and two new lifeguards would stay on until closing time at 8:00 PM. As I was gathering my bag from the snack bar, David walked in.

"Hey," he said.

"Hey."

"How was the day?"

"This place never changes."

"Yeah." He looked at me wistfully for a minute, as if he wanted to say something. "Did you bust out your mustard trick?"

"Yeah, still a crowd pleaser." I wiggled into my backpack.

"Hey, did you have soccer this morning?" I hadn't seen his car when I left, and he always trained with the Tech team during the summers to get ready for his fall season at Mercer.

"Huh?" He looked at me like I was speaking Swahili.

"Uh, soccer? You know, that thing you got a scholarship for?"

"Oh yeah." He nodded. "I was at practice."

"Was it tough?"

"What is this, twenty questions?"

"Take it easy. I was just making conversation."

"Yeah, well, don't bother if you're going to grill me. You're as bad as Mom."

"Great. See ya, sunshine." I didn't understand why he hated me so much. What had I done? We were supposed to be on the same side here. I got to my bike, knocked the kickstand up, and walked it angrily up the hill.

The gravel crunched, signaling the arrival of a car. I looked up to find Chris pulling into the lot in his black Jeep. It was a little ridiculous how good-looking he was in his Ray-Bans and white V-neck shirt—like a movie star on his day off. I blushed, remembering our run-in at Bootsie's.

He smiled at me shyly, as though he was just as surprised by the fact that he was sitting there. I realized that I was wearing giant, ripped athletic shorts and a tank top that had seen better days. I was also pushing my bike. If he flirted with me now, it would be a miracle.

"When did you take off last night?" he asked.

"Oh, I dunno. Around twelve-thirty, I think? What about you?"

"Probably a lil' after. It was a decent party."

"Yeah, it was good to see everyone."

He rolled his eyes. "I see those clowns all the time. I liked seeing you, though. You leaving?" he asked. A blush began creeping up from my chest.

"Yeah. Shift's over."

"What are you up to tonight?"

"Got plans with M.K." That was a lie. Why was I lying?

"Listen, would you want to go out sometime?"

I gulped in disbelief, but tried to cover it with a cough.

"Yeah, definitely," I replied, hoping to appear nonchalant if not a little bored by his invitation.

"Okay. Maybe Thursday night?"

"Oh yeah, sure."

"Great, I'll call you." What was I supposed to do now? If I let go of my bike, it would crash to the ground. Plus, he was still sitting in his Jeep. Was I supposed to hug him good-bye over the door frame? Shake hands? Wave?

"So, see ya, I guess," I offered, opting for no physical contact.

"Sounds good. I'm gonna see if I can finally corner your brother."

I jumped on my bike and wobbled off through the gravel and onto the street. Chris Fuller had just asked me out. Holy shit.

8

The early morning was my favorite time. No car engines or human bustle to drown out the birds and crickets chirping, the untouched grass glistening with dew. You couldn't help but feel hopeful when the world looked and sounded like that. I coasted down the hill on my bicycle, thinking about the drills I would run on my guppies. The first day of practice was always important. It set the tone for the rest of the summer. You had to be in charge, 100 percent. The minute you let their cuteness get the better of you, you were toast.

David was already in the water, winding the lanes through the pool. This was a tricky process that almost always involved some cursing and a little blood, especially if you did it alone. I hopped off my bike and made my way onto the deck to help.

The lane reel sat near the deep end like a giant's spool of blue and white thread. I unwound a bit of lane that had gotten caught on the edge of a diving block to give David more leeway.

"Thanks," he called out. "The wrench is on the diving board." I grabbed it to tighten the steel rope that ran through the plastic buoys and kept the lane in place.

David's head surfaced next to my hand. "G'morning, Ruthie." He looked so sweet for a second, like a little boy. None of that too cool for school attitude—just my brother David with his apple cheeks and blue eyes, his wet hair matted to his perfectly round skull.

"Hi," I replied, handing him the next lane. I'd just witnessed David's first non-scowl since I'd been home.

"Remember when we would play 'Abyss'?"

"Of course." We had seen that movie on TV when we were kids, and it had become the basis for that summer's obsession. David and I would swim out to the deep end with a handful of quarters and make ourselves at home by the diving blocks, pretending that we were ocean divers at risk of death by water monster. The quarters became the treasure we had to retrieve despite our horrible odds, and we would earnestly watch them plummet to the bottom in a shiny haze. Then, whoever's turn it was to dive would strap on goggles, give a stern nod to the other, and grab the block's handle before arching into a back dive.

"So did we just pretend that there was a monster lurking, or did one of us actually play the role?"

David shook his head with a smile. "You know, I'm not sure. I think we just pretended that we were in danger. We never played with anyone else, right?"

"No way. It was our own private geek-out game."

"Do you think any of these kids have any imagination anymore? Or are they all just too computer-and-cell-phone-ed out to bother?" he asked.

I handed him a rope. "I wonder about that all the time."

"I'm sure Mom and Dad worried about that with us. The next generation must always seem so out of touch with the world you grew up in, you know?" He dunked his head, and then resurfaced.

I couldn't remember the last time we had reminisced. The key was to not make a big fuss about it and scare him off. I wondered if I should tell him about Chris. Not now—this moment was too fragile. The smallest crack in the glass and it would shatter. Better to wait.

The gravel crunched in the parking lot as the parents rolled in to drop off their spawn. In a whirl of radio snippets and doors slamming, the perfect stillness of the morning was no more. David hooked the last lane, and I pushed the reel back against the wooden fence. It was time to put our coaching faces on.

I approached my huddle of guppies. They bounced around in their bathing suits like lottery ping-pong balls, some with their goggles already in place, the blue lenses fogged by the humidity.

"Good morning, team," I greeted them.

"Good morning, Coach Ruth!" they shouted back in unison as they all looked up at me. I felt like a giant version of myself, taller than the Empire State Building.

"Coach Ruth, somebody smells like cigarettes," declared Ali.

"Well, Ali, cigarettes are disgusting, and they will kill you. And forget about being a good swimmer when you smoke." Great, I was coaching The Bloodhound Gang.

"I know." Something about her tone seemed to suggest that she knew I was full of shit. Being judged by a six-year-old was a drag.

I looked for David, wondering if he had taken off. The older kids practiced in the next hour, so he was free to roam. I liked it better when he took off. There was something about knowing he was watching me coach that made me nervous. I didn't see him.

"All right, guys, let's get this practice started already. To start, we'll have the six-year-olds in lane two, the seven- and eight-year-olds in lane three, and the nine- and ten-year-olds in lane five."

"Coach Ruth, can you put my goggles back on me?" asked Ali. I suctioned them back onto her face. "There you go."

"Thanks!" She turned from me and jumped into her lane, barely able to contain her excitement.

"Okay, so we're going to start with kickboards." I retrieved them from the storage closet and handed them off. They were almost bigger than the kids themselves. "I'm just going to give you a little refresher course, so you know what you're doing."

I stripped down to my bathing suit and jumped in. As I demonstrated the art of holding on to a foam board and kicking one's legs, I noticed that none of them were actually paying attention to me. This was the hardest part about coaching the guppies. Nine times out of ten, when you were teaching them something important, they had their finger up their nose, their hand in their Speedo, or were running from an imaginary horsefly.

"Hey, let's go! Anyone that doesn't pay attention has ten extra laps at the end of practice."

In minutes, I had them all perched on their boards, with a foam of spray fanning out behind them as they triumphantly drove down the lane like human go-carts, smiling at me with pride. I ran the rest of the practice as a kind of Swimming 101 course—seeing who knew what they were doing and who had just graduated from water wings. I had an army of freestylers, save for some woeful breathing techniques, but the remainder of the strokes seemed to be a mystery to most of them. It was going to be a long summer filled with dolphin kicks and two-hand touches. At the hour's end, they gathered around me in their towels, exhausted.

"You guys look great out there," I said. They stared back, wide-eyed.

"Coach Ruth, how old are you?" asked Crystal.

"How old do you think I am?" They scrunched their foreheads in thought as they engaged their internal calculators.

"Twenty-four?" guessed Tyler.

"What?" I pouted in protest. "No way! I'm nineteen! How

could I be twenty-four if I just graduated high school? Y'all know better than that." They smiled up at me as if to say, *We know you're twenty-four, but it's okay if you want to be nineteen.*

"Go on, get outta here! See you goobers tomorrow."

"Goobers!" repeated Tyler, no doubt envisioning their chocolate equivalent. He giggled and lumbered off like a baby panda.

I collected my clothes and slipped them back on. The sun had thoroughly dried and baked me. The older kids were arriving, and David was sitting on top of one of the picnic tables.

"How'd it go?" he asked me.

"It's going to be a long-ass summer." I sighed dramatically. "But they're pretty damn cute. What about you—you ready for the hormone horror of your crew?"

"I am, actually." He hesitated and opened his mouth to say more, but then stopped. I knew that if I pressed, his mood pendulum would swing from open to defensive in seconds.

"Well, good luck. I'll see you later—I'm working the afternoon shift."

"Cool. See ya."

I walked my bike up the hill. Behind me I could hear him barking orders like a drill sergeant. I wondered about what he might have wanted to say to me just now.

Hey, Ruth, I'm sorry I was such a jerk this year and never called you.

Hey, Ruth, you really are a great coach.

Hey, Ruth, want to get a beer tonight?

The last one was a stretch. Open was one thing, but full-on buddy mode was another. I thought about my date with Chris. Would David be annoyed? I certainly had felt that way myself all of our lives as girlfriend after girlfriend of mine developed a crush on him. Yeah, excuse me, nineteen years of torture meant that he could deal for one summer.

I pulled into my driveway and put my bike away. M.K. and Jill were taking me rope swinging on the Escatawba in ten minutes. It had been a hard decision to agree to go because of the fact that it would give me no time to run. I could have gotten up before practice, but 7:00 AM had come and gone, and I hadn't been able to haul myself out of bed that early. As punishment for my laziness, I had skipped my cereal and planned on skipping lunch as well.

I unlocked the back door and entered the house. With no one in it, it felt so still and quiet—a giant, air-conditioned box of memories. Did it feel this way to my parents?

I stuffed a hotel towel into my backpack. My parents were big on those. Our bathroom had never seen a normal-size bottle of shampoo or bar of soap. Tiny toiletries were our specialty. A car honked in the driveway.

"What's up?" I slid into the backseat, and Jill backed out of my driveway.

"You ready to swang?" she asked with a twang.

"Sure as shit, ayam!"

"Are you hungry?" asked M.K.

"Girl, I've been up since the crack of dawn. I practically ate lunch already." *What is more exhausting*, I wondered, *not eating, or the energy it takes to pretend I am?*

"Well, too bad. We're going to Chick-fil-A for some breakfast biscuits."

"And you're eating three, whether you like it or not," added Jill.

"Forget it," I mumbled as I gazed out the window.

As we pulled into the drive-thru, I lit a cigarette and counted to ten slowly in my head. This was my favorite fast-food restaurant once upon a time. I was going to have to dig deep.

"Dang, this is so good," murmured Jill as she took a bite and the smell of fried chicken filled the car.

"Seriously," agreed M.K. "Wass, you sure you don't even want a bite?"

"Yeah, I'm sure." I pinched my stomach just above the waistband of my shorts. *No, Ruth. Not for you. Be strong.* In five minutes this would be over. I watched the clock on the dash. Seven minutes later exactly, the takeout bags were reopened and filled with empty wrappers. *Made it.*

We turned left off the main road, and any semblance of civilization disappeared. The road was not really a road at all, but rather a precarious ribbon of red dirt surrounded by trailer homes and pine trees. A few bedraggled children played in plastic pools in their front yards. A dog with its rib cage on full display and what appeared to be a nasty case of mange darted in front of the car.

"Yuck!" yelled Jill, swerving to her right. "This is some *Deliverance* shit."

"Ah, the Escatawba. As beautiful as the Riviera," I remarked. Not that I had ever been to the Riviera. We turned off onto an even skinnier path and slowly made our way to a small clearing to park. Through the pine trees I could see the murky water.

"What if that big-ass biscuit sinks me right to the bottom?" asked Jill.

"Wass can save you!" answered M.K. "We got ourselves a certified lifeguard on-site." She smiled at me. I put my arm around Jill's shoulder as we made our way to the river.

"You couldn't save a mosquito with your skinny ass." She grabbed me around the waist. "I'm going to have you knee-deep in chicken biscuits before this summer is over. Mark my words."

"Hey, does anyone have any weed?" I asked, willing the image of a chicken biscuit out of my head.

Jill pulled a packed bowl out of her jean shorts' pocket and smiled wickedly. "Shall we?"

She handed it to me, and I used my own lighter to ignite the bowl's green contents. As I inhaled, it turned orange and I felt the smoke fill my lungs. After we had passed it around three times, we nodded to signal its conclusion. Jill removed her shorts and set the warm bowl on top of them. She ripped off her tank top to reveal a neon-green bikini.

"Let's do this!" she yelled.

I opened my mouth to encourage her, but realized that my saliva had formed a preventative paste all around its inside. It was like speaking through glue. I motioned to M.K. to hand me her soda and took a giant swig.

"My mouth is a glue trap," I announced. M.K. giggled and took it back from me.

"Me too."

"But I'm high!" I clapped my hands.

"And so am I," agreed Jill. "All right, I'll go first!"

We approached the rope, which dangled in front of us from a very large tree. Whoever had taken the time to scale its heights and affix this toy was a prince among men. As much as its surroundings lacked in ambiance, the rope swing made up for it tenfold.

"Okay, here we go, bitches." Jill rubbed her palms together and grabbed the rope. A wolf whistle suddenly shattered our bubble of country bliss.

"What the—?" I asked and shaded my eyes to look out at the river below. Of course. Two rednecks in jean shorts leered up at us from the river. Upon closer inspection, it became clear that one of them had the Tasmanian Devil waving a Rebel flag tattooed over his heart. It also became clear as they began to yell various off-color remarks that they had maybe six teeth between the two of them.

"Shit." M.K. sighed. "I hope they don't ruin this for us."

"Go the fuck on!" yelled Jill. "Leave us alone." One of them held up his right hand, made a hole with his fingers, and then proceeded to stick the ring finger of his left hand through it repeatedly.

"Classy," I said.

"Okay, now's when we just ignore them and they go away," said M.K. "Let's sit for a while where they can't see us. Sooner or later they'll get bored."

Jill let go of the rope and plopped down on the ground. "We'll give them ten minutes. In the meantime, let's tan." I dug in my bag for my towel and unfurled it. The sun was spotty through the trees, but its warmth soothed my face. I closed my eyes.

"Wass, you're gonna get the gnarliest tan lines in that gramma suit," said M.K. as she untied her top.

"Oh, excuse me, I have a job to go to after this. Sorry I can't wear a bikini to save lives."

"But you will get a bikini this summer, right?" asked M.K.

"I dunno. I mean, I don't think my stomach has ever seen the light of day."

"Well, it's not like it's going to go up in flames, Wass. I think you're safe," said Jill.

"Will you go with me to buy one?" I asked. "Will you tell me the truth if I look like a fat-ass?"

Jill sat up and hovered over me. "You're not serious, right?"

I opened one eye. "What? About coming with me?"

"No, about thinking you could look like a fat-ass anything."

I grunted in response.

Jill grabbed my arm. "Wass, I can fit my hand around your entire upper arm." She gripped it tightly.

"Ow, Jesus!"

"I'm starting to think you might have, like, a disorder or something." M.K. was sitting up now too and nodded.

"Is everything okay?" she asked, her blue eyes searching

mine. "I mean, I know how much you wanted this—wanted to be skinny and all. And you do look pretty great."

"Too skinny. You looked great at Christmas," interjected Jill. "Now you look like a scarecrow."

"That's harsh, Jill," said M.K.

"It's not." She turned back to me. "I'm sorry, Ruth. I don't want to be a bitch, it's just that I love you so much and I'm worried about you. You are beautiful, you know? You've always been beautiful—skinny, not skinny, whatever."

"It's true," agreed M.K. "Don't you know that?"

"I'm fine," I said softly. "I'm just on a diet, you know? You don't understand because you're just naturally this way. You don't have to worry about every bite that goes into your mouth."

"Sure I do, Ruth. It's just not that important to me." Jill cupped my face. "You can let go a little. Relax the calorie counting for a while."

I removed her hands gently and shook my head. "I really can't."

Jill opened her mouth to argue with me, but I didn't give her the chance. "Listen, guys, I promise you that I eat. I really do. Like I said, I just have to be careful. I like looking like this," I explained, shrugging.

"I wish there was something I could say that made you understand that you can look the way you look, maybe even better, and ingest a fat gram every once in a while," said Jill.

"And if you're gonna work this hard for it, believe in the fact that you can rock a damn bikini," said M.K. "Okay?"

I nodded. Why was it so hard for me to admit out loud that I was worried about myself too? I feared that vulnerability the same way I feared French fries. Indulgence on any level would be the end of skinny Ruth, and skinny was the only thing I'd ever really been acknowledged for.

"Hey, are the river rats still there?" I asked, eager to change the subject. I crouched low and peered over the edge of the bank. "They're gone!"

"It's probably free skate day at The Roll," said Jill, making us all crack up. The Roll was a skating rink on the edge of town.

"Remember Kelly Ragstone's birthday there in the second grade?" asked M.K.

"Yes!" I said, laughing. "Her uncle had that crazy beer gut, and her grandmother was chain-smoking Kools?"

"Hey, Wass, I think that was the first time you'd ever been roller skating," said Jill. "Remember?"

"Oh man." I put my face in my hands. By the grace of God, I had finally managed to haul my sweaty, round body around the rink, only to realize that I was being watched by the entire party, who burst into applause at my finish. My eight-year-old self had been mortified, and I had spent the remainder of the party eating birthday cake.

"I think I kissed my first boy at that party," said M.K. "Robert Mitchell."

"Robertttttttt," we sang back to her.

"You loved him!" declared Jill.

"I really did. We went steady for about two weeks, and then I dumped him for Mark Kelly."

"Heartbreaker," I said.

"Yeah, well, easy come, easy go," M.K. said as she winked at us.

"Okay, let's get serious," said Jill. "It's rope-swinging time." We stood up. "I'll go first!"

We circled the thick rope. Jill gave it a few solid pulls and even hoisted herself up onto it to check for reliability. "Solid as a rock."

"Or a rope," I said.

"Very funny."

"All right, here we go," said Jill. M.K. and I clapped and whistled as she walked backward with the rope in her hands. When she had pulled it taut, she extended her arms and grabbed it at a higher point.

"If I die, tell Malik that he's the love of my life, please!" She ran forward and launched herself off the ground. The rope swung her over the water, and she hung in the air for a second like a hummingbird, before letting go and throwing up her middle finger as she fell into the water. We ran to the edge, to make sure she surfaced.

"That was awesome!" she yelled after her head broke through the water. "Wow!" She swam the short distance to the bank and hauled herself out. "Y'all, that was even better than I remembered!"

I looked at M.K. "You mind if I go next?"

"No, go ahead." She handed me the rope. I backed up with my heart racing. What if I cracked my skull open on a rock or some redneck's discarded commode? What if this was my last moment on earth? *So what.* I broke into a run and flew out over the river, watching it sparkle in the sun below me. I closed my eyes and hit the water, its coolness a welcome treat.

We spent the rest of the morning passing the bowl back and forth and taking swinging turns. Finally, when our river stink was at its peak, we piled back into Jill's car. In the backseat, I watched black dots swim in front of my eyes. I was sun-soaked, starving, and faint, but it didn't necessarily feel bad—just kind of like I was floating.

Jill drove up my driveway. "Great day, sweets," she said, turning around to say good-bye.

"The best. I'll call ya later. Hey, are my eyes super-red?"

"A little, but you can just say it's from the river," said M.K.

"Good point. Bye!" I shut the door and made my way toward the house. All I could think about was the bag of jumbo marshmallows waiting for me inside. I could taste the sugar on my tongue already. I opened the door to find my dad sitting at the kitchen table and eating a sandwich.

"Hi, Ruthie," he greeted me. This was going to be tough. I was stoned and marshmallow-obsessed. I prayed that his lunch hour was almost up. His office was close by, and if he didn't have a client lunch, he often came home to eat.

"Hey, Dad," I said. I dropped my bag on the floor and opened the cupboard by the refrigerator. There they were. Hallelujah. I grabbed the bag and ripped it open. Soft and supple, the marshmallow dusted my hand with white powder as I plucked and then popped it into my mouth. I moved to the table and continued my pluck-and-drop in gluttonous silence. Five 'mallows later, I took a breath and looked up to find my dad smirking at me.

"That's lunch?" he asked. "Sugar?"

"Oh no, I had lunch with Jill and M.K.," I lied. "This is dessert." I smiled weakly.

"You know, smoking marijuana before work is probably not a smart move, Ruth." He popped his last sandwich bite into his mouth and watched my reaction as he chewed.

"Huh?" I asked, feigning innocence.

"I'm not going to say it again." He gazed at me with disappointed eyes. "It's your job to keep kids safe at a pool, and you show up stoned?" He shook his head. "Shame on you."

He dropped his dish in the sink and left the house.

9

Sweat dripped from my brow as I jogged to a stop at my driveway. Panting heavily and feeling light-headed, I walked up the street to catch my breath. I thought about my dad's insight into my marshmallow binge yesterday. As far as I knew, he had never smoked weed in his life. Then again, I guess you didn't have to partake yourself to know that red eyes and maniacal face-stuffing were clues to such.

As if on cue, he walked out of the house on his way to the office.

"Dad!" I yelled. He looked up and frowned.

"Wait up!" I called, jogging back to him. He rested his briefcase on the top of the car and dangled his keys impatiently.

"Dad, I'm sorry about yesterday. I—well, I could lie and tell you that I hadn't smoked a little, but that would be pointless, right?" He raised his left eyebrow.

"It was just a little, I swear, and in the morning. I was fine by the time I got home. Just really hungry. Marshmallows are my weakness, you know."

He closed the door of the car and leaned against it. "Pot smoking is for losers, Ruth. You're not a loser."

"Dad, I think that's a bit extreme. I mean, I would venture

to say that 90 percent of the world population smokes pot. Are they all losers too?" I had statistics on my side—made up or not.

"Jesus, Ruth, you're not 90 percent of the population as far as I'm concerned. You're special. You're better than that. This is the same conversation we had about your drinking in high school. I just don't understand why you continue to sabotage yourself. You have so much potential, but you'd rather drink, smoke, and starve yourself into mediocrity. Why? It's such a waste."

I shook my head. "Dad, I think you need to relax. I'm sorry I can't be the paradigm of virtue you want me to be."

"I don't expect you to be perfect, Ruth. Really, I don't. I just wish you used your head more. The Ruth who came home from Michigan is someone I don't recognize." He laid his keys on the hood of the car and took my hand.

"Sorry, Dad."

"Yeah, I know. Promise me you'll start taking better care of yourself? I'm really worried. Your mother and I both are."

"Okay, no more reckless weed smoking. Scout's honor."

"And what about this food thing? I know I joke around about it sometimes, maybe make light of what you're eating or not eating, but it's only because I'm uncomfortable." I chewed the inside of my cheek as he spoke. "Should I be thinking about getting you some counseling?" He nudged me. "Look at me, Ruth." I tore my gaze away from the garage floor and faced him.

"Dad, it's just a diet," I whispered, feeling strangely like crying. "I swear."

"Really? What kind of diet calls marshmallows lunch?"

"I told you, it was a dessert. I had a salad earlier with Jill and M.K.," I lied.

"All right. I'm going to believe you because I don't know what else to do. Please talk to us—me and your mom—if you feel like this 'diet' is slipping out of your control, okay?"

"Okay." He hugged me.

"I'm gonna get your suit all wet!" I mumbled.

"Who cares." He released me. "See ya later, Ruthie."

"Bye, Dad."

I watched him get settled into his seat and thought about what it would be like to go back to the way I used to be. I couldn't do it. Not now. And it was stupidly easy to fool everyone, including myself, into thinking that this was just dieting. Deep down, I knew damn well that it wasn't. That it was a problem. But I was too scared of the alternative to do anything about it.

I glanced at my watch. Today was my first Khaki lesson, and I had five minutes to make it to her house. So much for appearing presentable. I jumped on my bike.

"So, what grade will you be in this fall?" Khaki looked up at me with the most convincing *fuck off* eyes I had ever seen from anyone, much less a nine-year-old. I'd arrived at her house to discover that her mother had completely blindsided her. Not only had Khaki had no idea that I was coming, but she'd also apparently had no interest in going anywhere with me. First she had refused to get dressed. Then she had deliberately riled her mother up by pairing a ratty, too-small Dora the Explorer T-shirt with sleep shorts instead of the matching pink outfit Laney had laid out for her. Finally, as her last act of defiance, she had opened up the back door and thrown her sneakers into the yard. She shuffled angrily beside me now in a pair of misshapen and bedazzled purple Crocs.

"I think fourth, right? And you're at Jacob Ray up the street?" She didn't answer me.

"I went to Jacob Ray too, you know. I had Mrs. Mason for fourth grade. She was tough, but I liked her." I looked down at the top of Khaki's head. Her brown hair circled it in limp waves. From this angle, I could see the way her stomach strained against the cotton of her T-shirt. She remained silent, but I continued on.

"So I figured we'd just take a half-hour walk or something—get to know each other a bit. Since we're going to be doing this all summer and all." Khaki came to an abrupt halt and put her hands on her hips. Or what would have been her hips.

"Do what now?" She looked up at me angrily.

"Me and you, all summer. Exercise buddies."

"Are you serious?"

"Well, yes. I think we'll have fun?" Her accusatory stare turned my statement into a question.

"Can we sit down for a sec? Just over on that curb over there?" she whined.

"Well, Khaki, I think that kind of defeats the purpose of our time together, you know? Why don't we walk and talk."

"Miss Ruth, can I be frank?"

Taken aback by her sudden morphing into a fifty-five-year-old accountant, I stammered. "Uh, sure, of course, I mean, why—"

"I need to sit down to process this, please. We'll get back up in two minutes and strap weights around our ankles or whatever the fudge my mother is paying you to do." This was the same nine-year-old who had thrown an epic tantrum ten minutes prior? The one in a Dora T-shirt and bedazzled Crocs?

"Um, okay, just for a minute." She shuffled over to the curb and plopped down. She sat Indian style, her hands cupping her chin. I hovered over her.

"You sit too, please. You're making me nervous." This was unreal. Who knew that Khaki Moorehouse was such a badass? I sat beside her in the damp grass. "Laney really outdid herself this time," she said.

"Laney? You call your mother by her first name?"

"Not to her face." She wiped the sweat from her pale brow. "Well, sometimes to her face, if she's really gone too far. Like now, for example. Hiring somebody to exercise me—like I'm a dog or somethin'—is going too far." She looked up at me. "Don't you think?"

"Well, I guess she thinks she has your best interests in mind, Khaki," I offered weakly. "She just wants you to be healthy and happy."

"She wants me to be happy, or she wants to make herself happy? I'm happy the way I am. She's the one who wants to die because she has a fat daughter." Beneath the bravado, her voice trembled.

"Hey, who said anything about fat?"

She rolled her eyes. "You're here because I'm skinny? Come on."

"No one said anything about fat, Khaki. Your mom just wants you to try to think differently about exercise. See it as fun instead of boring. And for whatever reason, she thought I would be a good person to help you with that." *Never mind that it's a warped case of the blind leading the blind.*

"I guess it could be worse." She up-downed me. "You seem all right. Better than the aerobics classes she drags me to sometimes." She winced. "Uch. The worst." I stood up and extended my hands to her to help her do the same. She grabbed them tentatively.

"We don't have to run or anything, do we?" She looked up at me, alarmed.

"Not right now. But maybe by the end of the summer, you'll want to." She cocked an eyebrow at me.

"Miss Ruth, get real."

~

I leaned against the sink, greedily gulping a glass of ice water.

"Ruthala!" My mom slid in beside me. She was a high school guidance counselor, and her summers off were her excuse to be as lazy as humanly possible and still maintain a pulse. "What are you doing home?"

"I have the day off." I rubbed the cold glass against my forehead.

"Want to go to the mall with your mama?"

"Oh, Mom, shopping? Now?"

"C'mon, I'll buy you a treat and we can grab a girls' lunch."

Saying no would have just been cruel. And to be honest, a new something for my date with Chris sounded pretty appealing. But lunch? What would I eat? *Shut up, Ruth. Just do this, please.* "Okay, sure. Why not?"

"Great. You ready?" She was practically behind the wheel already.

"Slow down there. I have to shower and, you know, get ready."

"Oh, okay. I'm going to be in my room. Just call me when you're ready." She got up. "But don't take forever, okay? It's the mall, not prom."

"What would I know about prom?"

"What exactly do you do that takes you so long?" my mom asked at a red light.

"You're already annoying me. I thought this was going to be fun." I stared out the window morosely.

"Honey, don't be so sensitive. I really am legitimately curious. You prepare yourself for a good half-hour, and when you finally emerge you look exactly the same."

"Thanks a lot."

"No, I don't mean it in a bad way! You look great. I just—I

know you're putting on makeup because I see it in your room, but I don't see it on your face."

"Hello, that's the key to good makeup. It's subtle. The key to looking good is appearing as though you've spent no time doing so."

"But, honey, you're nineteen. You don't even need the makeup." She glanced at me. "Well, maybe you do now. You never used to."

"What's that supposed to mean?"

"Ruth, a steady diet of sugar and air doesn't exactly provide a glowing complexion."

"Very nice, Mom. I'm glad you're perfect."

"C'mon, Ruth, it's not like you aren't aware of these things yourself, right? You're a smart girl."

"Mom, Dad already read me the riot act this morning. Can we please move on?"

"Oh yes. I heard about the grass."

"The grass? Is this 1969?" She pursed her lips.

"Okay, well, I apologized to him for acting so irresponsibly, and I'll apologize to you too."

"Thanks for the apology, but it doesn't change the fact that you did something really stupid."

"God! I know! This is like, some déjà vu shit. I had the talk with Dad, okay? I get it." Arguing with my parents took me from nineteen to thirteen at time warp speed.

"All right. We'll move on. For the moment at least." She sighed. "Are we looking for anything in particular today?"

"Not really. Maybe a cute top or a miniskirt. I'm not really sure."

"Are you going somewhere?" She pulled into a mall parking space.

"I have a date," I explained coyly. My mom had had a crush on Chris as long as I had, really, but not in a creepy Mrs. Robinson way. More in an appreciation of male charm kind of way.

"Oh, that's nice. With whom?"

"Mom, you're acting pretty nonchalant. I was hoping for more of a dramatic reaction. I think I went on a total of three dates during my entire high school career."

We began walking toward the entrance. "Sure, you didn't date much in high school, but that's because you had no confidence in yourself. It's different now. I'm not surprised at all." She put her arm around me.

"Mom, give me a break. The reason I didn't go on dates was not because of a lack of confidence. I was fat."

"Ruth Wasserman, you absolutely were not fat," she hissed. "I can't believe you're saying that."

"Mom, c'mon." We stared at each other. "You yourself told me I needed to lose some weight."

"Sure, a few pounds, but not anything extreme." She opened the door to the mall. "Oy, this air conditioning! And anyway, the only reason I said that was because you seemed so miserable about your weight. I wanted you to be happy."

I thought about Laney. Did she think that was all she wanted for Khaki as well? Was she blind to her own intentions? "Hey, Mom, it's okay to say that you wanted me to lose some weight for your own well-being. It's not a crime to want your daughter to be thin."

"Ruth, what are you talking about? Sure, I could have used one less shopping trip with you that didn't go on for hours on end with you in tears, but I honestly just wanted you to be happy. I suppose maybe I knew that your life would be easier if you were thinner . . . oh, who knows. I mean, God knows I'd like to lose a little weight." We made our way past an array of stores displaying bedazzled T-shirts, leather bomber jackets, and Crimson Tide paraphernalia in their windows.

"I just like food too much these days to be good. It's like I opened Pandora's box, except the box in question has Entenmann's written across its top."

"You never used to eat like that. Remember when you only ate grilled chicken for six months?"

"Grilled chicken and hard-boiled eggs. I looked wonderful." She sighed.

"And what about that cabbage soup kick you were on for David's bar mitzvah?"

"I had forgotten about that." She smiled wistfully. "I was practically down to my birth weight."

"God, you were such a bitch that year. You banned everything. The kitchen was like the Sahara."

"But did I look gorgeous or what? That photo of the four of us is a masterpiece." I rolled my eyes.

"Am I responsible for this?" She stopped midstride and faced me.

"Responsible for what?"

"This." She waved her hand in front of my waist.

"Mom." I reached out and put my hand on her goose-pimpled forearm. "No." The truth was that maybe she was partly responsible. She had always battled her body's inclinations with focused ferocity and tsk-tsked my own inability to do the same. I think she knew that, at least on a very basic level. Looking at her panic-stricken face now, however, I couldn't say as much. Besides, what would placing blame do? In the end, it was my choice what I ate, or didn't eat, every day.

"Are you sure?"

"Yeah. Relax."

"Good." We continued walking in awkward silence. "So, who is it?"

"Who's what?"

"The guy you're going on a date with?"

"It's Chris, actually."

"Our Chris?"

"That's the one."

"David's Chris?"

"Yes, ma'am."

She nodded slowly. "Well, I'll be damned." She smiled broadly. "He is really good-looking. And such a nice guy." She paused for a moment. "I'm trying to keep my cool here, you know that, right?"

"I know."

"Well, you know what this means. A new outfit, top to toe. This is serious business. What about these?" She held up a pair of shapeless pants. My mom had a soft spot for linen.

"Am I sixty-five?"

"Very funny."

"What about this?" I held up a purple T-shirt.

"Are you twelve?" I smirked. To say that we didn't have the same taste was a severe understatement.

In the dressing room, I surveyed myself in a black mini-dress. *Who the hell is this?* I wondered. I actually laughed—whether out of nerves or fright or happiness, I wasn't sure. The rational me saw the emaciated girl staring back and thought, *Yikes, you really are a nut job.* The crazy me saw a girl who could probably still stand to lose a few pounds around her mid-section. The rational me knew that there was no way in hell I'd be able to keep this up forever, and the crazy me said, *You'd better, because skinny is all you have.* It was a constant game of psychotic ping-pong.

My mom opened the dressing room door. "I'm so bored out there! Show me."

"So—"

"Oh, Ruth." She put her hands over her mouth, and her eyes widened behind her glasses.

"What, Mom?" I squirmed in front of her. "Mom! Come on!"

"Ruth, I—I just don't know what to say." She sat down on the stool beside me, and our eyes met in the mirror. "You're so thin."

I was trapped. I couldn't take the dress off and put on my baggier clothes, but I also couldn't just stand there and watch her fight back tears.

"You know what's really screwed up?"

"What?"

"Part of me actually thinks you look good!" She took her glasses off and rubbed her eyes. "How sick is that? Here's my daughter, looking like someone right out of Dachau, and there's part of me that's happy for her! It is my fault—all of this. I'm a terrible mother." I slid down the wall to the ground and sat with my back against it.

"You're not a terrible mother."

"What are we going to do?"

"Mom, this is not your issue. Cut the 'we' stuff. I've gone a little overboard with the eating thing, and I know that, okay? I'm trying to be more sane, I really am." *"Trying" as in I think about it but never actually act on it.*

"Do you promise?"

I nodded.

"Because if this gets worse. . . ."

"Mom, everything is going to be okay." I stood back up.

"Ruth, when you look in the mirror, do you see that you need to gain some weight? Five pounds would work wonders, you know. And this is coming from a woman who used to believe that a person could never be too thin. No longer. You're too thin, honey. Too, too thin."

What I wanted to do was scream, *But, Mom, five pounds leads to ten pounds, leads to thirty!* What I said was, "Yes, Mom, I see that."

"Okay." She exhaled deeply.

"Ruthala, remember when you were little and I found you stark naked in my bedroom, standing in front of the mirror and kissing your own shoulders?"

I laughed. "Yeah."

"What happened to that confidence? Where did it go?"

"Mom, I was three."

"I know, but oh—I wish I could have bottled that feeling for you."

"Mom, you have mascara all over your face." I licked my fingertips and rubbed it away as she waited patiently.

"Ruthie, you really promise that you're okay?" she asked when I was finished.

"Yes! Now scram so I can try on something that doesn't make you burst into tears."

"Okay, I'll wait outside for the next one."

She left, and I stared at myself in the mirror for another moment. I didn't want to live like this, but I also didn't know how to not live like this and look the way I wanted to look.

In the end we settled on a blue-and-white-striped tank top and some white shorts.

"Thanks, Mom," I said as the cashier handed her her credit card.

"You are very welcome." She looked at her watch. "Shall we go to lunch? You're going to eat something, right?"

"Yes, I'll eat something." *Get a freaking sandwich, eat half, and move on, Ruth!*

As we settled into our booth, my mom beamed like a beauty contestant. "I don't know if I've ever seen you look so excited," I told her. "Wow."

"I love lunch out," she confessed. "Your father will never indulge me, and it's impossible during the school year. There's something so wonderfully decadent about it." As I gave my order to a giant pair of braces attached to a fifteen-year-old boy, she nodded happily.

"No comments, please."

"Okay, I won't." She pursed her lips. "But I'm glad that you ordered a sandwich. Good girl."

"Mom, c'mon."

"Okay, okay. Let's change the subject." She took a long sip of her diet soda. "Where are you two going to go on your date? And when is it?"

"I'm not sure where we'll go. And Thursday is date night."

"I used to love going on dates."

"With Dad?"

"Well, sure, but with other people too. The whole idea of getting dressed up and being taken somewhere." She grinned.

"Where did you and Dad go on your first date?"

"Where did we go? I think it was to a dance or something. Or maybe we met at a dance and then our first date was to a party?"

"Mom! You really don't remember?"

"Honey, it was a long time ago. We were freshmen in college, for goodness' sake."

"Just like me now."

"Yep, just like you now." I took a sip of my drink and tried to imagine marrying Tony. Or Chris. It was impossible.

"Was Dad your first boyfriend?"

"Oh no. I dated a few boys in high school for a stretch. But he was the first man I fell in love with."

"And when you fell in love, did you know you were in love? Or was it just something you figured out later?"

"I'm not sure what you mean."

"I wonder if when you fall in love you're too busy experiencing it to fully realize that that's what's happening."

"I guess there's some of that. But mostly it just feels so different from 'like.' The thought of life without him seems unbearable. And then of course, at least for me, there was the whole sex part of the equation."

"Mom!" I blushed.

"What? We can't talk about these things?"

"Not if we're talking about it in relation to Dad." I thought about him asleep in his office.

Our waiter deposited our plates in front of us. My stomach dropped as I examined my BLT. As my mom futzed with the ketchup bottle, I discreetly removed the bacon and folded it into my napkin.

"Ruth, have you talked to David at all since you've been home?" she asked as she poured a pool of ketchup onto her plate.

"What do you mean? Like, really talked to him?"

"Yes, Ruth. Like a conversation."

"No. He hates me."

"He doesn't hate you!" She slapped her palm on the table, and her lemon wedge parachuted from the rim of her glass.

I rolled my eyes. "Whatever you say."

"Anyway, I'm worried about him. Something is off, but I don't know what it is exactly."

"Do you have actual proof, or is this just a mother's intuition thing?"

She chewed her burger and held her finger up. "Mother's intuition," she finally replied. "He's just acting differently. More secretive or something."

I chewed my own bite and tried my hardest to enjoy it, despite the mayonnaise that I detected. "He's the same as he's always been at swim practice."

"Is he? That's good to hear. It's just that he's always been so open with me and your father. These past couple of months, not so much."

"He's open because he's the favorite."

"Ruth, please." Her eyes widened above her burger bun.

"It's true. He's the soccer star on scholarship, and I'm the endearing screwup."

"I would hardly call getting into U of M being a screwup. You're being ridiculous."

"Geographic distribution saved my ass." I fingered the bread on my plate.

"Honey, that's just not true. And besides, whether or not he's the favorite is not what this conversation is about. Can we focus, please? If he says anything to you that's cause for concern, will you let me know?"

"I'll keep my ears open, okay?" Here I was, starving right in front of them, and they were sweating David's PMS. Typical.

My phone rang. It was Chris.

"Hello?" My mom stared at me like a frightened deer, her hands balled into fists on top of the table. To her, cell phones were for emergencies only. Every time one rang she was convinced that someone had died.

"It's Chris," I mouthed. "Relax." I slid out of the booth.

"How's it going?"

"Good. And you?"

"Decent. I have the day off."

"Nice! Uh, were you still into hanging out Thursday?"

"Yeah, definitely." I was loitering by the bar next to a woman who looked like a human cigarette. Gray and wrinkled, she appeared to be created out of ash. Her smoke languished in her ashtray as she drank a mudslide and gave me the stink-eye.

"Well, there's this bluegrass band that I like playing downtown. They start around nine. Would you be into that? Maybe supper first or something?"

"You know, I should probably eat with my parents, but I'm definitely into the music part." *Eat with my parents. Yeah, right.*

"Okay, cool. How 'bout I pick you up around eight-thirty then?"

"Sounds good." I looked back at our table. My mom was paying the bill. She cocked her head and stared into the distance as she calculated the tip. "Well, see ya later, Chris."

"Yep, take it easy." I considered asking human cigarette if I could bum a smoke, but thought again when I saw she was smoking menthols. I could wait it out. I made eye contact with my mom, and she began walking toward me. At the door I pocketed seven peppermints.

"Soooo?" she asked as we battled the heat on our way to the car.

"We're going to listen to some bluegrass on Thursday."

She clapped her hands. "That really sounds like fun, Ruthie." She beamed at me.

I smiled back. I was excited to go out with him, especially since we weren't headed to Chili's and miniature golf, the typical first date in our town. "Do you think David is going to care?"

"You know, it might make him uncomfortable for a minute or two, but it shouldn't be a huge issue. Think of all your friends he's flirted with."

"Yeah, that's what I figured."

"I would think that Chris had already told him about it," she said. "Although, with boys you never know."

"No, you never do."

"I had a nice time today, Ruthala," she announced with a smile. I reached over and cupped the top of her head with my hand.

10

The next afternoon I stood up on my bike pedals and pumped ferociously up the hill. I was working the afternoon shift, but wanted a cigarette first. At the top of the hill, I swung through my old elementary school's yard, crisscrossing back and forth from the sidewalk to the grass as I made my way to the back of the main building. I hopped off and parked before digging in my backpack for one.

I lit it and stared at myself in the reflection of a classroom window. I turned to the side, checking for any new flesh. I pinched my stomach, willing it not to grow via physical punishment. The rational me knew I was nuts. But of course, the crazy me would win out. The rational me knew that my arms looked like Barbie arms—the shoulder bone in each of them almost breaking skin—but the crazy me spotted a bit of a waddle when I raised it and waved. My collarbone may have been jutting out like a tree branch, but if I looked closely, I could see a bit of fat blurring the line of my jawbone.

I took a final drag and exhaled before grinding the butt into the ground with my purple flip-flop. Splashes and shrieks from the pool below cut through my thoughts. It was time to go.

I jumped back on my bike and flew down the incline, relish-

ing the warm breeze. I could smell the unmistakable, slightly
mildewed odor of my bathing suit, corn chips, and chlorine.
Intoxicating.

"Coach Ruth, Coach Ruth!" A school of guppies greeted me
before I even reached the snack stand.

"Are you working now, Coach Ruth?" Ali asked, latching
on to my leg.

"I am," I replied.

"It looks like it's gonna storm," Crystal informed me som-
berly. I looked up to survey the sky. While it had been bright
blue ten minutes before, now I spotted a gray curtain closing
in. Southern storms were legendary: one minute sun, the next
minute crackling thunder and lightning with pounding rain,
and then ten minutes later sun again, as though nothing ever
happened.

"Who's working with me, do you know?" I asked my min-
ions.

"David!" Tabitha exclaimed excitedly.

"Really?" I patted her on the head and began walking
toward the entrance. I never worked with David. Weird.

"Hey, hot stuff," greeted Jason. He was eating a Whopper
inside the snack bar, his tan chest and stomach still wet from
the pool.

"When did we start serving Whoppers?" The smell of meat
and ketchup made my stomach growl.

"Want a bite?" he asked.

"Um, no."

"Of course you don't. Skinny-ass."

"Hey, is David working with me?" I looked out to the lifeguard stand to find him already there, looking bored underneath the shade of the umbrella.

"Yeah." He crumpled up the Whopper wrapper and shot it
into the trash can.

"Nice, two points," he mumbled. "David is pulling a double because Kevin is sick."

"Kevin's sick?" I echoed. "Hungover or sick?"

"Do I look like a doctor to you? He said he's sick." Jason looked at the clock. "Sweet! Time for me to go. Looks like y'all are gonna get a storm." I retrieved my whistle from my basket and slipped my flip-flops off.

"See ya, Jason."

"Y'all don't kill each other today," he warned. "Be sweet."

I flipped him the bird behind my back as I walked to the stand. "Is that sweet enough?"

"Perfect."

"Hello," I mumbled as I climbed up the ladder to relieve David on the stand. "Are you a vampire or something?" I reached for the umbrella's lever and rotated it counterclockwise. It collapsed in accordance. David kept his eyes on the pool.

"It's not like you're going to get any sun anyway, Snooki," he replied. "That storm is going to hit in a minute." I looked up to survey the sky. A gray and purple bruise of clouds now sliced it in half.

"You want me to stay up here until the lightning cracks?" he asked. "Get everybody out?"

"I think I can handle it."

"All right, whatever you say." He hopped off the stand. "Keep your eyes on the sky."

"Keep your eyes on the sky," I mocked, surveying the pool. Only a few brave souls were holding on to what they knew would be the last five minutes of swimming before the storm hit.

There was Tyler, his giant goggles covering up half of his face. He was playing alone in the shallow end, tossing rings and making a dramatic show of sucking in his breath before submerging.

Crystal held court in the deep end, practicing her backstroke start off the blocks. Her friend Melissa acted as the stand-in starter, clinging to the side of the pool and telling her to "take your mark" with about as much enthusiasm as a CVS checkout girl. Crystal's brown arms clenched the starting block with impressive force; her face was set and determined. As Melissa yelled, "Go!" Crystal's arms swung back in an arc, and she disappeared beneath the surface, pulsing her legs in a butterfly kick for speed.

Crack!

I shot up, startled by the sudden bolt of lightning across the sky. It extended its menacing fingers toward me and then disappeared, leaving a faint outline of smoke in its wake.

I began to count in my head. The rule was that if you reached fifteen before thunder rumbled after a lightning strike, the storm wasn't coming toward you. But if thunder rumbled at any point before then, it was on its way, and fast.

Five, six, seven . . .

A roar filled the sky, seeming to shake the rickety wood beneath me. I put the whistle to my lips.

"Everybody out! Hit the bricks!"

Crystal, Melissa, and Tyler looked up, wide-eyed, before making a break for it. They quickly swam to the ladders and hauled themselves out of the water, pie-eyed with fright. I hopped down from the stand.

The kids dried themselves off quickly and then either mounted their bikes or ran to the phone, calling their parents for rides home. Faster than they could even wrap themselves in their giant Sponge-Bob towels, the cars pulled up, their honks piercing the humid, now almost pitch-black air.

"Bye, Coach Ruth! Bye, Coach David!" they yelled as they trudged up the hill to safety. They would be back as soon as the sun came out again, their parents more than happy to drop them back off until suppertime. We may have been called life-guards, but really we were tan babysitters in swimsuits.

"Well, looks like it's just you and me," David said. He was inside the concession stand, leaning back on the chair precariously with his feet propped on the ledge.

The first heavy drops of rain fell, splattering on the hot sidewalk. I opened the refrigerator to survey its contents of sugary junk. Skittles, Snickers, and individual corndogs wrapped in plastic stared back at me. I shut the door with a sigh and sat next to David. We watched the sky together in silence, its facade pierced by ferocious bolts of lightning.

"How's it going?" I asked after a few minutes. It was odd, making small talk with someone who used to arrange your dolls in compromising positions every time you left the house.

"Okay," he answered.

"That storm came in quick, huh?"

"They always do." Great, we were commiserating about the weather.

"You want to smoke?" David asked.

"Smoke what?"

"Smoke weed, Einstein." Smoking weed with David was something I never thought I'd do. Not in a million years. I'd never seen him touch the stuff.

"You smoke weed? What about soccer?"

"What about it?" He reached into his bag.

"They don't test you?" He didn't answer and began to pack his bowl, not looking at me.

"David? Hello?"

"What?" He looked up at me angrily with a glint of defiance in his eyes. "Shit, I don't go back to play for, like, two months. What are you, a narc?"

"Oh, I'm sorry. Excuse me for being even the slightest bit

taken aback. My brother is suddenly Willie Nelson, not to mention he's on the job, and I have the audacity to express disbelief."

"Ruth, take it easy. You're all riled up." He put his hand on my knee. "First of all, this weed is about as potent as a cigarette, and second of all, did you really think I didn't smoke weed just because you'd never seen me smoke weed? It's not a big deal, I swear. We'll be fine." He smiled at me.

"It's just weird to me, that's all."

"Yeah, well. I suppose it is." He got up and wrapped himself in his towel. "You want yours? Speaking of weird, it's actually cold."

"Yeah, thanks." He tossed my towel to me, and I covered myself with it.

"Hey, remember when we would dress up Maddie and pretend that she was a human?" he asked, changing the subject.

"Oh wow. Yeah, I remember. That poor dog."

"Yep." He sat back down and lit the bowl. "We would come home from swim practice, eat Pop-Tarts, and watch *The Price Is Right*." He exhaled.

"Remember to spay and neuter your pets!"

"Yep, and then we would dress her up in your doll clothes. Man, I was such a little girl!" He passed me the lit bowl, and I shook my head no. He looked at me for a minute as if to ask, *You sure?* and I waved it away. He shrugged his shoulders and took another hit.

"You were a little, er, sensitive," I agreed. "Speaking of dolls, remember Judy?"

"Oh man," he said, coughing a little as he exhaled. My great-aunt had found Judy at a yard sale and given her to me on my sixth birthday. Her hair had been either ripped or cut out— it wasn't entirely clear—and her face was one only a mother could love. My aunt's motive may have been to make sure that

I loved all babies regardless of their attractiveness, but it didn't work. I had felt a little bit guilty over hating the gift outright, but I had dealt with said guilt by shoving Judy in the back of my closet. Out of sight, out of mind.

David, however, getting wind of my cruelty, had rescued Judy, unbeknownst to me. It was only when I went charging into David's room months later to ask him about a missing pair of goggles that lo and behold, there she was. David had set up a high chair and a makeshift bed for her.

"Talk about issues," said David in a cloud of smoke.

"It was sweet. You were what, eight? A little strange maybe, but sweet." The rain continued to pound the pavement. "Are you high?" I asked.

"Yeah, a little." I could hear the saliva crackling in his mouth. "I'm thirsty."

He pulled four quarters from the cash box. "Whaddya want?" he asked as he walked to the drink machine.

"Diet Coke, thanks."

"Yech," said David. He dropped the quarters in the slots. "How do you drink that shit?"

"Oh, like that Sunkist is so much better. Do you know how many calories are in that thing? You're, like, drinking lunch." He handed me my can, and I popped it open.

"I don't think you need to worry so much about calories."

"Oh shut up."

"*We don't say shut up in this house!*" he yelled, mocking our dad's famous saying.

"Give me a swig of that," I demanded. He handed the orange can to me, and I gulped from it, relishing the sticky sweetness. I handed it back.

"Oh no, looks like the rain is letting up." The storm had been reduced to a drizzle, and the sun was breaking back through the clouds.

"Shit," said David, noticing it too. "How come you're not smoking? Don't you smoke at school?"

"I do. And I smoke here too. The other day I smoked with M.K. and Jill, and Dad busted me."

"No! How?"

"I mean, we smoked and I had to come home before work to eat, you know? He just happened to be on his lunch break, so I was pretty much caught red-handed."

"You had the munchies?" He laughed. "What did you do, eat frosting out of the can or something? Dip Cheetos in barbecue sauce?"

"Ew! Nasty! Who does that?"

He shrugged sheepishly. "It is pretty gross. But don't knock it till you've tried it. There's something strangely satisfying about it."

"Can you imagine me dipping Cheetos in barbecue sauce across the table from Dad like it was no big deal?" We laughed together.

"It wasn't that bad," I continued, "but I guess I was pretty obvious. I ripped into a bag of marshmallows and went to town."

"Oh no! You might as well have been wearing one of those pot leaf T-shirts and a hemp necklace."

"How dare you!" I was full on laughing now. "A hemp necklace!? Never." Our giggles petered out.

"Anyway, he got upset with me. I had to go into work that afternoon, you know?"

"Yeah, I mean, of course he has a valid point. But c'mon. By the time you went up on the stand it would have been a couple of hours already, right?"

"Yeah."

"God, they're so rigid, our parents." He shook his head. "I bet neither one of them ever smoked a joint in their lives. I bet they'd be a lot less miserable if they had."

"Since when do you think they're miserable?"

"Maybe 'miserable' is the wrong word. But I don't think they're happy. I never realized how high-strung or judgmental I was until I smoked weed. They could probably use a little relaxation, don't you think?" asked David.

"Yeah." What did David have to be anxious about? People swooned everywhere he went. I guess I could see how that came with its own set of issues, but certainly none that I could relate to.

"Do you think Mom and Dad made us that way?" he asked.

"Made us what way?"

"You know, anxious. Do you acquire it on your own, or is it something that's programmed from birth?"

"Good question. I don't know. Hey, can I ask you something?"

"Shoot."

"How come you're anxious? I mean, people worship you. You own a room before you even set foot in it."

"Ruth, nobody worships me in Atlanta. Nobody worships me here either for that matter. You've got a warped vision of reality."

"Are you kidding me? You were a high school soccer star! You're good-looking, popular, smart—the whole deal."

"Notice the key word you used. *Were.* Those days are over. I rode the bench all year. Guys like me are a dime a dozen." He slipped the bowl back into his backpack.

"I thought you got a lot of playing time. You were all over the field your freshman year when Mom and Dad dragged me out there for your games."

"They dragged you, huh?" He coughed again. "Freshman year, yeah, I played. This year—that was a different story."

"How come?"

"New talent came in, and mine was waning, I guess. And to be honest with you, I'd kind of lost my thrill for the game."

"Really? But you're so good. I've never seen anyone as effortlessly athletic in my life."

He covered his face with his towel. "Thanks, I guess. But I've been playing since I was in diapers, you know? I think I got kind of tired. And curious."

"Curious about what?"

"What else there was to me, I guess."

"I get that."

"But let's talk about something else, Ruthie. This conversation is getting a little too heavy for my taste." The rain had practically stopped, and the sun's rays were slicing through the mist.

David stood up and walked out from under the snack bar area. "Oh shit! Ruth, c'mere." I got up and walked over to him.

"Check 'er out," he said, pointing to the rainbow arching over the elementary school up the hill in front of us.

11

Like Batman's visage against the sky, the sun summoned every kid in the neighborhood back to the pool as soon as it returned. No sooner had David tossed his empty can in the trash than the parking lot gravel crunched with the wheels of myriad minivans and SUVs.

"Hey, I'll go up first. Are you okay?" I asked.

"Ruth, I'm fine. Take it easy." He put his arm around my shoulder and shook me gently.

"Okay, if you say so." I walked toward the stand as at least ten pairs of eyeballs bored holes in my back. They couldn't get in until I assumed the position and blew my whistle.

"Hey, Ruth, wait." David jogged back. "I forgot to tell you. Jason told me that we have a Kiddy Kare bus coming this afternoon."

"Kiddy Kare as in a group of kids in floaties with Kool-Aid mouths who can't swim?"

"You got it. They're paying a ton for the time, so the board okayed it."

"Oy." I nodded and took the stand. As I blew the whistle, I wondered just how many kids we were talking about.

Van Halen's "Love Comes Walking In" wafted over the

loudspeakers, and my thoughts drifted to Chris. Would we make out? Could it be possible that he would try to have sex with me? My lack of southern dating experience made me unsure. At school, the guy's hand would be down your pants before you could even say hello, but here, in the South . . . one would think that the approach was at least a little more gentlemanly. Then again, depending on your company, a trip to the Krystal drive-thru could qualify as a date, so who knew.

A white van pulled into the parking lot, the words KIDDY KARE emblazoned in red on its side. That was a pet peeve of mine—words misspelled for the sake of cuteness. What kind of example was that setting for the kids at the Kiddy Kare? They would grow up thinking that the "c" was obsolete. I braced myself as the kids began to spill out of the van. One, two . . . twelve, thirteen? Damn. That was a lot of kids.

Their teacher and what I assumed to be her assistant lined them up single file, but even from a distance I could see the excitement vibrating through them. They looked to be in the five-to-seven age range, a mix of white, black, and Latino. They grabbed each other's hands and snaked down the hill.

I watched David welcome them graciously. He seemed sober as he turned on the charm and made a little girl with braids popping up all over her head smile bashfully. The other kids in the pool watched their entry curiously, gripping the wall and peering out over it with be-goggled eyes.

Although most of them had been stuffed into their requisite flotation devices, they started in the baby pool. I thought it was smart of their teachers to do it that way—to get the kids used to the water before turning them loose on the real deal. The baby pool was kind of a joke to the members themselves—it mostly acted as a tanning destination for mothers on the weekends. They would submerge their chairs in the pool and then recline in the water. We secretly referred to it as "Sea World." Replace the buckets of fish with cans of Diet Coke and bags of Doritos and the resemblance was uncanny.

"All right, my turn," said David from below. He climbed up to join me. "There's a lot of 'em, huh?"

"I know. Looks like it won't be so bad, though. The teachers seem capable enough."

"Yeah." He looked over at the baby pool, where they were all splashing around with glee. "They're really cute." I climbed down and walked toward the snack bar, the concrete practically dry now from the sun's post-storm emergence.

"Hey, Coach Ruth." I looked down midstroll to find Tyler at my side.

"Hey, Tyler."

"I keep sinking when I try to do the butterfly kick," he admitted dejectedly.

"Whaddya mean?"

"You know when you said to make S's with your arms underwater? After you've already brought them out?"

I took my whistle off and laid it on the snack bar counter. "Yeah, like this, right?" I demonstrated the stroke to him. "You pull your arms out of the water along with your head and shoulders like this." I spread my arms wide and opened my mouth to simulate taking a breath. "And then you dive back in with your arms in front. Let me see you try."

He did the same and then stopped, looking at me for his next cue.

"Now what?" I asked.

"Well, this is where I get confused. I don't get the S's thing." He hung his head. "I just sink."

"It's not easy to get, Ty, don't worry."

I demonstrated the S's with my own arms, diving in and

then curving into my waist before sending them back out again. "See, this is what pulls the water under you and allows you to come back up again."

He gave it a shot, but the curve confused him. Although one of his arms was making a proper S, the other needed to create a backwards one. For someone just mastering the alphabet, I saw how it could be confusing.

"You know how sometimes they talk about a woman's body?" I asked. He cocked his head at me and wrinkled his freckled nose. "Like an hourglass?" I made the shape with my hands.

His eyes lit up. "Yeah! I've seen that in cartoons and stuff."

"Okay, so that's the shape you're making. An hourglass." I demonstrated the full stroke for him again.

He mirrored me perfectly and smiled broadly. "I get it now!" He repeated it, watching my face for approval.

"Excellent! Well done." This example didn't exactly bode well for his realistic perception of women, but that wasn't my problem. I was his swim coach, not Gloria Steinem.

"Now, another reason you might be sinking is because you're forgetting to kick." I looked around for a towel. "Here, grab that towel and I'll show you."

As he moved to grab his towel from the picnic table, I turned toward the pool. In the corner of the deep end, beneath the stand and off to the right, I saw something flutter. What were the odds? Seeing a butterfly while you were teaching the butterfly. I squinted to get a better look, and my heart stopped.

That was no butterfly. It was a white barrette, and the white barrette was attached to a black braid. One of the Kiddy Kare girls had somehow broken away from the pack. Her braid and its barrette waved on the surface of the water like a flag before submerging with the rest of her.

I reached down to bring my whistle to my lips just in time to remember that I had taken it off. Time froze. Tyler gazed at me in alarm, as he saw my expression change and my body tense. I looked back up at David. His eyes were on the other side of the pool. He had no idea that a little girl was drowning less than three feet away from him.

Move your feet, Ruth! Energy surged through my shaking limbs, and I broke into a sprint. Kids darted out of my way, and the few parents on deck looked up from their gossip magazines in shock. I saw the Kiddy Kare teacher make the connection just as I sprang off the side of the pool and into the water.

The pool was cloudy, but I could make her out in the near distance. *Swim, Ruth. Faster, Ruth. Faster!* Seconds felt like hours.

Finally, I reached her. I grabbed her around the chest and swam her to the surface. A crowd had gathered on land, watching in horror. David was at the ladder, his bloodshot eyes wide.

I ran through the lifeguarding rules in my head. *Keep the victim on her back.* Okay, fine, but how was I going to get her to land? And then what? I looked down at her. Her eyes were closed. Was she breathing? I couldn't tell. How could you even tell if black skin was turning blue? Did that even happen in real life, or just in the movies? How long had she been under? Somehow my head was on fire and my arms were in goose bumps simultaneously.

"Here, hand her to me," said David, who stood on the ladder, submerged up to his shins.

"You have to keep her steady," I said as I tread water.

"I know. C'mon." He motioned to me to hand her over, and I did. He put his hands under her armpits and pulled her up quickly. Her skin shone like onyx as the water ran off of it in rivulets.

As he placed her on the ground and I climbed out, I could hear the teacher sobbing behind me. David looked up at me, his face confused. He didn't have to speak—I knew that he couldn't remember what to do.

Shocked at his ineptitude, I got on my knees next to her head. "ABCs, David," I whispered. "Airway." I tilted her head back and her braids spilled all around like the spokes of a wheel. *Please, God, I know I'm not really religious, but if you could save this girl, I promise I'll get my shit together. I promise I'll figure out this food thing and not be such a jerk anymore. Please.*

I lifted her jaw, and just as I attempted to check for her breathing, she coughed. I sat back. One cough turned into several, and I helped her onto her side. She opened her eyes, and water spilled out of her mouth to pool on the concrete below.

"Hi," I said as tears spilled down my nose. "What's your name?"

She coughed again and looked at me with big brown eyes.

"Tanisha," she whispered.

"Hi, Tanisha, I'm Ruth." I sat her up. She looked around, dazed, and then reached for her teacher, who scooped her up in her arms.

"I don't know how that happened," the teacher said to me. "I don't know how she got away from me and over to the deep end." She spoke as though she was in a trance.

"I don't either." My breath was shallow. I put my hand to my chest as if to will more air into my lungs.

"Thank you so much," she continued. "Ruth, right?"

"Yeah, Ruth." I looked around at the group encircling us. David was nowhere to be found. "Did somebody call 911?" As if on cue, a fire truck's siren sang in the distance.

"I guess so," I said, answering my own question. "We better sit her down and make sure everything is okay." Tanisha was gripping her teacher with all of her might, so to detach her was no small feat. When we finally had her on the lawn chair, David appeared with a dry towel.

"Here you go," he said and wrapped her shivering body. "Ruth, that was amazing." He grabbed my hand.

"Holy shit," I whispered. "I think that took about twelve years off of my life."

The sirens came closer, and suddenly firemen sprinted onto the deck and toward us.

"Everybody out of the way!" they shouted.

"Is this the victim?" the EMT asked me.

"Yes, this is the one." I crouched down next to Tanisha.

"This is Tanisha. I'm pretty sure she's okay." She turned to me and promptly burst into tears again. I put my hand on her arm.

"How long was she under?"

"I don't know," I answered. "I saw her braid bobbing in the water and dove in."

"It couldn't have been that long," said David. "Ruth moved like lightning."

The EMT nodded. "Well, good job. Although with two guards on duty, I'm not sure why this would happen in the first place." I clenched my fists. *Thanks, guy.*

"We're going to have to examine her and take her to the ER, just to be sure everything is okay. Did someone call her parents?"

"I did," the teacher replied.

"Okay, call them back and have them go to the South Shore emergency room. That's where we'll be." He motioned to his colleague to bring the stretcher.

"Hi, Tanisha. We're just gonna take you for a little ride and make sure you're okay. Is that okay with you?"

She nodded as he checked her vitals. "It looks like you're

fine, but we just want to be sure. You're a very brave little girl, you know that?"

Soon she was strapped in and wheeled out—up the hill and into the ambulance, which had arrived directly behind the fire truck. The sirens resumed, and suddenly they were gone. The pool was silent, the water still. Everyone sat in the pool chairs or milled about aimlessly, unsure of what to do.

I collapsed onto the lawn chair and put my head in my hands. David sat down beside me.

"Thank you so much," repeated the teacher. Through my fingers I could see her knees, one of which was skinned. Behind her, the Kiddy Kare kids stood in a single-file line, their faces streaked with tears. I had forgotten about the rest of them. "Um, you're welcome?" I replied, sitting up. It felt strange to be thanked. "What's your name, anyway?"

"I'm Tiffany, and this is Monique." She pointed to her assistant. "I—I don't know what to say. You saved her life." The idea of me, screwup Ruth, saving anything had been ludicrous just that morning. But she was right. I couldn't believe how lucky I had been to spot Tanisha at all. One minute more and who knows where we would be.

"I'm going to take the kids back to the center, but then head to the hospital," she continued.

"Of course. We'll be there too," said David from out of nowhere.

"That's sweet of you, but I should warn you, her mom is—well, she's not exactly a walk in the park. Shit is going to hit the fan." Tiffany gulped. "I'm pretty sure I'm going to lose my job."

"No, you're not, T," offered Monique weakly.

And what would happen to us? Me and David? And the pool?

"Thanks for the heads-up," I said.

"Well, see ya there." She smiled as best she could and directed the kids off the deck, up the hill, and back into the van. We watched them in silence.

David stood up and blew his whistle. The remaining stragglers looked up.

"That's a wrap for the day, people," he said. "We're closing up." I put my head back in my hands and suddenly felt a clammy hand on my forearm.

"Coach Ruth," said Tyler solemnly. "You saved her."

"Thanks, Ty. I guess I did, huh?" My tears began to well as the force of the last half-hour hit me, but I swallowed them back. "We'll get that butterfly down, don't worry." He put his arms around my neck and hugged me. So much for holding back the tears.

"Looks like you've got a fan," said David as Tyler walked away, clearly shaken. He sat beside me on the chair.

"I know I shoulda had that, Ruth," he offered. I stared at him for a moment before putting my head back in my hands.

12

We should probably call Jason," I said to David from the passenger seat. His eyes were firmly on the road, and we hadn't spoken since his half-ass apology. I took a drag off of my cigarette and held it out the window.

"He'll find out from a parent or something. I don't feel like dragging him into this right now, do you?"

"I guess not. What about Mom and Dad?"

"Are you joking? No way. We wouldn't even be able to get the story out before they'd be yelling and blaming."

He had a point. A million bucks said that that blame would be placed on me. *David would never let a kid drown on his watch, but Ruth, well, Ruth was a different story.* Not this time, my friends. Believe it or not.

"I wonder what's going to happen at the hospital," I said. I tossed my cigarette out the window, watching it spark as it bounced off the road in the rearview mirror.

"You don't worry about it. I'll handle it."

"Why should you handle it? I'm the one who saved her."

"Yeah, I know you saved her, Ruth. On my watch." He stopped at a red light and looked over at me. "That's exactly why I want to handle it."

I stared out the window as pine trees whizzed by. "Do you think she's going to sue the pool?"

"Who? The mom?"

"Yeah."

"How could she sue the pool? Isn't drowning one of the risks you take when you send your kid there? And anyway, you saved her, for chrissake."

"I guess, but still. Everybody is so sue-happy these days, you know?"

"If she's going to sue anybody, she should sue those Kiddy Kare assholes. I can't believe they let her wander off." He shook his head in disgust. "I mean, how hard is their job?"

"You sure are judgmental for somebody who was smoking weed five minutes before he took the stand. I thought you said smoking made you less high-strung."

"Ruth, I told you I wasn't high! I was completely sober by the time that all went down."

I stared out the window.

"Ruth, goddammit, I'm talking to you!" he yelled. "If you think for one second that that had anything to do with Tanisha going under, you're out of your mind." We pulled into the hospital parking lot.

"Ruth, fucking look at me!"

I turned to face him. He was shaking. "If you're really so innocent, how come you're so angry right now?" I jabbed. He grabbed my right arm and shook me.

"Jesus! That hurts, asshole!" I punched him in his shoulder.

"I'm angry because this is ridiculous. I am telling you for the last time that I was not high. I don't give a shit if you believe me or not." He shoved me angrily as he released his grip. "If I was high, you were brain-dead from malnutrition."

"Oh, okay, that makes sense, Matlock. If I was so brain-dead, how come I saved her fucking life?" Passersby glanced into the car to see what the yelling was about. David stared straight ahead and gripped the wheel as though he were hanging from the ledge of a nine-hundred-story building; the muscles and bones in his hands were popping out of his skin.

"Ruth, I am begging you not to tell anyone about the weed. I swear that I wasn't high, but if people know that I was smoking, I'm dead." He rubbed his temples. "My time is almost up anyhow, but this would just put the nails in the coffin, man."

"What do you mean, your 'time is almost up'?" I yelled. "What the hell kind of cryptic talk is that? Wait, are you crying?" I was completely taken aback. I hadn't seen David cry since we were kids. What did I do now? Comfort him? I was angry at him, dammit! I leaned forward and tried to pry his hands from his face. "Listen, I'm not going to rat you out to anybody. Don't worry."

"Thanks. I really mean it." He wiped his eyes and sat back against the seat.

"But what the hell are these tears about? And what do you mean that your 'time is almost up'?"

"Nothing. It's nothing." He wiped his nose. "Just know that I feel bad about the kid, okay? I'm going to try to do whatever I can to fix this." He cleared his throat. "And part of that is talking to her mom."

I rubbed my eyes. I wanted to press the issue, but my energy tank was completely depleted.

"Do we know if there's a dad too?" I asked. "How come we just assume there's no dad?"

"So I'll talk to her dad too. Whoever I need to speak to, I will. Let me do this, okay?"

"Okay." I was scared. David had cried. We got out of the car.

"C'mon," said David, gently shoving me forward. We walked into the hospital, and I immediately wanted to leave.

The fluorescent lighting and Clorox and puke odor was a heady mix, and the pained faces of the people waiting to be seen made me self-conscious.

David went to shove his hands into his pockets before realizing that his athletic shorts would not afford him that luxury. "Do you see Tanisha or her teachers?" he asked.

I scanned the room, which seemed to be lit from below by a green lightbulb. "No, I don't see them."

"All right, let's go to the desk."

"Hello," said David. The woman at the desk didn't look up from underneath her hood of hairsprayed bangs. What a job this must be. Dealing with sick people and their neurotic, frightened relatives all day long. He cleared his throat. "Um, excuse me, please."

She glared at us. "What?" So much for southern hospitality.

"Yes, did a drowning victim come in here recently? A little black girl. Her name is Tanisha."

"Tanisha what?"

We looked at each other blankly. "We don't have a last name, unfortunately."

"You think this is Hollywood?" She growled. "Everybody only has one name, like Madonna?"

"No, of course not," said David as I stared mutely ahead. "I'm sorry, ma'am, we don't know her last name. We were lifeguarding at the pool where it happened," he explained. "We just want to make sure that she's okay, maybe talk to her parents if they're here."

"You were the lifeguards at the pool where a little girl drowned?" She shook her head in disapproval. "Guess y'all's lifeguard days is over."

"She didn't drown," I offered. "She—I saved her." She regarded me with an ounce more of interest.

"Listen, we don't mean to annoy you," interjected David. "We just want to see Tanisha. Maybe you could check the log and tell us where we could find her?"

She sighed heavily and began to flip some papers around. "Little black girl. Tanisha Green. She's here. In room 405."

"Is she okay?" I asked, my voice trembling.

"Seems to be."

"Thank you," said David, saving me from saying something that was sure to destroy the moment. "Let's go, Ruth." We got on an empty elevator. My finger shook as I pressed 4.

"You scared?" I asked. I backed up against the wall and then flinched immediately. This place was germ central.

"What's to be scared of? She said that Tanisha was fine. Don't worry, Ruth. I got this."

Ding!

We stepped off and were assaulted by mauve. From the walls to the front desk, to the chairs to even the undertone of the floor tile, it was like being trapped inside the wardrobe trailer for *The Golden Girls*.

We made a left and slowly walked toward Tanisha's room. As we passed open doors, I glanced inside, wondering if I would see spurting blood or women in labor, screaming for epidurals. No luck—all I heard was the faint drone of TV sitcoms and the occasional cough. At room 405, my heart froze in my chest.

"David, why are we here?" I asked, grabbing his hand.

"Because it's the right thing to do."

We lingered in the doorway. There was Tanisha, her gangly body lying on the bed with her braids spread over the green pillowcase. Four other people were in the room—a teenage boy flipping channels on the television, a tween girl perched on the windowsill and texting on her phone, a chubby boy about seven or so who was sitting on the bed with Tanisha and holding her hand. Her mother—at least I assumed it was her mother because of the resemblance, same cheekbones and bright eyes—sat in the mauve chair next to her bed, talking on her cell phone.

"Yes, she's fine. The doctor says everything is okay, thank God. Thank God." She paused, listening to the voice on the other end. "Yes, he was thorough! What you think this is?" She looked up at us with question marks in her eyes. *Who the hell are you?*

Tanisha turned to follow her gaze. When she saw me, she broke into a shy smile.

"I gotta go, Shirl. Somebody's here. I'll call you later." She stood up, a mama bear defending her cubs. "Can I help you?"

"Um, hello." David extended his hand. She glanced down and ignored it. He continued, undeterred. "I'm David, and this is Ruth."

"Hi, Tanisha," I said, waving to her from the doorway. She waved back timidly.

Sensing that we weren't a threat, her mother's tense posture dissipated a bit. "Okay. And?"

"We were the lifeguards on duty when Tanisha had her— her accident."

"Oh really?" Now she was practically snarling. I felt seconds away from having my neck severed.

"So you were the ones who weren't watching my baby? The ones who let her almost drown to death?"

"Well, actually, we didn't let her drown," answered David. I was impressed by his coolness. My voice had an annoying habit of rising several octaves when I was nervous. If I'd been the one facing off with the mom, glass would be shattering throughout the building. "My sister saved her."

I begrudgingly stepped out from behind him. "Hello."

"Tanisha, is that true? This girl saved you?"

"Yes, Mama. She pulled me up out of the water."

Her mother looked me up and down. "You don't look like

much of a lifeguard to me. Whatchoo gonna do if someone over sixty pounds drowns in that pool?"

"I'm stronger than I look," I answered defiantly. Now she was pissing me off. I saved her kid, and she was bullying me?

"I guess you must be." She extended her hand. "I'm Mary, Tanisha's mom. Thank you. I dunno what I woulda done if something had happened to my baby."

"And who are you?" she asked David. "You were the other lifeguard on duty?"

"Yes, ma'am. Tanisha slipped under right beneath my lifeguard stand, so I wasn't able to see her. Ruth saw her go under."

Mary sat down on the edge of the bed. "How you gonna have a lifeguard stand that doesn't let you see the whole pool? Sounds pretty ignorant to me."

"Yeah, well, the idea is that if you're in the deep end, you're more likely to be a good swimmer, I guess," he countered. As discreetly as I could, I pinched his oblique. It was time for him to shut up now.

"Oh, that's the idea, huh?" Sarcasm dripped off her tongue. "Sounds like a pretty self-satisfied way to manage a pool. 'Nothin' bad is gonna happen at this pool, no wayyyy. We all know how to swim.'"

"Mama," said Tanisha, sitting up from her pillows. "Quit bein' mean. Miss Ruth saved me."

"I know, baby. I just don't know what to make of this whole mess." She looked up at me and then back to her daughter. "You want to thank Miss Ruth, T?" She nodded.

"All right, go on." She stood up and motioned toward the bed. I sat gingerly next to Tanisha, who seemed even smaller now, on dry land. Her arms were as wiry as bobby pins.

"Thank you, Miss Ruth," she said. I took in her sweet face, her bright brown eyes, and the smoothness of her forehead. She smiled to reveal a missing front tooth.

"Hey, were you missing that before?" I asked. Her brother watched me curiously, inching up to me like a cat.

"I just lost it in the ambulance!" she replied proudly. "It was real loose befo', but then I guess I jes pushed on it or somethin'. Maybe with my tongue when I was underwater."

"Well, congrats. You look great without a tooth."

"No, I don't, Miss Ruth. I look silly."

"Tanisha, I'm so glad you're okay."

She nodded. "Me too. I shouldn't have been in the deep end. I was jes curious, though. Wanted to see how deep it really was." I nodded in understanding.

"What I can't figure out is how that dumb Tiffany let her wander away like that. How do you lose a child who can't swim at a pool?" asked Mary. "Now Monique, I thought she had a little bit more sense, but I guess not."

"They did seem pretty swamped," offered David. "That was a lot of kids for two women."

"Well then, you know what? They shouldn't have gone to the damn pool. Period."

"Mama," said Tanisha, "please don't git Miss Tiffany and Miss Monique in trouble. I love them."

"Sweetie, I love a lot of things that are bad for me, but you can't let two teachers who almost let you die go unpunished. It ain't right." Tanisha's lip trembled. "I'm sorry, baby. It's a hard fact of life."

She looked at us. "I might have to sue that Kiddy Kare." *Please don't say you're suing the pool. Please just leave it alone.*

"And yo' pool too. Might as well tell you now."

"I'm not sure that's such a smart idea," said David.

"David!" I hissed.

"What, it's the truth!"

Mary watched our exchange with a bemused expression. "You scared?" she asked. "You should be."

"We should get going," I said. Any more backtalk from David and the situation would go from bad to worse, I was sure of it. "Tanisha, I'm so glad you're okay." I hugged her gingerly. She still smelled of chlorine.

"Thanks for letting us see Tanisha," I said to Mary, who stood regally in the doorway. I could picture her in an Egyptian headdress holding court on the Nile.

"Thanks for not letting my baby drown," she said to me. She nodded at David, who had one foot out the door.

"Nice to meet you, Mary," he said. We turned to leave.

"Wait, can I ask you somethin'?" Mary followed us into the hallway. "Now, I know I can be confrontational, and that y'all are prolly scared half to death by the loud, angry black woman. I'm sorry for that. The truth is, I am loud. And in this case, I am angry. Justifiably so, I would say. There were four people supposed to be watching my baby—people I pay good money to—and still, she almost died. Think about that." She paused for effect.

"But what I wanted to ask you, though, is . . . well, it's a loaded question, but I need to ask it."

"Sure, what is it?" asked David.

"If my baby had been white, would y'all have been watching her more closely?" I looked to David, stunned. I thought I would let him take the floor on this one.

"Mary, the truth of the matter is that we watched your daughter more closely because she *is* black."

"Oh, so now you're telling me it's a given that a black child can't swim? It's a race thing?" Her nostrils flared. "Is that what's happening?"

"I think we're done here," I said. I gave a half-wave and pushed David in front of me.

"Don't look back," I murmured behind him.

"I won't."

13

Silence fueled the ride home. No radio, no cigarettes, no nothing. On the plus side, I had saved a kid's life. On the minus side, everything else. I was going to have to take David's secret to the grave and somehow not resent the hell out of him for it, and Mary was going to sue the free world. *Don't forget that Tanisha is alive.* Things could be so much worse right now, worse than I was capable of fathoming—or rather, worse than my privileged white mind was capable of fathoming, as Mary would probably say. The idea that we wouldn't keep an eye on Tanisha because she was black still burned me. It just wasn't true that her life didn't matter to me as much as a white child's would have. We pulled into the driveway.

"Do you think Mom and Dad know yet?" I asked.

"Yeah, I'm sure."

I took a deep breath. "Well, hopefully they won't be too nuts about it."

"You're kidding, right?" David cocked his eyebrow.

"Right." I opened the car door.

On cue, the back door opened, and my dad pushed open the screen. He held Maddie back with his left leg. A blur of white and caramel squirmed behind him.

"Are you two okay?" he bellowed.

"Yes, we're fine, Dad," I answered, stepping over the dog and into the house. Mom sat at the kitchen table, wringing her hands in her lap. She peered at us over the top of her glasses before jumping up to embrace us.

"We've been so worried about you," she said. "Jason called us about two hours ago to tell us the news, but you haven't been answering your cell phones."

"Which, by the way, is ironic considering we pay for those cell phones," Dad interjected.

"Honestly, Sam! Is this the time?" Her look of disdain could have melted steel.

"You're right. Not the point. Where have you been?" he asked again.

"And what happened at the pool?" asked Mom.

"Can we sit down first?" I asked. "Man." We collapsed into our respective spots at the table. To sit anywhere else always felt strange, like you were channeling the other person.

My parents sat down too, anxiety emanating off of them in waves. Maddie, sensing that something was amiss, curled at my feet. I slipped my flip-flops off and buried my toes in her coat.

"So, David, you saved a little black girl from drowning? Is that what happened?" Anger and hurt filled me in equal measure. *Of course. David saved her while I twiddled my thumbs.* I looked at him incredulously.

"No, Mom, Ruth saved her." Their mouths parted in shock.

"Ruth?" asked my dad. He looked at me. "You saved her?"

"What? Is that so impossible to believe?"

"No, of course not, Ruthie, that's not what we meant," Mom replied. She took my hand and squeezed. "We're so proud of you, honey. That's amazing."

"It really is," agreed Dad. He gazed at me with wonder. "Good for you."

"Did Jason tell you that David saved her? Is that what he thinks too?"

"I'm not sure. He was speaking so quickly, and we were so shocked. I'm sorry, Ruth." This was not how I wanted to behave—like a petulant child whose lollipop had been taken away. I wanted to be noble and dignified. Funny how you couldn't fight the role you were most comfortable playing when it came to family.

"I was on the stand, and the little girl—her name is Tanisha—the little girl fell into the deep end," David explained. "She was in my blind spot right beneath me. I couldn't see her." He paused. "But Ruth—Ruth saw her go under from the snack bar. She dove in and swam to her in, like, three seconds. It was pretty amazing." I stared down at the table.

"We're so proud of you." I nodded in response as my eyes welled with tears. To hear that they were proud of me was a rarity.

"Thanks," I mumbled. "It was pretty scary."

"I can't even imagine, honey." Mom got up and kneeled beside me. She hugged me close. "You saved someone's life today."

"Ruth, that's really something." Dad got up too and hugged me from the other side. I looked to my left, through an opening in my parents' entwined limbs, and watched David, who was staring at the floor.

"Well, it's not like David sat on his ass eating bonbons," I said, untangling myself. "As soon as he saw what was happening, he helped me pull her out." My parents went back to their seats and turned their attention to him.

"I would hope so," said Dad. "Let me ask you this. How does a pool have a blind spot? Isn't that playing with fire?"

"I guess it's never been an issue before," mumbled David. "Usually, if you come to a neighborhood pool and you're in the deep end, you know how to fucking swim."

"Language," whispered Mom.

"This was a black girl, this Tanisha?" asked Dad.

"No, she was a white girl named Tanisha. Come on, Dad." David stared at him belligerently across the table.

"Fair enough." He took off his glasses and massaged the bridge of his nose. "Who was she there with? Did she come with her parents?"

"She came with a Kiddy Kare group," I answered. "There were about thirteen of them with two teachers."

"Did the board know they were coming?" asked Mom. "Or did they just show up?"

"Yes, they knew they were coming. Fifteen nonmembers can't just show up unannounced," David said, his voice thick with annoyance.

"So why just two lifeguards on duty?" asked Dad. "With a group like that coming, you'd think that the board would take extra precautions."

"Dad, it's not like they were there by themselves," I answered. "They were being watched by two teachers too, don't forget."

"I thought that a majority of them would be able to tread water at least," added David. "Most of them were in floaties. Either they didn't put them on Tanisha, or she took them off herself when they weren't looking. The whole thing was a major liability."

Dad's ears perked up at the legal jargon. "A liability, huh?"

"Yeah, definitely. I guess the pool really needs the money or something." David arched his back and stretched.

"Did you have to resuscitate her?" asked Mom.

"Thankfully, no. Once we got her out, she started coughing up water. For a second I thought I would have to, but she was okay."

"Did you remember what to do?"

"Of course, Mom, I'm not an idiot."

"That's not what I meant at all! I just wonder if I would be able to remember all of the steps under that kind of stress."

"It's very impressive that you did," added Dad. I stole a glance at David. *He hadn't remembered.*

"So what happened after she came to?"

"David had called 911, so they took her to the hospital to make sure everything was okay. She was fine, we checked on her."

"Don't tell me you went to the hospital," said Dad.

"What's wrong with going there?" asked David. "Why wouldn't we?"

"You did, didn't you?" my dad barked. His chair shrieked over the tile floor as he backed it away to stand up.

"Dad, what's your problem?" I asked. "We wanted to make sure she was okay. It was the right thing to do!"

"Did you speak with her parents?" he asked. "Did they think it was the right thing for you to do?"

"We spoke to her mom," answered David. "It was fine."

"Was it fine? Because you know they're going to sue somebody, and it very well could be the pool. You shouldn't have spoken to them without a lawyer present."

"Dad, what are you talking about?" The pitch of my voice rose. "We did the right thing! How could we not go and see her? She almost drowned on our watch!"

"Exactly, Ruth. Any parent whose kid is endangered on somebody else's watch is like a ticking time bomb of guilt and blame. And I'm sure she wasn't pleased to see two white kids come strolling in."

"What the hell is that supposed to mean?" asked David.

"Exactly what you think it means. If you think for a minute that they're not going to claim some sort of racism, you're out of your naive little minds. A black child drowns at a white pool? Come on, David. Use your head." Dad began to pace.

"We watched Tanisha just like we would watch any other kid at the pool!" I yelled. Was I going to have to defend us to everyone? "The black thing wasn't even an issue! The issue was that we knew she couldn't swim because she came with a group of other kids who couldn't swim."

"Or was it that you knew she couldn't swim because she was black? And you were ticked off that a bunch of nonswimming black kids came to the pool and disrupted the day, so you said, screw it, I'm going to let my mind wander?" Dad replied, using what must have been his courtroom voice.

"All right, Johnny Cochran, take it easy," said David.

"Look." My dad sighed heavily. "I'm just telling you what's going to happen—what people are already thinking. What these parents may claim in court. Not everything is so—"

"Black and white?" I finished smugly.

"Simple. This is a complicated issue. At the pool and beyond, obviously. There's already commotion about the neighborhood changing. This is only going to fuel the fire."

"We wish you had called us," said Mom. "We could have at least voiced our opinion and maybe given you a different perspective."

"Jesus, do you think we should call you every time we have a problem?" yelled David. "Every time something goes wrong? We're not kids anymore."

"This qualifies as more than just a problem, David," said Dad. "This is serious."

"Why can't we concentrate on the fact that Ruth saved a kid's life today and worry about the other shit when and if it happens? You're the most negative people I've ever met in my life. No wonder we're so fucked up."

"What the hell does that mean?" asked Dad.

"It's always a worst-case scenario with you. Always."

"David, that's called being a goddamn grownup!" screamed

Mom suddenly, surprising everyone with the force of her conviction. We stared at her. "You have to plan for the worst and hope for the best. It's being a parent! It's having a career! It's living life responsibly! I am so sick of this entitled bullshit attitude from both of you."

"Whoa!" I said. "Where is this coming from?" I scooped my foot under Maddie's warm belly.

"I just—your father and I, that is—we just care very much about you, and when you make decisions without thinking about the consequences, we worry." She paused. "And David, we just feel like we don't know you at all anymore." She shrugged her shoulders. "You never talk to us, and you used to."

"Mom, what does that have to do with what happened today?" he asked.

"Easy. The old David would have saved Tanisha," I answered angrily. "And the old Ruth would have just, I dunno, stuck her thumb up her ass and watched." I stood up.

"Ruth, sit down," ordered Dad. "Let's not turn this into something petty."

"Now my feelings are petty! Great."

"You shouldn't take it so personally," said David quietly. "I don't really talk to anyone anymore."

"Is everything okay?" asked Mom. I sat down, defeated.

"Yeah, it's fine."

"Honey, are you depressed?" asked Mom.

"Nah. I'm just in a funk."

"You don't need a reason to be depressed, David. It just happens sometimes."

"Marjorie, he said he's not depressed," said Dad. "Leave the kid alone."

"Okay, as long as you know that we're here, and that we love you," said Mom. "And Ruth of course, you too. We love you more than anything. No matter what."

"And we're so proud of what you did today," said Dad. "Really and truly."

"Thanks," I mumbled, embarrassed.

"All right, are we done now?" asked David.

"Yes, we're done. But if you hear from Tanisha's family at all, let me know. I want to be involved. As a lawyer, and also as your father. Okay?" We pushed our chairs back and stood up without responding.

"Okay?"

"Okay," we drawled in unison.

I closed my door and sank onto my bed. What a day. I stared at the ceiling, too tired to take off my bathing suit but irritated by the fabric's pull across my body. It had dried completely— all evidence of my plunge into the pool now erased. I wondered what Tanisha was doing at this exact moment. Was she still in the hospital? Was she home? Where did she live? Was her mother plotting the pool's demise, as my father feared?

I got under the covers. My stomach roared at me angrily. When was the last time I ate? I looked at the clock. It was 8:07. The day had been lost in a blur of emotion. Hanging out with David post-storm had been so nice. So real. And then the consequences that my parents seemed to spend so much time worrying about finally presented themselves. How lucky was I that I had abstained from smoking David's weed? How lucky was Tanisha? My phone beeped, signaling a text. I pulled it out of my bag. Chris.

```
Heard about the pool. You okay, Super-
woman?
```

I smiled. This was the smallest town in the world.

```
Yeah, fine. Helluva day.
```

I attempted to take off my tank top, shorts, and bathing suit without actually getting out of bed. With some squirming and stretching, it wasn't so hard. Maybe I really was Superwoman.

```
We on for tmrrw?
```

Oh right, our date.

```
I think so. No, def. Def yes.
```

```
Cool, see you at 8?
```

```
Cool.
```

Was it right to go on a date when something so serious had just happened? I mean, what was the alternative? To sit at home and mope? I was going.

I placed my phone on the nightstand and curled into the covers, checking my stomach for pliable flesh. I thought of Tanisha, asleep in her room while Mary paced their living room and wondered what to do; my parents watching TV listlessly as their worry simmered silently; David face down on his bed next door, blocking out the guilt that I hoped was haunting him; Chris sipping a beer and maybe thinking about me, or the me he thought I was. I sighed deeply and closed my eyes.

14

S o, you're going out with Chris tonight," my dad said to me as I flipped through TV channels at the speed of light.

I looked up. "Mom told you?"

"No, it was on the local news actually." He sat down beside me on the couch.

"Very funny."

"Right after the segment on the latest whereabouts of the Crichton leprechaun. Did you know he opened his own hair salon?"

"Daaaaaaaaaaad!" I shoved him playfully.

"I like your hair like that."

I reached up to touch it. "What, you mean giant?" After an hour of trying to blow-dry it into submission, I had finally started all over again and just let it be. The current cloud of curl and frizz that sprung from my head was going to be pulled back as soon as it dried.

"It's not giant. It's nice. It's who you are. I don't know why you would want it to look like someone else's hair." I sat forward to get a glimpse of the kitchen clock. It was 7:52.

I cleared my throat. "I wasn't sure if I should go tonight,

considering everything that happened yesterday, but then I thought, why not? It's not like somebody died."

"No, it's not. Thanks to you." He patted my knee. "Does David know that the two of you are going out?"

"I haven't really had a chance to mention it to him. Well, I guess that's not true. I just didn't feel like mentioning it to him. In case it was weird or something, you know?"

"Are he and David still friends? I haven't seen him around this summer at all."

"I dunno. I think Chris mentioned that David hasn't been returning his phone calls for a while."

"Huh." He paused. "Does David seem distant to you too?"

"David always seems distant to me. We barely speak now. You know that."

"I know. I hate it."

"Join the club."

"He's always been pretty forthcoming with us, though, you know? Pretty eager to share. But this year—I dunno. He's changed. Your mother and I have been pretty worried. And then, with this whole 'blind spot' business . . . it just seems so unlike him to be asleep at the wheel like that."

"You mean for Tanisha to go under on his watch?"

"Yes. Exactly."

"Well, last night he pretty much admitted that he was depressed, Dad. You dismissed it immediately."

"Did I?" We watched the muted television together in silence. Two housewives stuffed into velour sweat suits sipped chardonnay from bejeweled wineglasses. "I guess I did," he admitted quietly. "I got too angry and lost control." He sighed. "The thing is, I want to help him, but I don't know how. Just like I want to help you. Between the two of you, and now this near-drowning business, your mother and I are going to our early graves."

I heard a car pull up in the driveway and froze. "He's here," I whispered. I sprang off the couch to check myself out in the bathroom mirror for the millionth time. As I pulled my hair back and twisted it into a bun, the doorbell rang. My heart was racing. *You look pretty, Ruth,* I whispered to my reflection. *You're not fat.* I took a deep breath and switched off the light.

I heard voices in the kitchen. Male voices. I walked tentatively down the hall. Wait, was that David's voice? I rounded the corner to find the three of them—Chris, David, and my dad—in an awkward huddle.

"Hey, Ruth," said Chris. He stepped out of the huddle to kiss me on the cheek. "You look nice."

"Thanks." I looked up to find David watching with a look of befuddlement on his face.

"You two are going out?"

"Uh, yeah, man. I'm taking your sister to that bluegrass benefit downtown," Chris sheepishly explained.

"Get the fuck out."

"David—your mouth," interjected my dad.

David ignored him. "Wow. You two are going out. On a date." He nodded. "Okay, well, Chris, thanks for asking me if I felt weird about it or anything. That was really cool of you."

"I tried to, man, but you didn't return any of my phone calls."

"Ruth, have a nice time," said David, now ignoring Chris as well. His eyes were glazed over, the sparkle completely dulled. I realized that he was high. He left us in the kitchen.

"Well, that was fun," said Chris.

"Yeah, a blast." I cleared my throat and looked at my dad, who smiled wistfully.

"Have fun tonight, guys." He opened the door, and we filed through. "Home by midnight, please."

"Dad, midnight?" I turned around to look at him incredulously.

"One o'clock and not a minute later."

"Yessir," answered Chris. My dad nodded and closed the door behind him. Alone with Chris, I felt a little dizzy. I half expected him to change his mind, jump in his Jeep, and drive away. He took my hand instead, and opened the door for me. I climbed in awkwardly.

"You okay?" he asked, as he started the engine.

"Yeah, I guess. I mean, what can we do?"

"Your brother has been acting strange for a while now," he said, backing out of the driveway. "We used to talk all the time, but this year he pretty much disappeared. I'd leave him messages, and nothing. I even went over to Mercer once with some buddies of mine, and you know, he didn't even call me back to meet up. It really bummed me out."

"How'd he act tonight when you just showed up at our door?"

"Oh, like everything was normal, you know? Like we just saw each other yesterday. I guess he assumed I was there to see him." He smiled.

"Yeah, I mean, why wouldn't he?"

"The look on his face when it was clear that I was there to see you instead was pretty priiiiceless," Chris said, dragging out the vowel.

"Ya can't blame him, I guess. We probably shoulda told him."

"Well, I really did call him a few times. I had seen him at the pool that day I asked you out, but I hadn't spoken to him in so long, you know? The timing seemed off. To tell him that we were going out, that is."

"Yeah, I can see that. Well, what's done is done, I guess. I'll apologize to him later. Or not." We stopped at a light, and he turned to smile at me. He smelled like suntan lotion and aftershave. Tony had always smelled like cigarettes and hot sauce. He liked to drizzle it on everything he ate.

"How are you doin' after the accident?"

"I'm okay, I guess. Sort of still shaken up. The whole thing was so surreal. And now, who knows what'll happen."

"Whaddya mean?"

"Oh, you know, like legal stuff. Her mother may sue the pool."

"No shit?"

"Yeah, no shit."

"But you saved her. I don't get it."

"Well, yeah, but she could make a fuss about the fact that it even happened at all. She went under in David's blind spot."

He whistled. "Man. I hope she doesn't sue. Sounds like that could be a big ole mess."

"Egg-zactly." I stared out the window. My nerves had subsided a bit.

"You like bluegrass?" he asked.

"I'm not so familiar with it, to be honest. But what I've heard, I like."

"Yeah, it's pretty authentic. None of that weepy country tear in my beer shit."

"How'd you get into it?"

"My dad left all these records behind, and one day I just flipped one on," he answered. Chris's dad had left his mom when he and David were in middle school. I vaguely remembered my parents talking about it in hushed tones when it happened. I'd seen his dad once or twice before then, in the stands at their Little League games, but we had never formally met. He had Chris's eyes, and they walked the same way—shoulders back, hands in their pockets, with a bit of a shuffle. Chris had seemed the same to me before and after his dad took off, but then again, my perspective was impossibly one-dimensional. Chris was an Adonis meant for worship, not character study.

"You have a record player?"

"I do."

"Where do you live, anyway?"

"Well, get ready to swoon, girlie. This guy still lives with his mama." He laughed uncomfortably.

"Oh." I paused to consider this. "Well, it's not like you're forty or something and still living at home. You're just a junior in college. And your school is here, so why not?"

"You don't have to try to make me feel better, you know." He reached over and touched my thigh, sending a current of electricity through my leg. "I know it's lame. I'm tryin' to save money, though, and it's just my mom in that big ole house, so there you have it. I basically have the whole second floor to myself." He laughed. "Look at me tryin' to make it sound better than it is! Tryin' to impress you."

He was trying to impress me? My face felt hot. "So you and your mom must get along pretty well, huh?"

"We do. She's really cool. Respectful of my space and stuff." He backed into a parking spot. "But I'm not a mama's boy, I swear."

"You sure about that?" I teased.

"Okay, maybe just a little." He turned the engine off with a playful smirk. "Just a touch." I laughed and reached for the door handle.

"Uh uh!" He reached across me and stopped me from opening the door. "I don't know what them Yankees have been teachin' you, but around here we open the doors for ladies."

I smiled. "Oh, because we're too dainty to handle it ourselves?"

"No, ma'am. Because it's the gentlemanly thing to do." He winked at me and got out of the car. I thought of all of the doors that had been shut in my face and all the lines at school I had been skipped in front of. The South had its benefits. He opened my door and took my hand.

Chris Fuller was holding my hand. I looked around nervously at first, and then proudly as I straightened my shoulders and owned the moment. Damn right he was holding my hand.

"Hey, Chris!" said a pair of very large breasts attached to a very blond head at the door of the bar.

"Hey, Larissa. This is Ruth." He gestured to me.

"Hi," I offered.

She cocked her head and batted her turquoise eyelashes. "Ruth? You're David's sister, right?"

"Yep, that's me."

"How is that boy?" She accepted Chris's money and stamped his hand with a Rebel flag. She motioned to me to put my right hand out. I held it limply in front of me as I gazed inside at the bras hanging from the ceiling and the giant papier-mâché cowboy boot in the center of the room. Not exactly the United Nations.

"He's all right," I answered.

"You tell him I said hey, okay?" She winked at me, revealing gold eye shadow that stretched all the way to her brow bone.

"Sure thing." We made our way inside.

"Who was that?" I asked.

"Larissa Rogers."

"She's very reserved."

"Yeah, a real lady."

We sidled up to the bar. "Okay, I know the decor here is less than glamorous, but don't be scared."

"I ain't scared!" I wrinkled my nose at him. "Who do you think you're dealin' with, anyway? Some Yankee snob?"

"Oh, I know who I'm dealin' with. Ruth Wasserman. The best rebound retriever this side of the Mississippi."

"Very funny." I stuck my tongue out at him. "What's with the stamp?" I held up my left hand and examined it. "The Rebel flag? Really?"

"I know, it's stupid," he agreed. "It's just kitschy, though. You know that."

"Is it, though? Some people around here really think that this flag is a symbol of the South's glory days. You know, like those dumb frat boys who hang them in the back windows of their trucks. Or the rednecks who fly them from their little shanty camps on the banks of the Escatawba."

He threw up his hands in mock surrender. "Yeah, but everyone knows those people are idiots. No one takes them seriously or anything." I raised my eyebrow. "My buddy James comes here with me all the time, and he has no problems."

"James is black?"

"Yep. Hey, what are you drinking?"

"Jack and Coke. Diet Coke."

"Why is it always the skinny girls who order the diet stuff?"

"Because that's how they stay skinny, Einstein." He laughed and turned to place our order. I wondered if, as he said that, he had stopped to think about the old me. The me who hadn't been skinny.

He handed me my drink. "To bluegrass," he said, lifting his beer. We clinked glasses.

"Looks like they're going on a little late," I said as we sipped.

"Yeah, this band isn't exactly punctual. Worth the wait, though." We sat down on barstools and surveyed the scene. I watched a group of people around our age smoke cigarettes at a picnic table in the corner, screeching and guffawing in a drunken haze. The girls were skinny, with arms like pipe cleaners. Did I look like that?

"Why are you pinching your arm?" Chris reached over and playfully swatted my hand away. "That looked like it hurt. You okay?"

"Oh yeah, yeah. Totally fine. I was just scratchin' it. Guess I got carried away." *Ruth, be normal.*

"So, are you worried that that girl's mom is going to sue?"

"Who? Tanisha?"

"Oh, that's the girl's name?" I nodded. "Oh." He took a thoughtful sip of his beer. "I didn't realize she was black."

"Yeah. She was. I mean, she is. You think that changes things?"

"Probably. I mean, there's more at stake now, you know?"

"Yeah, I guess. I just—me and David are the furthest thing from racist, you know? We're Jewish, for chrissake. We've been different here our whole lives too." I took a gulp of my drink. "I'm just nervous about the whole idea of a lawsuit. Really nervous."

"How come? Even if she does sue, it's not your fault the girl fell in. It'll be ugly, and it'll probably take a lot of hours you can never get back, but it's not the end of the world." *David was stoned, Chris.* God, I just wanted to tell someone so badly. The truth was burning a hole in my chest.

"I guess."

"The thing you need to be thinkin' about is that you saved a little girl from drowning. Ruthie. That's a big fucking deal. Excuse my language."

I drained the bottom of my cup with my straw. "It is a big fucking deal, you're right." He put his arm around my shoulders and pulled me into him.

We gazed at each other for a moment. "Do you think it's weird to be out on a date together?" I asked.

"I do. But not bad weird."

"No, definitely not bad weird. Good weird, even." I both wanted and didn't want him to kiss me. "The band!" I announced, a little too loudly, removing myself from his side.

"Yes, ma'am. I'll get us two more drinks and we'll move closer, okay?"

"Okay." Why did I have to be such a spaz? Tony had always

made fun of me. *Damn girl, you are jumpy as hell*, he would say, and pass me a joint.

Chris held up our drinks in victory and handed me mine before helping me off my stool. He moved ahead of me slightly, extending his hand backwards to lead me through the crowd.

"Did you like 'em?" asked Chris after a full set, encore, and three Jack and Cokes.

"I really did!" I swayed slightly.

"Whoa there, lady!" He put his arm around my waist to steady me. "You all right?"

"Yeah, maybe just a little drunk, though." He made the *I want to kiss you* face—his eyes almost misty and then, as he got closer to my lips, slightly crossed.

"You can kiss me if you want, Chris," I whispered.

He kissed my forehead instead. "You killed the moment. Can't do it now. Let's get out of here. I don't want your pops to skin me alive."

Later, as he pulled into my driveway, I popped my third mint. I was sure my dad would smell me coming from a mile away. Chris turned off the engine.

"I had a nice time with you tonight, Ruth."

"Me too. Can I ask you something, though?" I was emboldened by the whiskey coursing through my veins.

"Shoot."

"Did you ever want to ask me out before this summer?"

"Sure, I thought about it. But this town is so small. I didn't feel like dealing with the gossip. Or David."

"C'mon, you can tell the truth, Chris."

"What?"

"I wasn't pretty before."

He furrowed his brow. "Huh?"

"I wasn't pretty before," I said, slower this time. "I was fat."

"Ruth, you were always pretty. The skinny thing is new, yeah, but that's not why I asked you out."

"Not even a little?"

He was flustered. "I mean, you look great, yeah, but I don't think I consciously registered the skinny thing." He shook his head. "You're being rude, I think."

"I'm sorry, Chris. I just wanted to know, I guess. I've always been attracted to you, but never would have thought you'd be attracted to me. I was just curious."

"That's messed up that you would even ask me that."

"I know, I'm sorry. I'm drunk."

"You were always attracted to me?"

"What? Oh, yeah. Didn't you know that?"

"Nope." He moved toward me, but this time I kept my mouth shut. His lips on mine felt nice. Like warm, spearmint pillows. I had imagined kissing him a thousand times but had never really taken into account the physicality of it. I was kissing him, yes, but it was more like I was watching him kiss me instead of actually engaging. He put his hand on my waist, and I jumped.

"Whoa, you okay?"

"I better get inside." I had felt my stomach folding over my waistband where he had touched me. "Give me a call."

"I will." He smoothed my hair back from my face. " 'Night, Ruth."

"G'night." I got out, stumbling a little, and made my way carefully to the back door.

15

Out on the road today, I saw a Deadhead sticker on a Cadillac. . . . A little voice inside my hea—

"Everybody out!" Dana's raspy voice over the loudspeaker jackhammered my Don Henley moment to bits. Jason was a huge fan of classic rock, so 104.5 FM was our summer soundtrack. It didn't matter where I was the rest of the year, if a Led Zeppelin or Genesis song came on, I was instantly transported back to heat, the smell of Doritos, and the sound of splashing water.

"Awww, man!" yelled a couple of kids in the shallow end who were engaged in a heated match of water basketball. I blew my whistle, and they looked up at me in anger.

"Move it or lose it, boys." I hopped off the stand as they swam to the steps. It had been a long day of sun, and now we had our first swim meet. Usually, meets were held on Thursdays, but in light of the accident, we had closed the pool the day before and moved the meet to today, Friday. The other team had graciously complied, for which we were incredibly grateful. Getting thirty to forty kids and their parents to rearrange their schedules on twenty-four hours' notice was no small miracle.

It had been a strange day at work—quiet even. No one had

really spoken about Tanisha, but the accident hung in the air. I mean, what had I expected to happen—a surprise party thrown in my honor? *Congratulations, Ruth! She's alive!* scribbled on a sheet cake? The truth was that I had been secretly looking forward to some sort of fuss being made over me. Maybe a parent or two commending me on my valor or asking for a photo. Alas, nothing. Now, if David had done the saving, that would have been a different story. There would have been a parade, balloons, a band—the works.

We had canceled practice that morning because of the meet, and David and I hadn't talked about our approach—hadn't spoken at all, actually, since he had run into Chris in our kitchen. The thought of seeing him now added a layer of anxiety on top of the nervousness I felt about unleashing my timid little guppies into the world of competition.

As I made my way into the snack bar area, my stomach screeched like a cat in heat. I had overslept and missed my run that morning, so I had skipped lunch. *Tit for tat.* Now I was starving. The smart thing to do would have been to call home and ask my mom to make me a salad and run it down to me. I decided to do the stupid thing and eat my weight in Skittles. Easy energy. I ripped open a bag and emptied a handful into my mouth.

"Y'all gonna use the flags tonight?" asked Dana. She turned the radio dial to pop, and Peter Gabriel was replaced by Ke$ha.

"I love her!" she howled.

"Really?" I swallowed a giant glob of rainbow-colored sugar. "I think she's trashy. And not talented."

"You're such a tight-ass, Wasserman. This isn't Pop 101. Just enjoy the song, girl!" She shook her tan hips, which peeked out over the very low waistband of her hot pink athletic shorts.

I took a swig of water from my bottle. "We are using the flags. Jason and David should be here any minute, but let's go ahead and string those across now."

I looked at the clock. We had an hour and a half to transform the place from unassuming neighborhood pool into official competition zone.

Making this happen involved pulling the heat board and timers out of the storage closet, unfurling the lanes, rigging the sound system so that the race announcer would replace the music, turning our normal snack bar into Snack Bar 2.0, and setting up two tents for the teams to sit, eat, nap, and play cards under. I remembered those tents from my own days as a swim team kid. We'd lay our towels out underneath according to our social caste and then settle our backpacks, goggles, and swim caps all around us just so. I was always on the fringe of the cool kids—not disliked but not exactly liked either. David, on the other hand, was a god. I would sit on my towel in between heats, hungrily eyeing another kid's Little Debbie snacks and self-consciously adjusting my suit over my round tummy while David held court in the very center of The Cool Kingdom, calmly listening to his Walkman as everyone around him clamored for his approval.

The next hour was a whirlwind of preparation. Before I knew it, we had a half-hour left before go-time. Most of my little ones had already arrived. I looked up from putting the final touches on the heat board to find them encircling Tyler and whispering to each other excitedly. I realized that they were talking about the accident, as Tyler was the only one who had actually witnessed the fabled event. He pointed to the deep end for reference as he spoke. I wondered how tangled the story had become in less than forty-eight hours. It was like that game "Telephone" we used to play at slumber parties. You'd start with something like *Monkeys like bananas* and end up with *Kerry is a slut*. The older kids trudged in one by one, reeking of McDonald's, J Lo perfume, and hormones.

"I was thinking we should have a little team meeting. You

know, talk about the accident real quick and get it out of the way," said David, appearing rather suddenly at my side. He was soaked with sweat from the tent setup, his white T-shirt smudged with rust and dirt.

"Sure, that sounds good."

"All right, come on." He blew his whistle, and all of the kids came to attention. *David Wasserman: Swim Team Whisperer.* He motioned to them to follow us to the tent.

"Hey, guys," he said. They had settled their towels and gazed at us expectantly. "We wanted to talk to you about the accident."

"Just to get it out of the way," I added.

"Yeah, I'm sure you've probably heard all sorts of rumors," said David.

"Did a kid drown?" asked Derrick, his voice cracking.

"Nobody drowned. Ruth saved her."

"Good job, Coach Ruth!" exclaimed Julie, standing up from the picnic table. She began to clap, and everyone followed along. The little ones jumped up and wiggled around in excitement, elated by the energy.

Embarrassed that the recognition I had been hoping for was coming from six-year-olds, I motioned with my hands for them to stop. "Thanks, guys. That's really sweet of you. I'm just glad she's okay."

"Was it scary?" asked Tabitha.

"You know, I'm sure it was, but I had to move so quickly that I don't even really remember. I saw her go under, and then that was it. I dove in and swam over as quickly as I could."

"It was a black girl, right?" asked Julie.

"It was," I answered.

"Figures," mumbled Derrick.

"What the hell does that mean?" snapped David angrily. The little ones gasped at his language.

"Uh, it means whatever."

"And what does 'whatever' mean?"

"Nothin'. Forget it."

"I'd like to know what it means, Derrick," I added. "I really would."

"It means that black people can't swim," he answered finally. Tyler snickered beside him.

"Oh, is that so?" I asked. "Is that the way it is? No black people can swim? It's just a rule?"

"Well, yeah."

"Derrick, you are so dumb," said Julie. "Seriously. That is so rude."

"Derrick, why would you say something like that?" asked David.

"I dunno." He picked at his towel. The pimples on his face glowed as his face reddened.

"What do you mean, you don't know?" I asked.

"It's just what I think, okay? I can have an opinion."

"Yes, everyone is entitled to their own opinion, but ignorant talk like that won't be tolerated here. You got that?"

"And anyway, if black people can't swim, how do you explain the black families who belong to the pool, dumb-ass?" asked Julie.

"They shouldn't be here, anyway. That's what my dad says."

"What is this, 1955? Everybody is welcome here, Derrick. Your dad is wrong." My voice shook.

"Don't talk about my dad!"

"All right, everybody take it easy," interjected David. "Derrick, you need to keep your opinions to yourself. Period. Especially if they have no basis in fact whatsoever."

"Ooooooooooh," murmured the older kids. "He told you." A few of the little ones giggled, but most of them kept their eyes locked on me, confused about how to react properly to the tension.

"The fact is, a lot of kids can't swim, and Tanisha just happened to be one of them. She was here with the Kiddy Kare group and somehow wandered away from them," explained David. "She didn't almost drown because she was black, she almost drowned because she broke the rules and left her teachers."

Derrick looked bored. I wanted to knock that pathetic mustache right off of his pimply face. If all black people couldn't swim, what was it that all Jews did? Drink the blood of children at their Passover seders? Once, in elementary school, my father had visited my class to speak about the holiday, and my teacher had asked him that very question. I would always remember the look of horror on my dad's face as he attempted to explain that *no, no, Mrs. Moron, that is not the case at all.*

"Is she okay? The little girl?" asked Ali.

"We saw her yesterday at the hospital, and she was fine," answered David. "We just wanted to clear the air in case you had any questions or anything. We're all okay." I nodded. How come David and I weren't taking Derrick aside right now and arguing the racism out of him? Were we lazy or just realistic? "Everybody stretch out and get ready. We have a swim meet to win!" The kids grinned halfheartedly. Our odds of winning were slim to none.

David and I walked away, and I punched his arm softly. "Nice work back there."

"How come we're the ones responsible for talking some sense into these kids? What does that say about their parents and their prejudices? I felt like I was talking out of my ass."

"Nah, your mouth."

He grinned at me. "Very funny."

Hours later, after we had been soundly trounced by the Fairhope Flounders and the last chlorine-soaked kid and be-

draggled parent had driven away, David, Jason, and I surveyed
the damage. Everything had to be put back the way it was. I
guzzled a Diet Coke and gnawed on a hotdog bun for energy.

"Shit," said Jason.

"Tell me about it," answered David. "Well, the sooner we
get this over with the better. Ruth, as soon as you finish that nu-
tritious meal packed with essential vitamins and minerals, why
don't you start on the flags and stuff? Jason and I will get the
tents." I opened up my mouth to reveal a glob of white dough.

"Nice. Very nice."

I made my way through my various chores, thinking about
my college friends. What was Meg doing right now? And Tony?
A million bucks said that they were not hosing pizza barf off of
a pool deck. I had emailed and texted a bit with Meg since we
had left, but that was it. She had threatened to come visit, but I
had pushed her off. I liked my life to exist in separate compart-
ments, like a TV dinner tray.

"Man, I am tired," announced Jason as we all sat slumped
on the picnic benches.

"Me too," mumbled David. I sat with my head on my right
forearm, staring through a crack in the table at a family of ants
crawling along the wet sidewalk below.

Jason grabbed change from the cash box and walked over to
the drink machine. "Listen, the board wants to have a meeting
about what went down with Tanisha," he said with his back to
us. David and I looked at each other. The board consisted of a
few parents and the family of the pool's original founders.

"Shit, man, why?" asked David.

"Dude, why do you think? A kid almost drowned here.
They want to hear about what happened and figure out this
whole Kiddy Kare mess."

"Are Tanisha's parents thinking about suing?" I asked.

"I dunno, Ruthie. I guess there have been some rumblings

about that." My stomach churned. "Anyway, it's at five next Wednesday night at Miss Carol's house. I see from your schedules that both of y'all can make it, so that's that."

"Why can't we just call her Carol, for God's sake?" I asked, annoyed.

"Oh, cool Yankee girl with her Yankee ways," teased Jason.

"How is that a Yankee thing? I mean, it's ridiculous. 'Miss Carol.' Seriously?" Jason burped loudly in response.

"Hey, Jason, I got a question for you," said David.

"Shoot."

"That wall over there, between the bathrooms. It's so blah, man." Jason and I redirected our gazes to the aqua wall.

"Yeah. And . . . ?" said Jason.

"Well, I was thinkin' about painting a mural there, if that was okay with you. And with the board and stuff."

"A mural?" Jason laughed. "That's some Da Vinci shit! Wheredya get that idea?"

"I dunno, I just thought of it. I've always messed around with drawing and painting and stuff, you know that." I watched him curiously, surprised by his request. He had been very into drawing and painting growing up—taking some classes at the community college on the weekends when he wasn't playing soccer and, of course, since there was nothing he did that he didn't excel at, winning a few contests in the process—but I thought he had since moved on. Our parents hadn't exactly encouraged a fine arts major. He gnawed on the cuticle of his right thumb.

"Hmmm." Jason stood up. "Well, what would you paint? Some kids in the pool? A giant portrait of me?" He looked at me. "Ruth's ass?"

"You're a regular comedian. David's good. I swear. I think it's a cool idea," I said. David gave me a smile as thanks.

"I'm sure he's good, Ruthie—it's not that. I just wonder what the board will say. And when would you work on it anyway, David? After work?"

"Yeah, sure, whenever I can fit it in. And you know, I'd paint stuff that has to do with the pool. I wouldn't do anything weird."

"All right, I'll just tell the board. Screw asking. They've got enough on their plate right now with this Tanisha business. You're right, it would spruce up the joint."

"Thanks, Jason, it should be cool." David was smiling. Jason got up to gather his things, and I stood up and stretched my arms to the sky.

"What are you going to paint?" I asked.

"Not sure yet."

"Remember when you won that craft show contest in elementary school and some lady bought your painting for, like, sixty bucks?"

"Yeah. It was a charcoal drawing, actually. Of a blue heron. I thought I was a millionaire." He smiled.

"Hey, can I get a ride home?"

"Shit, Ruth, I'm sorry. I'm going out."

"Seriously?"

"What?"

"You can't drive me home when it's, like, a minute and a half out of your way, tops?"

"Dude, you have your bike here! What's the big deal? You'll be home in two seconds."

"Maybe I'm tired!"

"Ruth, what the hell?"

"Hey hey, Wassermans!" Jason approached us with the keys in hand. "No cursing. Peace and love."

"Jason, can you give this little baby a ride home?" asked David.

"Fuck you." I grabbed my backpack and walked out.

"I thought you would want to ride your bike—you know, to burn off the imaginary calories from your nonexistent dinner!" yelled David as I walked my bike up the hill. I wished that I had the strength to tackle him to the ground and scratch the life out of him the way I had when we were kids. It was amazing how he could be so endearing one minute and then a completely self-ish prick the next. I got on my bike, but immediately thought better of it and turned around. Jason and David were getting into their cars.

"Oh shit, you're not going to shoot me, are you?" asked David, throwing his arms up to the sky in mock surrender.

"You're a totally subpar artist, by the way!" I yelled. "I was just being nice. That mural is going to be a joke!"

I hopped back on my bike and wobbled away, tears rolling down my cheeks. Why had I yelled that? It wasn't even true. What was true was that I had saved his pot-smoking ass from who knows what by rescuing Tanisha. This was how he repaid me? By embarrassing me in front of Jason and then refusing to go two minutes out of his way to drive me home?

I made a left and headed toward M.K.'s house. My exhaustion was replaced by a manic rush of adrenaline. I tore up her driveway and parked my bike as the garage light went on. The back door opened, and M.K. appeared in a green face mask.

"Wass?" She came closer. "You've been crying! What's wrong?" She went to hug me, but I bobbed out of her grasp.

"Easy, Kermit," I sniffled.

"Oh! I totally forgot about this crusty thing! Come in, come in." She held the door open for me, and I followed her into the kitchen. The counters were strewn with face masks and nail polishes. "It's beauty night," she explained. "Sheila's on a date. Here, make yourself at home while I wash this mess off in the bathroom."

I dug in her purse and grabbed a cigarette while simultaneously opening the fridge to look for alcohol. Pink wine. Perfect. I poured myself a glass.

"I'm on the back porch!" I yelled. I sat on the swing and lit up.

"So, Wass, what's the deal?" M.K. joined me, her face scrubbed and glowing like a nightlight. "You okay?" She took a sip of my wine.

"I just—David is such a jerk." I fought back another round of tears with an inhale of nicotine.

"What happened?" I explained the story to her as we rocked. "See, now when I tell it, it sounds like I overreacted," I said when I was done.

"Maybe a little. But he's really been acting like a douche."

I put my cigarette out in the ashtray and sat back with a giant exhale. "There are just so many things that suck about our relationship. Other brothers and sisters don't act like this."

"How do you know?"

I sighed. "I feel bad for saying that about his art. That was rude."

"Yeah, but who cares. Jason would let him paint the Mona Lisa on his ass if David asked. He's, like, in love with him."

"True."

"Do you think he'll ice you out now?"

"Who knows. I guess I should probably apologize."

"Why should you have to apologize? He was the dick. Make him sweat it out."

"Are we talking about my brother or my boyfriend?" I shook my head. "What is wrong with me? Why do I care so much?"

"Because you love him, I guess."

"I guess."

M.K. lit a cigarette, and we swung.

16

I lay in bed, staring at the ceiling in the early morning light. I had another Khaki lesson today. My second foray into the world of an exercise and diet coach, and my stomach was empty save for a handful of Skittles and maybe some leftover globs of hot dog bun. I slowly sat up. Tiny white stars danced in front of my eyes.

I pushed my sheet off and placed my feet on the floor. Immediately, they were licked by Maddie's sandpapery tongue.

"Maddie." I reached down, scooped her up, and kissed her on her wet nose. "Mornin'." I put her on the bed and lay down beside her. "I haven't been paying enough attention to you."

She panted, patiently waiting for a more profuse apology. "I'm sorry, Maddie Mae." She flipped onto her back and offered up a pink belly for scratching.

I ran my fingers back and forth in her fur and listened to my stomach growl. "Okay, that's a wrap." She looked at me accusingly. "Sorry, Mads, I have to eat some breakfast before I keel over and die."

I stood up, closing my eyes for a moment in an attempt to clear my head. I made my way to the kitchen with Maddie following behind me—her nails tickling the tile floor.

"Morning, Dad." I made a beeline for the refrigerator. I grabbed the milk, cereal, and a bowl. I wistfully measured my one cup of flakes, then carried the bowl to the table.

"I love cereal," I announced breathlessly three minutes later when every last flake was gone.

"I can see that." He pushed his own empty bowl away and grabbed his basket of pills. He pulled a bottle of multivitamins out and unscrewed the cap.

"There are a whole lot of bottles in there, huh?"

"Yes, ma'am." He patiently unscrewed each bottle, extracted a pill, and placed the pills in a precise line.

"How come you don't get one of those weekly pill containers? You know, the ones with a pod for each day of the week?"

"Too depressing. Besides, I like the ritual." He eyed my bowl. "You gonna drink your milk?"

I looked down at my bowl and then back up at him. "Of course." I dutifully poured its contents into my mouth.

"Are you working today?" he asked.

"Later. But you're never gonna guess what my new side gig is."

He raised his eyebrows. "Please tell me it's legal."

"Very funny." I took a sip of his water. "You know Laney Moorehouse? From the pool?"

"Does she live up the block? Over on Maple?"

"Yeah. With the frosted hair?".

"What does frosted hair mean?"

"Never mind. She drives that convertible Beemer?"

"Oh yes. The one with the Saban/Palin sticker plastered across its bumper?"

"Dad! You're joking."

"Wish I was, Ruthie. Wish I was."

"Shit." I sighed. "She's asked me to walk her daughter a couple times a week."

"Walk her daughter?"

"Yeah, take her for walks, maybe a bike ride or two. She wants me to get her excited about exercise and stuff."

"Her daughter is overweight?"

"Yeah. Strange, right?"

"It doesn't sound strange so much as sad. That poor little girl is probably tortured by her mother night and day about her weight." He shook his head and began placing his bottles back into the basket. "Did we ever make you feel badly?"

"Dad, I've already been through this with Mom." I looked up to meet his eyes, which glistened back at me.

"But did we do this to you? Make you obsessed with food?"

I had thought about it a bit since the mall and come to the conclusion that my mom wasn't the only Wasserman at fault, that it had a little to do with all of them. How many times had David made fun of my belly or my dad demanded I go on a jog with him? They'd never made me feel fat per se, but they'd definitely instilled in me a general embarrassment about the way I looked.

"I mean, yeah, you guys weren't exactly shy about mentioning my weight, but I know that you were only trying to help. Plenty of other people gave me grief, don't worry."

"We were trying to help, that's true, but maybe it wasn't for us to say that you even needed it. When you're a parent, sometimes you just want your kids to be happy so badly that you don't stop to think that maybe they can figure out their happiness on their own." He smiled weakly at me and let go of my hand. "I love you so much, Ruthie."

"Dad, I love you too!" I stood up, my chair scraping loudly on the tile floor. "And by the way, I'm fine! It's called a diet, for chrissake! I don't know why everyone is so dramatic about it." I hugged him. "Now, if you'll excuse me, I'm off to walk a kid."

"Ruth, would you come to services with me next Friday?"

He looked small and tired, shrunken somehow by our conversation. How could I say no?

"Sure."

He lit up. "That's great. Very good. I'll talk to David and your mother too. We'll make a night of it—services and dinner."

"Okay, Dad." I smiled at him and trudged back to my room to change.

"So, if you were an animal, what would you want to be?" I asked Khaki as we rode our bikes side by side down the street.

"Hmmm. A dolphin, I guess. They're super smart and cute, and everybody likes them."

"That's true. Good call."

"What would you want to be?"

"I'm not sure." I stood up and pumped the pedals vigorously. "Maybe a leopard? Or a lion?"

"No offense, Ruth, but that's pretty predictable." I'd told her to lose the "Miss."

"Excuse me?"

"Well, it's true. Every girl wants to be a cat of some . . . sort," she panted as she tried to keep up. "Bor-ing."

"Are you kidding me? A nine-year-old is schooling me on being boring?" I reached over and wiggled the handlebar of her bike.

"Hey! I'm gonna fall!" she shrieked, laughing.

"Okay, you're right. That is boring. What about a giraffe?"

"That works. Much better." She snuck a sideways glance at me. "You have a long neck." A steep hill loomed in front of us. Khaki came to a stop.

"Come on, let's tackle this," I urged, circling back. She looked at me with wide eyes.

"I don't wanna."

"C'mon," I ribbed.

"I said I don't want to." She dismounted completely and released the kickstand with an angry shove. I got off my bike too.

"So what do you suggest we do instead? Walk up?"

"I guess." She pouted.

"Seems like it would be a lot faster if we rode it. Probably would take about half the time."

"Yeah, for you," she mumbled.

"What does that mean?"

"You're skinny!" she whispered accusingly.

"I'm not—" I stopped myself from arguing. She looked up at me with tired eyes, her cheeks flushed crimson from exertion. "Well, I haven't always been skinny." She considered this while a car approached behind us.

"C'mon, let's pull over and cop a squat," I said. We wheeled ourselves over to the shoulder and planted ourselves in a lush yard. "I was just like you when I was little."

"Yeah, right."

"I swear. Scout's honor."

"Then how come you look like this now?"

"Well, first of all, I grew into my skin. My mom called me a late bloomer."

"That's what mine says I'm gonna be."

I nodded. "See? So there's that. But I also exercise and watch what I eat." *That's one way to put it.*

"But I like food," she whimpered. "I don't want to eat those dumb salads my mother makes me, or have an apple for dessert." She pulled a clump of grass out of the lawn, leaving a brown, bald patch behind. "I hate almonds," she declared.

"You don't have to eat almonds. And you can still have dessert sometimes. You just have to be more mindful about what you're putting in your body. And you have to—*have to*—

exercise." She sighed heavily. "It's not so much about losing weight, Khaki, it's about feeling better."

"I feel fine."

"Do you?"

"No."

"What do you feel like?"

"I dunno." She stopped pulling the grass and splayed her hand out on top of the ground. Something about the combination of her chipped blue nail polish and seemingly knuckle-less digits made my heart break a little bit. "I feel loose, I guess."

"Loose, huh? What does that mean?"

"Like when I'm walking or something. My thighs rub together. They're *loose*." She looked up at me. "I get a rash from it," she whispered. "And my pants—the ones with the buttons? Sometimes they hurt my stomach."

"I know what that feels like," I said. "They hurt so badly by the end of the day that you can't think about anything but taking them off."

"Yeah." She sighed. "And at school I always get picked last for stuff," she confessed.

"Like what?"

"Kickball and Red Rover and stuff. Nobody wants me on their team. They think I'm fat."

"That's not true. Maybe they don't pick you because they're intimidated by you."

"Give me a break."

"Well, I picked you to be my exercise buddy."

"Laney paid you to pick me. It's not the same."

"Well, fine. I guess that's technically true. I would pick you anyway, though. And that's why we're out here together, you know? So you can feel less *loose*. Biking and walking will make you feel better in the long run, I promise. Stronger. Tighter even."

"It's not making me feel stronger right now."

"I know, it's no fun in the beginning. But that's the thing about exercise. The more you do it the easier it becomes." She eyed me warily. "I swear. Practice makes perfect. Well, not perfect. No one needs perfect. Better, though." I thought about my dad and the way he would try to make me train for soccer season in high school. *C'mon, Ruth, let's run around the block*, he would say as I sprawled on the couch watching pregnant teenagers on MTV and eating fat-free Pringles. I'd roll my eyes and turn the volume up. Later, as I panted and wheezed my way through drills with the team, I would curse my own laziness. I had said no to him out of stubborn self-consciousness. *You think I'm out of shape and need to train, huh? I'll show you.*

Khaki touched my hand. "Okay, let's try this stupid hill."

"That's the spirit, Khak. If it doesn't work out, so what? We'll stop and walk the rest of the way."

"Okay," she mumbled. "But if I feel like stopping, I'm stopping!"

"You got it." We wheeled our bikes back into the street and began the slow trek together.

"Hey, you want the umbrella?" Kevin gazed up at me from below the stand, his hand shielding his eyes from the sun.

"Nah, I put on a ton of sunscreen. Thanks, though."

"No problem. Although I don't know how you do it. When I come up, I'm definitely rollin' it out."

"It's the whole olive skin thing. I don't roast as easily." He regarded me with his token blank expression. I shifted focus to my crotch, suddenly paranoid that it was hanging out of my suit.

"Yeah, well, I'll be back in thirty. See ya."

"See ya." He walked away and blew his whistle at Crystal, who was standing on the side of the pool, bossing Melissa around. She jumped.

"I wasn't doin' nothin'!" she screeched in protest. Kevin kept his eyes ahead, unfazed by her reaction. She pouted and then jumped in, attempting a toe touch.

"That was good, Crystal," Melissa said to her as she came up from the water. She nodded as if to say, *I know.* I wondered if Khaki had any friends.

Jill's VW bug turned into the pool parking lot. Malik, his dreads unmistakable, was in the passenger seat. They got out and waved. Jill didn't have a membership, but I always let her in. She loved to lie out more than anyone I had ever met. Her method of doing so went beyond OCD into a whole new realm. Once her sunscreen was applied evenly to the entire surface of her body—even those spots in no danger of sun exposure—her towel was adjusted just so, her chair was angled so that no rays would escape her, and her drink was positioned for optimal sippage, she would collapse in a heap of bliss. She roasted each side evenly, setting her flip to her phone alarm. I had always wondered secretly if her obsession with tanning went hand in hand with her preference for black men. I waved back.

As they made their way toward me, I scanned the crowd for any glances of disapproval.

"Hey, Wass!" Jill climbed up the ladder to give me a hug. "Thanks for lettin' us come here to tan."

"Sure, no problem. Hey, Malik," I added.

"Hey, Ruth. Long time no see," he shouted up. "You look good!"

"You don't think she's a lil' skinny?" asked Jill. "I mean, come on."

"Damn, girl! You can be salty as hell sometimes." He scowled at her and then looked back at me. "You look great."

"What? I don't say anything behind Ruth's back that I don't say to her face. Right, Ruth? We've been that way since first grade." She smiled up at me in her Ray-Bans.

"Yeah, for better or for worse," I answered. "Go grab some seats, and I'll come talk to you later. I kind of have to keep my eyes on the pool here."

"Of course. Ruth, you know I love you, right?"

"I know, Jill." She and Malik sauntered off to find seating suitable to Jill's optimum sun exposure standards, and I refocused on the diving board. Derrick was climbing the ladder—his adolescent awkwardness emanating from every pore. Slumped over like a ninety-year-old man, he carried himself as though he were apologizing.

"Do a flip, fat-ass!" yelled Julie from the shallow end. I blew my whistle.

"Language!" She looked at me and put her hand over her mouth in apology, her glitter nail polish glinting wildly in the sun. "Sorry, Coach Ruth! My bad."

"Yeah, watch your language!" Derrick yelled, straightening his posture now that somebody was on his side. "You should sit her out," he called to me.

"I think I can handle my job without your advice, thanks." He took a running start and leaped off the board, rounding his gangly body into a somersault before crashing into the water's unforgiving surface on his back. The sound of his skin slapping water made me wince.

"Nice one, genius!" yelled Julie. Derrick surfaced, his face contorted in pain.

"Owwwwwww," he moaned. Crystal and Melissa watched him, wide-eyed.

"My turn," said Kevin. He had snuck up on me again.

I climbed down and continued to watch the pool as he took

his seat. "Can you hand me the umbrella?" he asked. I hoisted it up to him.

"Is that Jill Dobbs over there?"

"Yeah." He made a face as the umbrella unfurled. "What, not a fan?"

He shook his head.

"Naw. And not of her boyfriend either."

"Really, why?" My stomach turned as I anticipated his answer.

"Has she always been a nigger lover?"

"C'mon, Kevin!"

"What?" He looked at me in complete innocence, as though I was the one who was an asshole.

"She's my friend. And so is he."

"Well, that's your choice, ain't it? You'd think after one of them practically drowned here that they'd know where they weren't wanted." I stared at him for a few seconds and then just walked away, ashamed by my cowardice but too much of a wimp to take him on. My face burned.

"Hey, Wass, come talk to us!" said Jill as I passed by their chairs, my head hung low.

"Gotta get back to the snack bar," I mumbled. "I promise I'll come hang in a little."

I was a horrible person. Worse, a spineless wimp. Why was I intimidated by Kevin? Did his thinking I was cool really trump defending basic human rights?

I sank into the plastic pool chair and stared morosely over the snack bar counter. Kevin was sprawled out in the umbrella's shade, twirling his whistle around his index finger. I wished he would say something stupid to Malik and that Malik would flatten his face with one punch. This wasn't the pool I had grown up at. Or was it? And what did Kevin mean by "weren't wanted"? Did he think that David and I were racists too? Did he even know that we were Jewish? Jesus.

A sharp rap on the wooden counter jolted me out of my spiral.

"Earth to Ruth! Come in, Ruth." David smirked at me, and held up two large cans of paint by their handles. "I went down to the art supply store and bought some stuff for the mural," he explained excitedly.

"Cool," I replied unenthusiastically.

"What's up your ass?" He shook his head and walked away.

Great. Leonardo da Vinci was here. Meanwhile, I had saved a kid's life to almost zero gratitude from David or anyone else, and a Klan member was watching the pool. I looked at the clock. It was almost time to relieve Kevin.

"Hey, guys," I said as I passed Jill and Malik. Jill was reading an *Us Weekly* and Malik's eyes were closed. He opened one.

"You're blocking my sun, babe," said Jill. "Move a little to the left."

Malik shook his head. "She's obsessed. Forgive her, it's beyond her control. How you likin' Michigan?"

"It's cool. I like it a lot, actually."

"Helluva football team. They actually sent a recruiter down to talk to me, but my mom would have killed me if I had gone that far away."

"She lives for her precious Malik," added Jill, rolling her eyes.

"How's FSU?" I asked.

"Good. I like it down there. It's hard balancing classes and football, but I'm trying."

"Do you miss Jill like crazy?"

"I do, I do." He put his hand on her brown belly, and she smiled.

"It's not easy, but we're makin' it work," she said. "At least that's what he tells me. I'm sure there's no lack of hoochies swarming."

"All the hoochies in the world can't compare to you."

"Awwwwwww." Jill grabbed his hand.

"Okay, I'm going to go puke now." I smiled. "See ya when I get down."

"How long do you go up for?" asked Jill. "And what's your brother doing over there?" She shielded her eyes with her hand.

"Half-hour, and he's painting a mural."

"A mural? Cool. But what about your back?"

"What about my what?"

"Your back? You're up there for half-hour shifts all summer long, but your back never gets tan! Don't you hate that?"

"Somehow I carry on." I waved and continued walking.

Kevin looked down at me. "You're just in time. I was about to burst into flames."

"Hey, Kevin?" My heart beat like a drum in my chest.

"Yeah?"

"I don't want you to ever say that word around me ever again."

"What word?" I furrowed my brow. "Nigger?"

"I said, don't say it."

"I can say whatever the hell I want about whoever the hell I want. I don't need your permission." He climbed down, and I kept my eyes on the pool. "And besides, Jill doesn't even have a membership."

"So you're okay with being a racist?"

"Sure am."

"You know I'm Jewish, right? And that David's Jewish?"

"Yeah, so?"

"So don't you hate on us too at your Klan meetings?"

He shook his head. "I've never said shit to you about being Jewish."

"But obviously you've thought it."

"This conversation is boring. Watch the pool." I wanted to kick his pointy teeth right into his smug little mouth. He walked away and then circled back.

"You know, we've always been cool, Ruth. Let's keep it that way."

"I meant what I said. If I ever hear you say that word again, or you so much as look sideways at Jill, or Malik, or any other nonwhite person who comes here, I'll—"

"You'll do what? Tell the board? Good luck with that." He sauntered off, and I fought back tears of frustration and disbelief. I hated him. I hated him—but for a change, I liked me.

17

On my run the next morning, I rehashed yesterday's conversation with Khaki. Was I inadvertently awakening the crazy Khaki that lurked inside of her? I desperately wanted to teach her the sane way to handle food and exercise, but would it backfire? She was so smart. Maybe she'd be able to lose weight and not spend the rest of her life calculating calories at twenty paces. Then again, I was smart and look what had happened to me. A loud honk made me catch my breath in fright. I turned around to find M.K. on my tail, grinning broadly.

"Need a ride, sweetie?"

"Follow me home!" She nodded and waved me on.

"Are you stalking me?" I asked. She leaned against the hood of her car in my driveway, drinking a Diet Mountain Dew. Her bottle's contents glowed chartreuse in the bright sun.

"Maybe. Where have you been? You don't call, you don't write."

"I'm sorry, Reed." I walked over to her. "Things have been sort of nuts around here."

"So I hear! Hello, Lifeguard of the Year!" She put her arm around my damp shoulder. "Uch, sweathog." She wrinkled her nose.

"Yeah, that's me all right. Lifeguard of the Year," I replied.

"You workin' this morning?" she asked.

I shook my head. "Nope, I have the day off."

"Nice, I'm kidnappin' you for a little bit."

"Technically, I think that kidnapping involves no prior warning."

"Okay, smart-ass, get in the car. I need some company runnin' somethin' over to Dwight's real quick. We broke up again."

"Wait, what? What happened?"

"Oh, just the usual shit." She rummaged in her purse for a cigarette while starting the ignition. "We're takin' a break."

"Are you okay?"

"I'm fine, Wass. You know we do this every couple of months or so. It keeps things interesting." She exhaled smoke as we backed out into the street.

"But why? What are all of these breaks even about?"

"It's usually a jealousy thing. Either he's talking to some girl, or worse, sleeping with her, or he swears I'm making eyes at, like, the Burger King drive-thru guy."

"Sounds like your grievances are a little more serious than his." I stared out the window for a second before continuing. "Reed, why would you stay with someone who cheated on you?"

"Oh, he doesn't mean it, Wass. He's a guy. He can't help it."

"You buy that?" I asked. "That his dick is beyond his control?"

We stopped at a red light, and she looked over at me with sad eyes. "No."

As the light turned green she added, "But I love him, Wass. What can I do?"

"M.K., it's not like this is the only guy you'll ever love in your entire life! There will be others who actually respect you and treat you right. You've never even tried to meet one."

"You sure do talk a lot for somebody who's never really been in a happy relationship either." I looked at my lap. "That Tony guy didn't exactly sound like a prize."

"Okay, fair enough, but we dated for what—a semester? We're talking about years here with you and Dwight."

"Wass, honestly. Enough. It is what it is." She winked at me. "I know you hate that saying. That's why I used it." I stared out the window, pouting.

"Thanks," I replied.

"Can we quit gabbing about dumb Dwight and talk about you, please? Tell me about the accident. You didn't tell me anything the other night." I recounted the story for her, minus David's weed.

"I can't believe that David Wasserman was asleep at the wheel. That's so unlike him," she said when I had finished.

"Yeah. It is."

"Did he thank you profusely or what? You saved that little girl and his ass in one fail swoop."

"Yeah, I guess so. In his David way."

"Well, that's bullshit. He better step up." She made a left onto Dwight's dirt road. His parents lived in a giant house in the country, filled with wooden ducks and plaid wallpaper in various shades.

"Is the little girl so cute? What's her name?"

"Tanisha."

"Tanisha," she repeated. "I'm telling you, some of these names. Remember our friend Tequila in the third grade? I mean, c'mon. Tequila?"

"I hardly think Tanisha is as bad as Tequila," I replied. "Maybe it's got something to do with black culture that us crackers are totally clueless about." If M.K. revealed her own hidden racism reserve right now, I would lose it.

"Mmm, maybe." We pulled into Dwight's driveway. His

enormous beige truck sat in front of the house—a vehicular version of a giant penis.

She turned off the engine. "A hundred bucks says that there are a ton of idiots up there talking racist crap."

"You mean at the pool?" I asked with relief.

"No, at your house. Of course the pool, dummy."

"You want that hundred bucks in twenties or tens?"

She shook her head. "That is nasty. Ignorant and nasty." She looked over her shoulder into the backseat. "All right, time to hand off the bag."

"How many times have you two handed each other the same damn bag?"

"Do I look hot?" she asked, expectantly.

"You're on fire," I answered.

"Okay, be right back." She got out of the car and adjusted her cutoffs, which were dangerously close to exposing ass cheek. I held my tongue. As she walked away, I lit a cigarette.

I watched her fidget as she rang the doorbell. Dwight opened it shirtless, his impressive beer gut straining against the waistband of his basketball shorts. He leaned on the doorjamb as she handed him the bag dramatically, turning to leave as soon as the handoff had been made. He grabbed her arm, and they took turns making wide eyes and gesturing at each other. I could see the same scene ten years from now—a couple of kids loitering in the doorway, M.K. inside and Dwight on the porch, begging for forgiveness. It was depressingly easy to envision. Where would I be in ten years? Not here. That was for sure.

She turned to leave again and this time went through with her departure. I watched Dwight watch her walk away. He gawked at her backside as she gave me a victory wink.

"Oh, Wass, don't be such a stick in the mud," she said as she got in.

"What?"

"I see you, you know. The look on your face."

"I'm sorry. Ignore me." She started the car. "I just think you can do better, I guess."

"Yeah, yeah. Hey, have you gone out with Chris yet?" she asked as we headed home.

"Yeah, actually. Right after the accident."

"I can't believe you didn't tell me!" She punched me in the arm.

"Ow! I'm sorry, I've just kind of had my head in the sand, I guess. We just went to see this bluegrass band play downtown. It was fun."

"Did y'all do it?"

"No, we did not *do it*. We did kiss, though."

"What was that like?"

"Really nice." I took a swig of her warm soda. "I'm seeing him again tonight."

"Ooooooooohhhhhhhhh, Ruthie has a boyfrienddddd!" she teased. "What are y'all gonna do?"

"No idea. I was thinking about canceling, but I guess I won't."

"Canceling? Why?"

"It's been an intense couple of days," I answered. "I feel like just curlin' up into a ball and takin' a break for a little bit."

"Sweetie, you can do that when you're dead. I'd love to hear what he has to say about your brother."

"What do you mean?"

Her face froze. "What do you mean, what do I mean?"

"Reed, what are you talking about?" Did she know about the weed? Had I told anyone unknowingly?

"Shit. I thought you knew. Or at least had heard the same rumor."

"What rumor? You're bugging me out." She stared at the road ahead, refusing to look at me.

"Jesus, Reed! What is it?"

"Okay, fine. I heard he left school."

"Who left school?"

"David. Your brother. I heard he dropped out about a month into last semester."

"What the fuck are you talking about, Reed? That's impossible. He's still playing soccer."

"I mean, I don't know the whole story, but I heard it from a sorority sister."

"How would your sorority sister in Tuscaloosa know about David dropping out in Atlanta?"

"No, not someone at school with me. Someone in my sister sorority at Mercer. We all know everything. It's like the Mafia," she explained matter-of-factly.

I stared out the window. "I love how you're being so blasé about this. Just dropping this bomb on me like my brother secretly dropping out of school happens every day."

"Wass, come on, this may just be a crazy rumor. I thought you knew. And by the way, people dropping out of college *is* something that happens every day."

"Not to us! Not to David Wasserman especially. C'mon, Reed, what about soccer? His scholarship?"

"Honey, I really don't know." She made a left into our neighborhood. "I'm just telling you what I heard, which unfortunately involved no details whatsoever." She glanced over at me and put her hand on my knee. "Want to come over?"

"No, I should get home." I sighed.

"Are you pissed at me?"

"No, I'm not, I swear. I'm just confused. I mean, if it is true, my parents are going to go nuts."

"Like I said, it could very well just be a rumor that someone started."

"Why would someone make up a rumor that he dropped out of school? How does that make sense?"

"I don't know." She pulled into my driveway. "Listen, you know how tiny this town is. I mean, you walked into Bootsie's party a couple—okay, a lot—of pounds thinner and everyone and their gramma was convinced that you were a coke whore. It's probably not true. I'll call you later, okay?" I nodded and got out, slamming the door behind me. She began to pull away, but stopped and stuck her head out of the window. "Maybe you could ask Chris if he knows anything?"

"Maybe." I waved a limp hand in good-bye.

In my bedroom, I shut the door, leaving an outraged Maddie outside. Why would David drop out of school and lie to my parents about it for an entire semester? I mean, my classes weren't easy, but it wasn't like I was a physics major at MIT. How could David's be any harder? And he was smarter than me! A hundred times smarter. He was third in his graduating class. And how had he managed to keep our parents in the dark? These were people who smelled beer on our breath a week before we drank it. And what about soccer? How do you just throw a scholarship in the garbage? Wouldn't there be letters to my parents and meetings with coaches? You couldn't just walk away so neatly, could you?

Or could you? He was walking neatly away from the accident. No one would ever know about the weed, thanks to me. Is this the person David had become? Someone who covered his tracks without a second thought? I flipped over on my stomach and relished the feeling of my ribs pressing into the mattress. No, that wasn't him.

The truth was that the rumor didn't seem so far-fetched. He hadn't spoken about soccer once this summer; he smoked cigarettes and weed, which I had never seen him do before; and he was acting strange and withdrawn—so much so that he had my parents seriously worried. I had taken Psych 101—these were the habits of a stressed-out, possibly depressed person. And maybe he was stressed out and depressed because he had something to hide. I buried my face in my pillow.

My shorts felt tighter than they had the last time I'd put them on. The rational me knew that they had just been washed, but the crazy me said that I had gained weight. They battled like two yapping terriers inside my head. There was a knock at the door.

"Yeah?"

"Can I come in?" It was my dad.

"Sure." I sat up and tried to compose myself. I had managed to avoid my parents and David since M.K. had dropped me off. Investing an obscene amount of time in the way you looked awarded you that privilege. Chris was picking me up in a half-hour.

"Hi," he said as he entered my room. "You look nice." He sat down on the bed next to me.

"Thanks. Having a bit of a meltdown. Nothing looks right on me."

"Ruth, everything looks great."

"Righto." I rolled my eyes. "How's it going?"

"Fine. I'm handling a tough case at the office right now, so today was a pain in the neck."

"Oh yeah, what about?"

"Just a family contesting their dead mother's will. Ugly stuff." He shuddered. "But I wanted to talk to you about the accident."

"Dad, I thought we went over this. What else is there to say?"

"You're right, you're right, there's nothing else to say right now. I just wanted to know if the board had made any moves yet."

"We have a meeting tomorrow night."

"Who's we?"

"Me, David, Jason, and the board, Dad. God."

"I don't know why you're so annoyed with me. I'm asking you pretty basic questions here."

I rubbed my temples. "I know. I guess I'm just anxious about everything."

"Did anything happen that you're not telling me about?"

"What do you mean?"

"Exactly what you think I mean." *Sure, two things to be exact. One, David smoked a bowl of weed about ten minutes before he assumed the stand, and two, it is entirely possible that he's dropped out of school and has been lying to you for an entire semester.*

"No!" I exhaled sharply. "What is this, *Law and Order*? You're my dad, not a private fucking detective." My internal Jacuzzi of nerves pumped bubbles of heat through my bloodstream.

"Your mouth is like a sewer!" He shook his head. "I thought you were an English major. You can't think of a better adjective?" He paused. "So you're sure? Nothing with David?"

"Dad, I told you already! Enough!" I stood up.

"Hey, Ruth." He took my hand. "I'm not trying to upset you, I promise. It's just that if this girl's parents do move to sue you two, or the pool, we need to know everything."

"The only reason you're making such a big deal about this is because you still can't accept the fact that David screwed up. It's inconceivable to you!"

"Honey, I'm telling you that that's not it."

I pursed my lips and jutted my chin toward him as if to say, *Right.*

"Okay, if I'm being really honest, yes. Maybe there's a part of me that's having a hard time understanding how David could be so out to lunch. Who knows, maybe it's because he's been so strange this summer, period." He raked his hands over his scalp. "Part of my job as a lawyer is to ask the questions that everyone wants to know the answers to. The bottom line is that David's track record makes his irresponsibility suspect."

"And my track record makes irresponsibility a given. If I had been on the stand, everyone would have just shrugged their shoulders and said, 'Eh, that makes sense.' But since it was David, everyone assumes that some sinister secret lurks beneath the surface. It's so messed up, Dad. I got busted for drinking beers a couple of times in high school and my reputation is soiled for life? What's the big deal? That's what every normal kid does." He looked at me. "Except David," I added.

He put his arm around me. "I'm sorry if I've upset you. Your mother told me to take it easy, but I charged in here anyway." He threw up his hands. "I can't help it." He pulled me into him.

So much was swirling in my head. What if this rumor was true? It would mean, among other things, that David had been lying to my parents for months. They hated lying. Once after kindergarten, when my mom and dad were still at work, I had climbed up on a stool searching for sweets in a high cabinet and fallen—taking my mom's crystal decanter with me. It had crashed to the ground, and I had spent what felt like a million years picking up each individual tiny shard in an attempt to cover my tracks. When she got home, of course she discovered the few pieces that I had missed.

"What is all this glass from, Ruthie?" she had asked.

Panic produced my very first lie. I had told her that I picked it up off the playground because I was worried about the other kids getting hurt. She had put her hands on her hips and given me her *really?* face. A few hours later, when my dad came home, they had gathered David and me for the first of many talks about the dangers of lying. Talks like that had had absolutely no effect on my rather illustrious lying career thus far (other than a profound sense of guilt), but David—as far as I knew David had never told a lie in his life. Until now. And if this rumor was true, he had really saved up his reserves wisely.

The doorbell rang, and I sat up suddenly.

"What's wrong?" asked my dad.

"I'm so nervous," I confessed.

"Sweetie, he should be the nervous one. You could eat poor ole Chris Fuller for lunch."

Lunch. I had skipped dinner. I nodded at my dad, gave him one last hug, and grabbed my bag. I turned off the light and jogged to the door with Maddie at my heels.

"Hey, Ruth." Chris smiled mischievously at me.

"Don't you look guilty," I said, smiling back. "Do you have a body in your trunk or something?"

He laughed. "Just happy to see you, I guess."

I patted Maddie good-bye and closed the door behind me. I hugged him hello, relishing the warm firmness of his chest and the impressive musculature of his back. The faint odor of cigarettes lingered underneath his crisp, citrusy cologne. I fought back the surprising urge to lick his neck.

"Hey," he whispered. "You smell good." His breath tickled my skin.

I pulled back and looked him in the eyes. "Thanks. Let's hit the road, shall we?"

"So, I've been thinking about the accident," he said in the car.

"Yeah?"

"You ever wonder what it was that made you look over there?"

"What do you mean?"

"You know, the whole concept of destiny and all that."

"Whoa, this is a surprise. Chris Fuller asking me about destiny." I laughed. "I wouldn't think you'd go for that kind of stuff."

"What, you don't think a jock from the country can be sensitive? I do yoga. I know what's up."

I laughed. "You do yoga?"

"Yep. Well, I had a girlfriend who was into it. I went a couple of times with her." I tensed at the mention of a former girlfriend. Who was she? What did she look like? Was she blond? When she sat up, did her stomach stay flat? Did she like sex?

"Your boys know about that?" I teased, hoping that sarcasm would mask my neuroses.

"Ruth Wasserman, you don't know me at all. I don't give a rat's ass about what my boys think. Never have."

"All right then. I stand corrected." He looked forlorn. "Hey, I'm sorry. I guess there's a lot we don't know about each other. And I haven't really thought about why I looked where I looked. Except that I was worried about David."

"Why were you worried about David?"

"Oh, not worried," I backtracked. "That's not the right word. It's just that there were a lot of Kiddy Kare kids near the pool."

"Oh yeah. It must have been pretty hectic."

"It was."

"Do you feel different now, now that you can say that you saved somebody's life?"

"Not really. I've been thinking about it a lot, though, that's for sure. About that and, you know, the South."

"What about the South?"

"Well, she's a black girl at a white pool, you know? I've heard some pretty awful opinions."

"I bet. But can you say that's necessarily a southern thing?"

"What, racism?"

"Yeah. I don't think that kind of stupidity is ours alone."

"That may be true. I guess it's just more expected here."

"I can see your point. I'm sorry that we've met your expectations, though. That's bullshit."

"It's interesting that you say 'we.' Like you and the South are one and the same."

"Well, we are. It's in my blood. My parents were born and raised here, and my parents' parents, and so on and so on. Y'all are different."

"Who's 'y'all'?"

"The Wassermans." He grinned. "You come from New York. It's a different thing, even if you've lived here all of your life."

"That is true," I agreed. "Plus, the Jewish thing."

"Yeah, that too. You don't exactly blend seamlessly."

"Rude!"

"You know I mean it in the best way, Ruth. That's something I loved about my friendship with your brother. As easily as he was embraced here, he was always different. In a good way."

"Different how?"

"I dunno. His sense of humor, the way he looked at things. That crazy bar mitzvar he had."

I laughed. "Oh my God. That was nuts. Remember the theme?"

"*Seinfeld*, right?" We both burst into a fit of giggles. "I mean, how is that a theme?"

"Why is that a theme is more like it." I laughed. "To be honest, I think my parents got a little desperate. David was the last of his age group to go. The other three thirteen-year-old Jews in town had already monopolized the sports market. Nothing was left."

"I don't remember David even watching *Seinfeld*," said Chris.

"Me either." I shook my head. "Sam and Marjorie cracked under the pressure."

"I think I was sitting at the Kramer table," said David. "We all got bubble gum cigars or something."

"Oy."

"Did you ever have one?"

"Have what?"

"A bar mitzvar thing. Wait, is that what it's called?"

"It's bar mitzvah, actually. That's what a boy has. The girl has a bat mitzvah."

"Oh. Well, did you have one?"

"Nah. I didn't really care about being Jewish back then, you know? I thought the whole bat mitzvah thing would be a waste of everybody's time. Plus, I didn't want to go dress shopping with my mother." Dress shopping as an overweight tween was torture. Nothing was designed to make you feel worse about yourself than a dress. Once, my mom and I had spent every weekend for four months searching for an eighth-grade dance dress, finally settling on a peach bridesmaid monstrosity. Horrifying.

"Huh. Wasn't David super into the whole Jew scene around that age, though?"

"Yeah, he was. It was really annoying, actually."

"Yeah, what was that group called? BBY something?"

"BBYO." David had spent his early teens as a super Jew. BBYO stood for B'nai B'rith Youth Organization and was, in a nutshell, a national (if not international, I certainly didn't know) group of Jewish kids who got together to do charity work and read the Torah. Or something like that. My interest level had been zero, much to my parents' chagrin. One look at his BBYO leader, who had a ponytail, high-waisted pleated shorts, and a

Dodge Neon plastered with Dilbert stickers, and even the re-
motest chance of my participation was destroyed.

"You weren't into that?"

"Not even a little bit."

"How come?"

"I dunno. Maybe because it made me feel even more different than I already did. And who wants to feel different in high
school?"

"Aw, c'mon. Everybody liked you."

"I mean, maybe I was liked, but I had to work double time
at it. Because I was Jewish." *And fat.*

"Ruth, no offense, but I think that's bullshit. You don't
think your sense of alienation is as much your fault as it is the
South's?"

"How so?"

"You've always had a little bit of a chip on your shoulder,
girl. Always a little bit better than everyone else."

"Get outta here! All I ever wanted was to fit in!"

"Well, that may be so, but it didn't seem that way from the
outside."

"You're bullshitting me."

"Nope."

"No way. How could that possibly be true?"

"That's just the way I saw it. Maybe I'm the exception to
the rule."

"You're trying to tell me that if I had just been 'sweet,' my
phone would have been ringing off the hook? I've always stood
out like a sore thumb here, and not in a good way. Whether you
admit it or not, the South is a pretty homogeneous place."

"So how did your brother defy the odds?"

"He's an athlete! And he's super good-looking!" I covered
my mouth with my hand. "Oh wow, I'm yelling. Sorry. I'm
really sorry."

"It's okay. But I think there are some big holes in your argument here. Just sayin'."

"I need a drink."

Chris laughed. "I can get you that drink."

"Where are we going, anyway?"

"How do you feel about bowling?"

"I'm not sure that anyone actually feels a certain way about bowling, but I'm game." Honestly, I despised bowling. But being with Chris was taking my mind off of David somehow, even though we were talking about him. It was almost like the more we spoke about the David I had always known, the less possible it became that this new rumored David could even exist. "And I'll try to remove my shoulder chip before we strap on those ridiculous clown shoes."

"Do that," he replied. "See what happens."

18

I swung around the corner on my bike, nursing the pit of dread in my stomach with some deep breaths.

In . . . hold for five-four-three-two-one . . . outtttttttt. In . . . hold for five-four-three-two-one . . . outttt.

I was on my way to the house of Miss Carol (or Carol Cummings, as the rest of the world knew her) for the board meeting. I wasn't sure why I was so terrified—I mean, really, what was the worst that could happen? It had already been established by the sibling code of silence that I was never ratting David out. Whatever consequences stemmed from that decision were par for the course: a jail sentence, an afterlife in the pits of hell, a guilty conscience that sat on my shoulders like an iron cloak. All of it was worth it, right? For this wonderful relationship with a brother who was completely open with me and loved me beyond a shadow of a doubt. Right.

Here I was, expected to put it all on the line, and he was living a full-on secret life. Maybe that's why he had no trouble ignoring the facts and claiming sobriety—he'd been spinning his own cobweb of lies for months. This wasn't how the Wassermans operated. I was the endearing fuck-up who couldn't lie

my way out of a paper bag but always attempted to nevertheless (*No, Mom, I didn't sneak out—I have no idea why the
window screen is broken / No, Dad, I wasn't drinking, I just
smell like this because everyone else was / No, this isn't a new
shirt that I bought with your credit card last week—I've had it
forever*), and David was the perfect son. He never lied because
he didn't have to. He made excellent grades, he didn't drink or
do drugs, and he could always be counted on. If those tenets of
his persona were erased, who was he? Who was I? Who were
the Wassermans?

I stopped in front of Miss Carol's house. Jason's and David's
cars were parked outside already, along with the familiar cars of
the board: a navy blue Volvo for Cynthia Sherman (her family
had built the pool and she was my favorite of the bunch—a
no-nonsense, crimson lipstick–wearing former debutante with a
liberal streak); a silver minivan for Bill Whitaker (dad of Tyler
and beleaguered member of every board in town courtesy of the
bossiest wife I had ever encountered); and a giant black Suburban for the infamous Dusty Forsythe (co-head of the board
along with Miss Carol and the most good-ole-boy-iest good ole
boy there ever was).

I parked my bike and rubbed my sweaty palms on my shorts.
Here we go. I rang the doorbell.

"Well, heyyyyy, honay," Miss Carol said, opening the door
to a foyer filled with War Eagle paraphernalia.

"Hey, Miss Carol." I smiled down at her. She was as broad
as she was tall—the human version of a potbelly pig. Standing,
she came up to my collarbone, and at least three inches of that
height was teased blond hair.

"Come on in, we're all just sittin' around and talkin' about
nothin'. Are you hungry, darlin'?" She beckoned for me to take
the lead.

"Oh no, I'm fine, thank you."

"Well, if you change yer mind, I've got chips out for y'all." I heard her stop behind me. I turned around to make sure she hadn't been eaten alive by the giant macramé eagle adorning the wall.

"Let me git you somethin' to drank, at least."

"A Diet Coke would be great, thank you."

"You're welcome, sweetie. I'll git it for you. You go on in. I'll be right there." I followed the hallway down to the wood-paneled living room. Everyone was sitting together on a giant, forest green couch, but they only filled three-quarters of it. It was one of those circular couches with pop-up footstools that made laziness optimal at every angle.

"Hey, Ruth," greeted Jason, obviously desperate for an out from the conversation he was having with Bill. Bill was in standard form, wearing a white golf shirt, khakis, and boat shoes, the bald top of his head gleaming like an ice cube. He had the bad luck of being pear-shaped—a phenomenon I had never before witnessed in a man. It was unfortunate, but very fitting considering Bill's personality. If there ever was a man who fit being pear-shaped, it was him. He had the machismo of a toy poodle.

"Hey, Jason," I replied. "Hey, Mr. Whitaker."

"Hey there, Ruth. How are you?" He struggled to get up, but the depth of the couch fought him like quicksand.

"Oh please, don't get up! That's okay. And I'm fine, thanks."

"Hi, David," I said curtly. He was sitting at the far end with a handful of chips and a glass of soda at his feet. He gave me a tight smile and shoved what appeared to be ten chips into his mouth. His chewing sounded like road construction.

"Hey, Mr. Forsythe, hey, Cynthia," I said. Cynthia had ordered me to drop the "Miss" the first time we were introduced, thereby cementing my fondness for her immediately. I attempted

to perch daintily on the couch's edge. It was useless, though—
the sheer volume of the seat affected the gravity of the room.
Against my will, I was soon reclining.

"Ruth, you're what, nineteen now? I think it's okay to call
me Dusty, sweetie." He was a giant bear of a man, standing six
feet four inches tall and weighing what had to be 285 pounds.
Even the couch looked small underneath him.

"I'm sorry, I always forget!" In contrast to Bill, Dusty was
the epitome of maleness, at least by southern definition. Wealthy,
sporty, heterosexual, and Republican.

"Dusty, if I didn't know any better, I would think you were
flirtin' with her," interjected Cynthia. She rolled her eyes and
smiled conspiratorially at me. Her silver hair was pulled into a
loose bun, and she was wearing a men's chambray work shirt
and white jeans.

"Here's Ruth's drank!" Miss Carol came bustling in with a
glass of ice and soda and handed it to me with a nervous smile.
"I thank we're all here, right?" She sat down in a rocking chair
facing us. The room was silent except for the whir of the ceiling
fan blades.

"Yes, we're all here, Carol," said Dusty. "Let's cut the small
talk, shall we? We're all in a world of shit right now." I glanced
at David. His face was obscured by his drinking glass.

"It looks like this Tanisha's mama is gonna sue the pool."

"Are you kidding me? How? How is this our fault?" asked
Jason. "She almost drowned and Ruth saved her! She saved her
damn life! These people should be kissing our asses, not riding
them."

"Jason, I know tensions are high, but if you could not curse,
I'd appreciate it," scolded Miss Carol. "You too, Dusty." She
looked to the wooden cross adorning the wall as if to guilt them
into submission.

"Apologies, Miss Carol. I'm not myself at the moment." Jason smiled at her. "But, Dusty, on a legal level, do they even have a leg to stand on? You're not assured 100 percent safety at a swimming pool, I mean, gawleeeeee. Let's get real. Shi—, I mean, stuff happens."

"You have a point, Jason. I'm not sure if this lawsuit will even take shape, but I know that we need to be on point if it does."

"We need to know exactly what happened," added Cynthia. "We want to make absolutely sure that everything is on the table."

"No surprises," added Miss Carol.

"There are no surprises," said David, his mouth finally chip-free. "She was in my blind spot, she went under, Ruth saw her, dove in, got her out of the pool, and saved her. There was no resuscitation necessary." I detected a spark of irritation beneath the buttery surface of his speech.

"Ruth, is that what happened?" Cynthia asked me. Her blue eyes searched my face like a flashlight.

"Yes, that's what happened," I answered, forcing myself to maintain eye contact and keep my voice level.

"You sure nothin' went on before the Kiddy Kare got there that would have impaired your ability to watch the pool? Y'all were on point?" Dusty asked both of us. My mouth went dry.

"We're sure," answered David quickly. "Why would you think that?" He appeared completely calm and at ease, as though his outright lie had soothed him somehow.

"Aw, I know y'all didn't do anything wrong, son," said Dusty. "I just want to be sure that we're all on the same page. We all know that they're gonna get some nigger lawyer who hoots and hollers all over the place."

I cringed and opened my mouth to say something, but Cynthia beat me to it.

"Dusty, I will not have that language spoken in my presence, do you hear me? And you sure as hell better not use it in regards to this case."

"Oh, c'mon, Cynthia. All due respect, we know exactly how this is gonna go down. I apologize for that word. That was ugly." He reached out and put his hand on her knee. "Old habits die hard, I guess."

"Don't you know that this is how we're going to be expected to react? To be the racist jerks they perceive us as being? To say something derogatory about black people and swimming pools and prove their point that we didn't care about their child the way we would have cared about one of our own?" Cynthia was practically yelling.

"She's right, Dusty," agreed Carol. "We need to defy expectations."

"I know that's what Tanisha's mom is thinking, but I swear that wasn't the case," I said. My voice sounded strange to me—like it was coming from the bottom of a well. "The fact that she was black had nothing to do with her accident, at least on our part."

"Not at all," agreed David. "The truth of the matter is that Tanisha couldn't swim. If anyone should be sued, it's those Kiddy Kare people. They're the ones who let her wander off. And without floaties."

"And what about her mama?" asked Mr. Whitaker. "Obviously she knew that her daughter couldn't swim, but agreed to let her go to a pool anyway. Surely she would have had to sign a permission slip. She knew about the risk she was taking, and now she wants to cry wolf?"

"That's a damn good point, Bill. A damn good point," said Dusty. Bill swelled with pride at the compliment.

"Have y'all reached out to a lawyer?" asked Jason.

"Yes, I have a friend who's agreed to take this on if need

be," answered Cynthia. "He's quite reputable." I thought about my dad's offer to defend us. By not telling him the whole truth either, we'd be asking him to lie on our behalf. I wondered if David's conscience would get the better of him if our father was on the line. I certainly hoped so, but watching him lie so effortlessly here made me doubtful.

"Cynthia, if they do sue, will they sue the pool as a whole, or will they single out David and me?" I asked.

"We're all in this together, Ruth. All for one and one for all." She gave me a sad smile.

"Are we all set then?" asked Miss Carol. "For now?"

"I believe we are," answered Dusty. "Ruth, I want to commend you again on a job well done. You saved a little girl's life, and we're lucky to have you on our team."

"Yes, absolutely," agreed Cynthia.

"Thanks," I replied. I couldn't think of anything else to say.

"Well, I guess we'll take off then," said David. "Miss Carol, thank you for hosting."

"Yes, thanks, Miss Carol. I'm taking a cookie to go," said Jason, grinning.

"Please, Jason, take the bag! My behind doesn't need any more of these, believe me." She got up to get them from the kitchen.

"You are such a kiss-ass," I whispered.

"Don't say 'ass'!" he whispered back. "Jesus doesn't like that word." He pointed to the cross.

"You guys ready?" asked David. He stood up and loomed over us.

"You all right?" asked Jason. "You look about as nervous as a whore in church."

"I'm just ready to get outta here, man." He popped his knuckles.

"Here are your cookies, Jase. And David, here are yours."

She handed them Ziplocs filled to bursting. "Ruth, I would have offered some to you, but I know how good you are." She winked at me. "I wish I had half the self-control that you do."

What if I did want a damn cookie? It was ironic that I had started not eating to look like everyone else, but had ended up sticking out even more. We waved good-bye a final time and wandered into the yard.

"You want a ride?" asked David.

"I can't. I rode my bike."

"I'll drop your bike off in my truck," volunteered Jason.

"No, that's silly," I said.

"But it's far. Seriously, it's no problem."

"Well, if you're sure, Jason. I am a little tired."

"You got it." He picked up my bike and deposited it into his truck bed with a clank. "See ya'll. I'm headed to the pool to see what's what." He climbed into the driver's seat and started the engine. ACDC poured out of his truck's speakers, the beat shaking its body and, seemingly, the pavement beneath its wheels. "I'll just park yer bike in yer carport, 'kay?"

"Great. Thanks." He drove off, leaving David and me in awkward silence.

"What did you think about the meeting?" he asked as we walked to his car.

"Mmm, I guess it was productive. I mean, nothing was really resolved or anything. But really, what could be resolved at this point?"

"Yeah, it was more about getting ready for battle, I guess," he answered. We opened our doors and got in.

"Battle?"

"Yeah." He started the engine. "Battle."

"That's a pretty aggressive way of phrasing it."

"What else would you call it? If they sue the pool, it's on."

"I guess." We pulled into the road, and I watched Miss Carol's house grow smaller in the rearview mirror. "I just don't see how they would really have a case, though. And why spend all that money if you don't have a case?"

"I think they could make a case pretty easily, actually. People love that shit."

"What shit?"

"The race card and all that goes with it." He glanced at me. "Why do you look so surprised?"

"I guess I just can't believe that they would accuse us of being the kind of people that would wish a kid dead because she was black."

"Whoa, that's a little over the top. Take it easy."

"What? In essence, that's what they would be saying, isn't it? That we didn't watch Tanisha carefully because she was black, right? That we didn't care if she drowned?"

"Well, yeah, if you put it that way."

"But how could that even stand up in court? We're Jewish. You were the freakin' BBYO crusader in high school. Didn't you spearhead that whole trip to New Orleans after Katrina?"

"That has zero relevance, believe me. Just because I helped some black people build houses doesn't not make me a racist. And you, you don't even have that to hide behind."

"Are you kidding me? I have black friends! I'm not a racist."

"Congratulations. You have black friends. You're a regular civil rights crusader."

"Well, I mean, think about the alternative. People like Kevin and Dusty."

"What does Kevin have to do with this?"

"He called Jill's boyfriend the 'n' word the other day."

"Malik? Shit. Where?" David frowned.

"When he was up at the pool." I shook my head angrily. "We have a black president, for chrissake, and this is still happening here."

"The only thing worse than being black in the South is being Jewish in the South," said David.

"What? Are you serious? I don't think that's true, David."

"Oh yeah? Well, if you don't think that Kevin hates us, you're nuts." He stopped suddenly as a squirrel darted in front of us.

"Give me a break. He probably does, but let's get real. Black people have had it a lot harder here. Getting converted to Christianity at your locker is one thing, but having a separate bathroom is another. C'mon now." I couldn't tell if he was serious or just trying to get a rise out of me.

"Ruth, you c'mon. At least black people are liked by other black people. Jews are hated by whites and blacks alike, and there are only, like, five other Jews here to like them back. Think about it."

"You're nuts."

"Oh, I forgot, you have black friends." He rolled his eyes. "Ruth, I'm not a racist by any stretch of the imagination. I'm just calling it like I see it."

"You really are out of your mind."

"Maybe the reason it makes you so mad is because you see a little bit of truth in it," he said smugly.

"Oh, fuck off, David." We rode along in silence.

"I mean, look at stupid Dusty back there," I said a few minutes later. "The 'n' word rolls off his tongue like nothing. It's just a word to him—a word he probably uses daily. And it's wrong! It's horrible!"

"It is horrible. I agree. This place is filled with Dustys and Kevins. That's why Tanisha's parents would have a case. To not be a racist on some level is an exception to the rule. It's just the way it is. Same thing for Jews. People might pretend to embrace us, but believe me, they all think we have tiny horns beneath our hair. They just might not say it as much." I stared out the window.

"David, people made fun of your Camp Maccabee T-shirt a couple of times. It's not like they burned a cross in our front yard. Relax."

"Yeah, sure, that's all they did. You think you know everything."

"What?"

"They beat the shit out of me in the third grade. You don't remember?"

"No."

"Well, it's true. A bunch of rednecks ripped that shirt right off of my back and beat me up. Plus, every sports team I was ever on as a kid had some asshole there to flick pennies at me or wisecrack about Jesus."

"Really?"

"Yeah, really. So don't tell me that I don't know of what I speak, okay?"

"How come nobody ever told me?"

"You were little. It didn't matter. Besides, that stuff pretty much all stopped once I got good at soccer. Athleticism trumps all else, I guess."

"I never knew all that."

"Now you do." Had they kept that from me on purpose, or had I just been too clueless to see it? "So, you don't still think I was high, do you?" he asked. I didn't answer.

"Do you?" I stared out the window. "Jesus, Ruth!" He pounded the steering wheel. "I told you I wasn't! What the hell do you want from me? A urine sample?"

"Listen, David, obviously I'm not going to tell anyone about it. I just would really like it if you admitted to me that you were. Because we went through this together, you know? I think you owe me some honesty." He kept his eyes on the road, but his knuckles were white on the wheel. "I'm your sister. You don't have to lie to me. About anything."

If he could just admit this to me, then maybe the dam would break and all of the lies would come rushing out. I wanted to help him despite my anger toward him, but as long as he was locked in his prison of denial, I couldn't.

"You know, for someone who is a pro at lying, you sure are high and mighty over there. You lied your ass off in high school, and you're living one whopper of a lie right now."

"What do you mean? Because I told a few fibs about drinking beers, I'm a lying pro? There's a giant difference between that kind of lie and the kind of lie that almost kills someone, David."

"So you never got behind the wheel when you drank? You never got in a car with someone who was drinking? Huh? That's the same thing, genius."

"Oh my God, this is ridiculous. You're gonna spin this until you're blue in the face." I sighed heavily. "You're never going to come clean about it, I can see that. And if you expect me not to resent you for it, you're nuts."

"So c'mon then, ask me what I mean about the lie you're living now."

"What?"

"The whopper of a lie I was referring to."

"Because I don't care," I hissed.

"You have an eating disorder, and you won't admit it, and you won't get help. So don't talk to me about honesty, Ruth. Talk about killing someone—you're killing yourself."

"Oh Christ, suddenly it's an after-school special." My lip trembled. I would not cry.

He pulled into our driveway. "Go ahead, make light of it. But what I said is ringing true, and you know it. Quit being such a hypocrite and open your own damn eyes."

19

otherfucker!" I whispered as the coldness of the water connected with a tooth on the top right side of my mouth. The pain was indescribable—like someone had plugged my entire head into an electrical socket. I had been ignoring that tooth for months now, despite the fact that I was pretty sure I had lost an entire piece of chewing gum to the hole inside of it. I hated the dentist. I grabbed the bathroom counter and waited for the pain to subside.

"You done in there or what?" David yelled at me from the other side. I turned on the water.

"Just a minute, dear!" I yelled back. Jackass. I would stay in here as long as I wanted. I surveyed myself in the mirror. This was not how you were supposed to feel on your way to Friday night services. You were supposed to feel warm and charitable, loving and gracious. Yeah, right. Did anyone ever want to go to services? If you asked me, it was just another form of torture we were asked as a people to overcome.

I opened the door to find him pacing in the hallway. He glared at me. "What the hell do you do in there?" he hissed. "Make yourself puke?"

"All I have to do is think of your face, and it all comes right up." I gave him a fake smile and let him pass. He slammed the door behind me.

"Glad to see everyone is in as good a mood as I am," said my mom as she marched past.

"Oh yeah," I answered. I sat on my bed and strapped on my sandals. It had been a long, hot day at work, and Kevin had tweaked my last nerve by continuing to ask me all about the Tanisha debacle. I kept waiting for him to say something racist and awful again, but surprisingly, he had kept his mouth shut. I wondered if Jason had warned him to keep his opinions to himself as we waited to find out if her parents were suing. If someone overheard him spouting nonsense, we could all be in trouble. My head started to ache just thinking about it.

"Ruthhhhh! Let's goooooooo!" yelled my dad from the kitchen.

"Comingggggggggggg!"

"We're going to be late," he warned as I ran past him. David and my mom were already in the car, their faces glum. I opened the back door and toppled in. My dad followed, and we backed out of the driveway in silence.

"Can we turn the radio on?" I asked.

"No," my dad replied. "Let's talk to each other for a change."

"Great," I mumbled. I watched David out of the corner of my eye. He was looking out the window with his chino-ed legs spread in front of him like a colt. The smell of his aftershave hung over us like a cloud. My mind drifted back to the days when grape Bubblicious was the predominant scent of our car rides together. I could still hear him prodding and popping it like the cud of a cow, right in my ear. On cue, my tooth began to throb.

"Hey, Mom," I said. "I need to go to the dentist."

She turned around. "What's the matter?" she asked, eyeing me with concern. "Do you have a cavity?"

"Yeah, I think so. It really hurts."

"Okay, sure. I'll call Dr. Cooper tomorrow. Let me know your work schedule and we'll figure it out, okay?"

" 'Kay."

"David, how are your teeth?"

"Fine, no problems." He smirked at me, and I made a face back.

"Ruth, do you floss every night? You know how important that is," said my dad. "You have to really get in there."

"Oh yeah, every night." I couldn't remember the last time I had flossed. What I did remember were all the Swedish fish I had consumed while stoned at school, and the fact that I often passed out with their red jelly remnants swaddling my enamel.

"I always floss, Dad," volunteered David. He smiled at me. "Never miss a night."

"Great, let's get you a medal." I rolled my eyes. "This is a fascinating conversation."

"How's training going, David?" asked my mom. "You haven't talked a lot about it this summer." I tensed up reflexively and continued to stare out the window. We passed the 7/11 where I had almost been arrested for buying a six-pack of Schlitz when I was fifteen. How I had escaped that one unscathed still boggled my mind.

"It's fine," he answered. "Same as always." I listened for a change in the tone of his voice—for anything that would convey just a touch of guilt on his part for lying outright to them. On the way to services nonetheless. Nothing. I glanced at him, hoping to see him nervously fidgeting with his fingers or chewing his lip. Zero. He was as cool as a cucumber. Maybe it really was a rumor. I heard a rustling and looked down. David's leg was bouncing spasmatically. *Then again.*

"Is Coach Foster checking in with you?" asked my dad.

"Uh, yeah, he sends emails and stuff."

"So what kinds of drills are they running?"

"Hey, Dad, do you mind?" David asked. "I don't feel like talking about soccer right now." I watched my dad react in the rearview mirror. His eyebrows went up, and he pursed his lips like a duck. This was his trademark expression of concern. He glanced at my mother, but I couldn't see her face. I guessed that she was widening her eyes and rolling her hands over in her lap to expose her palms as if to say, *Give it a rest, Sam.*

"Okay," he answered.

"Did you tell them about your mural?" I whispered.

"No," he whispered back.

"Why?"

"I dunno. Didn't think they'd be interested, I guess." He shrugged.

"What are you two whispering about back there?" my mom asked. "No secrets."

"David's painting a mural at the pool," I said.

"You are, sweetie?" asked my mom. "That's great! Where?"

"On the wall between the bathrooms," he mumbled.

"Nice," said my dad with a noticeable lack of enthusiasm. David had wanted to be an art major in college, but that hadn't gone over well with either of my parents. *Major in business and take a couple of drawing classes,* my dad had said. *You can't live on a hobby.* It was the only time I had seen David fight with my parents. The argument had gone on for weeks until finally David had given in.

"What's it of?" Dad asked.

"It's a surprise," David answered. "Nobody knows."

"How are you keeping it covered up?" asked my mom.

"I've rigged up this elaborate tarp system. And all the kids know that if they touch it, they're dead."

"When do you paint?" asked Dad.

"In the mornings. Early."

"Before soccer?"

"Yeah, before soccer."

"When will you unveil it?" asked my mom.

"At the end-of-season banquet, I guess," he answered.

"Can we come?"

"Yeah, sure, why not?" His leg was still.

"When is that?"

"When is what?"

"The banquet."

"I don't know. It should be right before we leave for school, I think."

"That doesn't give you much time," my mom warned. "We're already halfway through summer—which I cannot believe, by the way." She shook her head. "You two both go back mid-August, right?"

"Uh, yeah," mumbled David. *Back to what?* I wondered.

"I'm here until, like, the last week of August or something. Next week is the Fourth, right?" I asked.

"Listen, I'll get the mural done, don't worry," David interjected. He sighed. "Could we can it with the twenty questions now? Why can't we ever just 'be'? It's always the Spanish Inquisition around here."

My dad began to answer, but my mom put her hand on his leg. "Okay, okay. Enough." We pulled into the synagogue parking lot and stopped beneath an oak tree.

"You're not worried about bird crap, Sam?"

"It's too hot for birds to crap." We piled out of the car.

"Is that the Wassermans?" a voice trilled behind us. I turned around. Mrs. Kahn. Great.

Mrs. Kahn was the mother of Rebecca and Ruby Kahn. Rebecca was a year younger than me, and Ruby two or three—I couldn't remember exactly. She had arranged a playdate for us when I was ten, much to my chagrin. They reminded me of dachshunds, with their long dour faces and lanky hair that clung to their heads save for the giant, starched bows perched on top. The day of our dreaded date, I was handed off to them in the synagogue parking lot after Sunday School. As I watched my father drive away, Ruby had grabbed my stomach with her bony fingers and asked, *What's this?* In response, I had bent her fingers back so fiercely that she had burst into tears. For months afterward, I had lain awake at night thinking of the ultimate comeback—hoping that my chance would come again. Naturally, it never had.

"Well, hey, y'all," droned Mrs. Kahn. "Don't y'all look gorgeous!" My mom winced as she went in for the cheek kiss. I stared her down.

"Ruth Wasserman, you get any skinnier and Miss Tyra Banks herself is gonna come on down to recruit you!" She gave me the up-down. *I hate you*, I thought to myself as I fake-smiled in response.

"Ruby could take some pointers from you, but don't tell her I said so." She smiled conspiratorially. "There's a girl that just loves her McDonald's, let me tell you." *Ah, karma. Bless it.*

"How have you been, Sandy?" asked my dad.

"Oh, just fine, thank you. Barry wasn't able to come tonight, and gettin' the girls to forfeit a Friday night is like tryin' to deep-fry a pickup truck, so it's just me, here all by my lonesome!" She fingered her pearls nervously. My mom grunted beside me. I made eye contact with her, and we shared a look of distaste.

"Well, I'll see y'all inside," said Mrs. Kahn. "Good Shabbas!" *Good Shabbas* said with a southern accent was priceless. *Good Shabbas, y'all!* or *Y'all come on down for a Good Shabbas!* I liked it, actually. I'd heard enough nasally Long Island accents at school that year to not take it for granted.

"She's got a lot of energy," said David as she teetered away on her high heels.

"That she does," said my dad. "But no gossip now. Not on Shabbas, okay?" I opened my mouth to make a smart-ass reply, but his grave expression made me hold my tongue. I would try to be a good Jew. One night wouldn't kill me.

We entered the synagogue and were greeted warmly by Mrs. Ginsberg, who had been the synagogue secretary for at least as long as I had been alive and probably for my parents' lifetimes as well. She also hailed from New York and had never lost her accent or her brass. She was a legend—well, a legend here at least.

"Hello, dears!" she said. "Marjorie, you look beautiful. I swear, you never age."

"I could say the same for you, Sylvia. You look fantastic." She didn't, but it was nice of my mom to say so. The little hair she had left was teased into a hairspray halo, and each of her front teeth was shellacked with her mandarin lipstick.

"David, you look so handsome," Mrs. Ginsberg said. Her hand shook as she touched his arm. The contrast between her veiny, liver-spotted, and pink-manicured claw and his supple, tan, and blond-haired forearm was jarring.

"Thanks, Mrs. Ginsberg," he replied, unfazed. "I knew you were going to be here tonight, so I put in a little extra effort."

"Oh you," she said. "You're a lady killah." She smiled up at him adoringly.

"And Ruthie," she said finally, coming closer and looking me right in the eye. "You're a vision." I blushed. "You're too skinny, but I guess that's how they like 'em these days."

"Thank you, Mrs. Ginsberg," I replied. She smelled of White Musk, hand lotion, and Altoids.

"You're giving your brotha a run for his money," she added.

"Good to see you, Sylvia," said my dad. He was beaming. I realized that this was what he lived for—this unit that was the Wasserman family out and about, charming everyone in our path. Team Wasserman. He and David retrieved their tallit, recited the prayer inscribed on their collars, and draped them around their necks as my mom and I gathered prayer books.

We settled into the pew, and the rabbi gave my father a head nod in greeting. Old Sam Wasserman was a regular Frank Sinatra around here. I settled in, looking around for entertainment. The crowd was sparse, to say the least. I wondered if rabbis were pissed 98 percent of the time. Unless they were converting or about to be bar mitzvah-ed, it seemed to me that Jews showed up only on Rosh Hashanah and Yom Kippur. My dad was the one exception to the rule. He said it wasn't really about God so much, it was about identity and community.

The thing was, I really didn't identify with anyone here. Sure, you were probably going to find the only brunettes or curly-haired people for miles within these walls, but other than that, I really didn't feel a connection. I felt more of a bond with M.K. and Jill, and they were about as Jewish as Dolly Parton. We didn't look alike, and our families were like night and day, but we spoke the same language somehow. With someone like Rebecca Kahn, it was like pulling teeth to find a common thread. That common thread was usually our hair, which was not exactly soil for a flowering bond.

David read along in the prayer book on the other side of my mom. He had had more Jewish friends than I did growing up, but that was because the number of guys in our age group tripled that of the girls. Had it been a question of proximity, or did he legitimately relate to them? I'd never asked.

Mom read along as well, but I knew that she was watching the clock. I couldn't think of one Jewish friend she had, but that wasn't exactly her fault. Most of the ones who were her age were all versions of Mrs. Kahn.

And my dad? Well, I wasn't sure. He certainly knew everyone here, but I couldn't say if they were his friends. It was hard to tell if his openness was born out of a need to socialize or garner clients. He might say that those two things were one and the same, and I guessed I could see what he meant. It was hard to not have an ulterior motive, socially speaking.

I fingered the strands of his tallis. When I was little, I would occupy myself by braiding them over and over. Each time we had to stand, my work would be destroyed and I would have to start all over again. This was especially difficult on Yom Kippur, as the standing outweighed the sitting.

Ruth, pay attention, my dad would say, and I would look up at him with feigned innocence. *I ammmmm*, I would whine, and then go back to braiding.

David always kept his focus, except for once. It was one of the first moments I could remember being funny—when what was coming out of my mouth was almost as exciting as anticipating the response. I must have been eight or so, and our cantor at the time bore a striking resemblance to Rick Moranis. As he sang, I had leaned over to David and whispered, *Honey, I shrunk the Torah!* He had burst into full-fledged laughter, and I had been so delighted by both my joke and his response that I laughed too. My dad had grabbed me by the wrist and pulled me over to the seat on the other side of him, where I languished in the glory of a joke well delivered. Making my friends laugh was one thing, but making David laugh was quite another.

The rabbi launched into Veshameru, and I sang along quietly. When was the last time I had made David laugh or vice versa? That afternoon at the pool had been the only time our hang hadn't been fraught with tension, and that was probably only because David was high. Or not high, depending on whom you asked. He was much tenser this summer than he ever had been before, now that I thought about it. Maybe that was the price he paid for keeping so many secrets.

I stared up at the stained-glass windows and thought about

Tanisha. Was she scared of the water now? I hoped not. I wanted to see her and talk to her about what happened. I was curious about what it felt like to be suspended helplessly like that. I had always thought that drowning victims flailed and screamed, but Tanisha had slipped under as easily as a cracked egg yolk into a bowl. I could still see her last braid submerging like the telescope of a submarine. Were her eyes open? Was she worried? Was she confident that someone would save her? Did she panic when she realized she couldn't breathe? Not questions I could really ask a little kid obviously, but I was curious. All I did in life was fight against whatever was threatening me. The concept of surrender was as foreign as Christmas.

Mom tapped me on the leg, and I looked at her. "Is it over yet?" she mouthed. "I'm starving." I looked at my watch. We'd been there forty-three minutes.

"I think so," I mouthed back. The rabbi segued into announcements, which meant we were about ten minutes away from freedom. I wiggled my eyebrows at her in euphoria. She made a victory fist at her side.

"Tonight I see David and Ruth Wasserman here, and I just wanted to take a moment to welcome them home for the summer." *Oh no. This is not happening.* David leaned forward and glanced at me in mortification before changing the entire landscape of his face and waving back at the rabbi appreciatively. I smiled in accordance.

"Looking good, guys," the rabbi continued. I studied the blue carpet in horror.

"He means well," my mom offered.

"Jesus," I muttered.

"And now, we're going to close tonight's service with 'Adon Olam'."

"Please just do it the old-fashioned way," Mom whispered beside me.

"What?" I asked.

"Please," she said again.

"But tonight, we're going to change it up and sing it to the tune of another song we know and love, 'Take Me Out to the Ballgame'!"

"What?" I said too loudly. My dad shushed me.

"Don't shush me," I whispered. "Is he serious?"

And with that, he and the cantor—a new one, Rick Moranis was long gone—began to butcher one of the only prayers I knew by heart. Dad attempted to sing through his laughter, and this sparked my own incredulous giggling, which broke down Mom's indignant reserve and finally evoked a snort of absurdity from David.

If this was what Dad meant by community and identity, maybe I was a fan after all.

20

Okay, so let's do some sit-ups." I sat on the grass in front of Khaki's sneaker-clad feet. Each of her ankles was encircled by an angry chain of mosquito bites. "Well, c'mon, get down here."

She sighed heavily and fell to the ground. "I hate sit-ups," she declared.

"Who doesn't? Do you think anyone actually likes doing these things?"

"So why do them?" She eyed me defiantly as she pulled a dandelion out of the grass and twirled it between her fingers. Why did a nine-year-old need to do sit-ups? I had no idea. And who cared if her stomach was flat?

"Sit-ups make you stronger, you know? They work your core muscles. And those are the muscles that allow you to stand up straighter and carry yourself more confidently. I mean, who doesn't want to be stronger?"

"We have to shop in the women's section for my jeans," she confessed softly, crushing the petals in her fist.

"I did too when I was your age." I touched her leg.

"Did not." She looked up at me.

"Did so."

"Really?"

"Really. My mom and I would set out on these epic shopping voyages every season. Being built the way I was made it tough to find clothes."

"Whaddya mean?"

"Well, I was sort of like a potato on toothpicks."

"What?" She giggled and put her hand over her mouth.

"You know, like Mr. Peanut. That's where I hold my weight—in my tummy and boobs. Well, eventually they became boobs. For a long time they were just extra flesh." Khaki eyed her own chest suspiciously.

"Am I a Mr. Peanut?"

"No. You're Khaki." She cocked her head and grinned at me.

"You're not a potato on toothpicks anymore, Ruth. You're a toothpick on toothpicks." Thinking about my mom's infinite patience with me on those shopping trips made me ache a little. Even then, I had wanted so badly to fit in. I had to wear the clothes that everyone else was wearing, despite the fact that they didn't fit. We would search and search for the equivalent in bigger sizes, and not once did she snap.

"When I was your age, they did this weird thing sometimes with clothes. We'd be in the juniors department, and instead of sizes, they would label the clothes with ages. So, let's say I was nine, and I was wearing something that said it was for age fifteen. It was awful."

"Did you cut the labels off?"

"I did. As soon as I got home."

"That's what I do too," said Khaki. We sat in silence for a bit as gnats swarmed around us in the morning heat. "Do you wear clothes in your real size now?" she asked hopefully.

"I do." Well, not really. Whose "real size" was a zero? From age fifteen to age zero. It was as though I was erasing myself.

"Ruuuuuuuuuuuuuth?" My mom yelled from the other side of the house. I didn't answer.

"Ruuuuuuuuuuuuuthhhhhhhhhhhhhhhhh?" Honestly, how could she not know how annoying that was? I put my pillow over my face in frustration.

Flip-flop, flip-flop, flip-flop. She plodded down the hallway toward me. "Ruth! I'm calling you!" I stayed still on my bed with the pillow firmly in place and a slight smile on my face. She was annoyed with me. This pillow was going to hit the floor courtesy of her hands in about five seconds. Sure enough, I felt a sharp tug.

"Ruth Wasserman, hello?" I opened my eyes and squinted up at her. Buttery twilight flooded my bedroom.

"Mom, you know how much I hate it when you bellow at me from the other end of the house."

"Oh, I'm sorry, Princess Ruth. Sorry to have disturbed you. Let me assure you it won't happen again, miss. May I get you anything while I'm here?" She smirked and sat down next to me. Maddie appeared in the doorway. She cocked her head playfully and took a flying leap onto the bed. The three Wasserman ladies.

"Hey, Maddie," I murmured, gently clenching the roll of skin between her tiny neck and torso. She licked my face.

"I called Dr. Cooper," said my mom. "He can see you at five today." I whimpered in response. I had just gotten off work and felt like the human equivalent of dried fruit.

"Listen, you have to go. Your tooth is only going to get worse, and believe me, tooth pain is nothing to mess with." She stood up and grabbed my hand, pulling me up as well.

"Pleeeeeeeaaaaaseeeeeee, nooooooooooo."

"Let's go, Ruthie. You can take my car." She cringed as she

said this. I was not what one would call an excellent driver. Learning how to back out of the driveway had almost killed my father and me. I just could not grasp the fact that turning the wheel one way made the car turn the other.

"Really?" I hadn't driven all summer. All year, actually. I crossed my fingers for no highways en route. Merging terrified me.

"Yes, really. Do you know how to get there?"

I shook my head. "Mmm, not really."

"We must have driven there a hundred times together."

"Yeah, I wasn't paying attention. Sorry." I held my hand out, and she pulled me up. Maddie jumped off of the bed and stood at attention at our feet.

"Okay, I'll write down the directions while you get dressed." She turned to go.

"I have to get dressed?" I whined.

"You cannot wear a bathing suit and gym shorts to the dentist. Put on some clothes."

"Are you kidding me? I've seen men in tank tops at church here! Suddenly there's a dress code?"

"Ruth, please. What do you know about church?"

"In the parking lots, driving by. I've seen 'em!"

"Get moving," she said as she stood up and walked out.

"Fine, maybe I haven't seen it. But I know it happens," I called after her. I closed the door and peeled the top of my bathing suit off—removing it with my shorts in one fell swoop. I pulled on some nicer shorts and a clean T-shirt, happily noting the fact that they were loose again. There were no scales in the house, so numbered notation was impossible. Weighing myself was ritualistic, to say the least. At school, I had kept my scale hidden in my closet. When Meg left for her 8:00 AM class on Tuesdays, I would pull it out, strip down to nothing (including the removal of my earrings), and weigh in, my heart pounding in anticipation and dread. If I had lost weight, it would be a great day. If I was the same, it would just be okay. If I had gained even one-quarter of a pound, forget about it: terrible day.

"Okay, Mom, I'm ready." I stood in front of her like a peace offering.

"Here are the directions. Very easy. Just take a right on Woodbridge and—"

"Mom, I can read. I've got it, don't worry."

"Please don't fuss with the radio while you're driving. Keep your eyes on the road." I snatched the paper from her and headed out the door. En route, I realized that I did indeed remember how to get there. I'd been going to Dr. Cooper since I was in baby teeth and he would fill my mouth with fluoride trays that should have tasted like frosting but absolutely did not.

As I parked, my phone vibrated on the passenger seat. A text from Chris. I hadn't seen him in almost a week.

Beach tomorrow?

Beach. Bathing suits. Water. Sex.

Can't, swim meet,

I typed back on my way into the office.

But I have the day off on Wednesday.
You?

I continued.

I don't at the moment, but I will. Pick
you up at 10?

Sure.

And then, because I wasn't sure what else to say,

☺

I put my phone in my purse and continued inside. Wearing a bathing suit to work was one thing, but wearing it on a date was quite another. Shifting its material to flatten out unsightly bulges and wrinkles was harder when you were sitting right next to someone.

"I'm here for my appointment," I announced into the circle cut into the plastic reception window. The receptionist didn't look up.

"You know I can hear you just fine, right? You don't need to yell through the circle," she said, not taking her eyes off the paper in front of her. Her blue eye shadow melted into her dark eyebrows like one of those puffy oil stickers that separated upon contact.

"Right, sorry," I replied through the circle. I winced, realizing my mistake. "Shit, sorry."

She rolled her eyes. "And you are?"

I stopped myself from leaning forward. "Ruth. Ruth Wasserman?"

She consulted her appointment book. "He'll be out in a few minutes. You can just have a seat."

"Thanks." I sat down on a mauve chair and examined the pile of magazines on the coffee table in front of me. They were all *People*s and *O*s from three years ago. Old magazines depressed me.

"Ruth?" I looked up to see Dr. Cooper. He was tall and thin with a full head of silver hair that sat on his head like a schooner. He gave me a giant smile, revealing the whitest, straightest teeth I had ever seen.

"Hey, Dr. Cooper," I replied, standing up.

His smile faded as he gave me an up-down. "Ruth, good Lord! You've lost so much weight!"

"Yessir, I did." He ushered me through the door without adding further comment.

"Have a seat," he said. I settled into the dental Barcalounger, and the plastic squeaked beneath me. I looked up at him nervously.

"My assistant Andrea will give you a proper cleaning and take care of some X-rays first, okay?" I nodded. "Then I'll come in and tell you what's what. Sound good?"

"Sure, no problem." I smiled weakly as Andrea entered the room. Thirty minutes of poking, scraping, buzzing, and lead robe–wearing later, she was done. My mouth felt unnaturally clean—as though it had been scrubbed with Comet.

"Okay Ruth, I'll send Dr. Cooper in now," said Andrea. She handed me my free toothbrush and tiny floss dispenser.

"Thanks," I replied, fidgeting nervously with my paper bib.

"So where were you at school this year? Was it Michigan?" Dr. Cooper asked, as he entered the room. He pulled the rolling stool over and sat down next to me.

"Yessir, that's right."

"Big football school, huh?"

"Yup, huge." *I had been to one game.*

He glanced at his chart. "So, Andrea says you've got a tooth botherin' you, huh?"

"Yessir, on my top right side."

"Well, all right, let me have a look. Okay, open wide for me." He pulled up his mask, and I closed my eyes as he explored my mouth. I was freezing. I clenched my fists and moved them under my behind for warmth.

"Mmmm hmmmm," he murmured. The feel of metal against my enamel made my skin crawl. I shut my eyes tighter and crossed my ankles. Every muscle in my body was tensed. He gently probed the tooth that bothered me—setting off fireworks of pain in my skull. My eyes welled up.

After what felt like an eternity, he sat up and pulled down his mask. "Well, sweetie, you have six cavities, and the tooth that's botherin' you needs a root canal and a crown." He shut the door. "And I wanna talk to you about something."

"Okay."

"Now, the last time you were here, your teeth were normal." He pointed to my chart. "You had one cavity and some tartar buildup. Not a big deal."

"Yessir."

"You also weighed what I'm estimatin' is about thirty pounds more. Is that fair to say?"

"Yeah—I mean, yessir." *Thirty-five actually, but who's counting.*

"Ruth." He raised his eyebrows. "You have the mouth of a ninety-year-old." I examined the pastel rendering of a sailboat that hung on the wall in front of me.

"The enamel on your teeth has reduced significantly, which is why they're fallin' apart. Now, do you know why your enamel is in trouble?" I shook my head.

"Well, it's probably a combination of the fact that your body isn't getting any nutrients and the fact that whatever nutrients it is gettin' are bein' thrown up."

I gulped. "I don't throw up," I said weakly.

"Okay," he answered. "But you're not eatin'. That's clear. And let me guess—whatever you do eat doesn't sit well, right? You have a lot of acid reflux?" He was right. I nodded.

"Now, Ruth, I'm just a dentist. I'm no nutritionist. That said, I've known you since you had baby teeth, and I've been practicin' a long time. I know an eating disorder when I see it. Teeth don't lie."

"You're not gonna call my parents, are you?"

"Well, I don't know. I'm sure they have the same concerns I do. If my daughter came home from college and she weighed ninety pounds soakin' wet, I'd get real nervous." He paused. "The fact is though, you're nineteen, and as a doctor, I can't tell them anything if you don't want me to—"

"I don't want you to."

"That's what I figured." He sighed. "Ruth, you're a smart girl. I want you to get help for this. You can get better. It doesn't have to be like this."

"I'm scared," I whispered.

"I know. But if your teeth look like this, think about the rest of your body. Your organs, your blood, your muscles. They're all sufferin' now, and I am sincerely worried about what the future holds for you if you don't get help. I can tell you for sure that your teeth are just going to get worse. I know you don't like comin' here, and I don't take it personally, darlin', but if you keep this up, you'll know this office like the back of your hand."

He patted my arm again. "Now, we're closin' up for the day, so I can't fix that bad tooth right this minute, even though I'd like to. You gonna be okay for a couple more days?"

I nodded as he patted my hand.

"Good girl. Go on out there and make some appointments with Charlene. We'll try to knock these out as quickly as possible." My eyes widened. "Not knock out your teeth! Just git 'er done as quickly as possible. Pardon the pun." He smiled and left the room.

I moved my fists out from under me and unclenched them in my lap. What did he know about me?

I wobbled uneasily down the short hallway to Charlene. I made my appointments and left the office in a daze. Outside, the sun's sizzle had subsided. *He does know what he's talking about. He's a doctor. He saw your insides and reported back from the front lines. You're falling apart.*

I started the car. How come none of those Hollywood chicks who so obviously starved themselves ever got sick? Where were the magazine covers showing girls with busted teeth and straw-like hair instead of the Photoshopped bullshit they all fed us? I mean, it wasn't like I never ate anything. How could one year destroy all of my teeth? I still got my period, for chrissake. I wasn't even a real anorexic. *Come on, Ruth. One year and your body is breaking down? You don't think he was being a little dramatic?*

I wanted a cigarette. I'd drive to the elementary school and go to my usual spot, since handling one behind the wheel would only mean bad things for my mother's upholstery and the road at large.

I turned into my neighborhood and almost directly into a familiar backside trudging up the hill in front of me. I rolled my window down.

"Khaki?"

Her mouth was set in a determined scowl. Purple head-phones covered her ears, clashing dramatically with the bright red hue of her face. I honked my horn a few times to no avail. Finally, she turned, with an expression of incredulous irritation. I waved obnoxiously.

"Geez, Ruth!" she said as she removed her headphones. "You scared me."

"What are you doing?"

"What does it look like I'm doing? I'm going for a walk."

"By yourself?"

"Yeah. Quit grinnin' at me like that! You're freaking me out."

"Am I? Okay, I'll stop. I'm just so happy to see you, I guess. Out here exercising on your own."

"It's just a twenty-minute walk. It's not such a big deal."

"But it is. I'm really impressed. Especially since we already went out this morning."

"I've been going out twice all week," she confessed. "Just a little walk in the afternoon. Nothing crazy." A car pulled up behind me, and I waved for it to go around.

"You look great, Khak. You want a ride home?"

"That kind of defeats the purpose, don't you think?"

"Fair enough, smarty-pants. Get home safe." She clamped her headphones back on her sweat-soaked head. As I drove off, I watched her in my rearview mirror with a small pit in my stomach. Laney Moorehouse, my own mom, and now me. Did you encourage a kid to diet because you wanted to spare her the taunts and teases, but end up robbing her of any sense of self-worth—fat or thin—in the process? Would Khaki look back on her summer with me fondly, or would she mark it as the beginning of her obsession with every calorie that she consumed? I really wanted to make sure it wasn't the latter. How, was the question.

21

Coach Ruth?"

I turned around and lowered my gaze. Tyler rubbed his belly as his Speedo dripped on the concrete below. He looked up at me through long, wet lashes rimmed by the red imprint of his goggles.

"Tyler! Third place, buddy!" I put my hand on his wet head.

"Third place!" he echoed, beaming.

"I'm so proud of you. Your backstroke was terrific. I saw you counting."

"I didn't bang my head on the wall!"

"You sure didn't. Good job, champ."

"Hey, Ruthie, guess what?" asked Jason, putting his hands on my shoulders from behind.

"What?"

"Tanisha's mom ain't gonna sue!" I whipped around to face him.

"What?"

"I just heard from Dusty."

"Get out! That's great news!" I hugged him tightly as the next batch of swimmers plunged into the pool beside us.

"I know it. That was a close one, for sure."

"What made her change her mind?"

"Dusty said that she decided to nail the Kiddy Kare instead. It's a better case or something."

"Hey, geeks," David said, passing by us.

"Did you hear the good news?"

"I did." He grinned. "I'm so relieved." *You should be.*

"No shit," agreed Jason.

"Plus, we're actually winning this thing. Did you know that?" His eyes darted back to the pool. "C'mon, Julie, push it!" he yelled and moved on, taking Jason with him. I stood there alone on the pool deck and took a deep breath, letting my gratefulness wash over me. *Thank you*, I whispered. I had been carrying the threat of the lawsuit around like a backpack filled with lead.

"Coach Ruth!" I turned around to find M.K. walking toward me. Her blond hair was pulled into a high ponytail, and it swung with her as she approached. In the twilight, she could have been twelve again.

"Hey! I was just drivin' by and saw all of the excitement. Figured I'd come down and cheer on the team."

"Where's your cheerleading outfit?"

"Please, I couldn't even get that past my pinky toe. Maybe I should give it to you. You can grow into it." She rolled her eyes.

"Derrrrrrrrrrr. Good one." I turned back around to face the pool. "I just got the best news." She raised her right eyebrow at me. "You know Tanisha's mom?"

"The mom of the girl you saved?"

I nodded. "She's not gonna sue the pool."

"That's awesome!" She enveloped me in a hug.

"And we're winning!"

"The Sharks are winning? Can this other team not swim or somethin'?"

"Nah. Half of the other team's been wiped out by the chicken pox. But still!" My littlest swimmers were crowded around the heat board, clutching their race cards cluelessly. "Listen, I gotta go take care of them, but stick around. This is the last event, and then maybe we can hang at your house or something?"

" 'Kay. I'm gonna go buy one of them ring-pops at the concession stand. I used to love those things."

I jogged over to the heat board.

"Coach Ruth, we're winnin'!" said Tyler. He was so excited that I became concerned he might pee on the ground in front of me.

"I know," I whispered. "But don't jinx it. Let's just keep up the good work, okay, guys?"

"Okay!" yelled Crystal. She danced around in a circle in her blue swim cap, clutching her pink card with red-tipped fingers.

"Coach Ruth, are you married?" she asked, stopping abruptly.

"No, Crystal, I'm not married." She looked at me with pity and gave me a consolatory pat on the knee.

"All right, let's go! Over to the blocks!" I stood to the side as they all handed their cards to their timers and climbed on top of the blue-carpeted pedestals. Ali stood at the bottom of hers with her lip trembling.

"Hey, Ali, what's the matter?" I asked, kneeling down.

She shook with tears as she looked at me with blue eyes. "I don't wanna do butterfly," she whimpered. "I hate it."

"Ali, I know you can do this. You've been doing so well in practice. You've come so far. Are you sure you don't want to do it?" Her shaking continued.

"It's okay if you don't wanna, baby. You can do it next meet." I reached for her hand. Her shaking was now a slight tremble, and her tears had stopped.

"You think I can do it?" she asked softly.

"I really do," I answered. "The way you've been practicin', I know you can."

"Okay," she whispered. "I'll do it."

"That's my girl!" I kissed her on the cheek and held her hand as she ascended her throne.

As the announcer yelled "Go!" they threw themselves off the blocks with unabashed enthusiasm. It didn't matter how many times you went over the starting dive when they were this young. They were just so excited to get into the water—it didn't matter whether it was a full-fledged belly flop or a jump or a cannonball or even a recognizable relative of the dive. As long as they were wet, they were happy.

Ali butterflied her way down the pool with surprising precision, and I did a little victory dance in my head. Seeing her tiny body undulating like a dolphin as she made her way toward the wall, her head and arms breaking through the water with strength and confidence, made me swell with pride and happiness. *I taught her that.*

After the last heat had swum, David and I gathered the team under the tent and waited for the scores. We held court in the middle of our circle of toweled kids. The last I'd checked, we were ahead, but the idea that we might actually have won the meet was so far-fetched that I couldn't fully conceive it. I looked around at all of them and felt a surge of maternal protectiveness.

"Is this thing on?" Jason asked into the microphone. "Testing, one, two—"

"It's on!" yelled David.

"Oh good. Thanks." He cleared his throat. "Well, I wanna thank y'all for comin' out tonight, especially the Bayside Barracudas." He paused to clap, and we all joined in reluctantly.

"Just announce it already," I muttered.

"The scores have been tallied, and I had to read this twice

I was so surprised, but I'm happy to say that the Sharks have won! Congratulations, y'all! You won a swim meet!" The circle erupted in squeals and shouts of victory. I surprised my own self by jumping up and down. Suddenly I felt arms around me. It was David, hugging me with all of his might.

"We did it!" he yelled.

"We did!" I yelled back. I felt like we were little again. There were no secrets and no resentment—just unabashed love for the person who always had your back. My legs were soon being hugged by what felt like thousands of little hands, and my shorts were practically being tugged off.

"Coach Ruth, we did it! We won!" my guppies yelled. Even the sullen teenagers were jumping around like maniacs, high-fiving me and David with abandon. Hands grabbed me under my armpits and another set took my feet. I craned my head back to see Jason laughing maniacally.

"Ready to take a victory lap, Ruthie?" he teased.

"Nooooo," I screamed in protest. Julie had my feet.

"Let's go, girl! In the pool with ya!" I looked around for David. Kevin, Derrick, and Mike were carrying him.

"Dude, take off my shoes! Please!" he begged.

"No way, man. All or nothin'!" They carried us kicking and screaming to the pool.

The kids surrounded us and started chanting, "Coach Ruth! Coach David! Coach Ruth! Coach David!"

"One, two, three!" they yelled in unison as they threw us both into the deep end. I hit the water laughing. Once I was under, I looked around for David. He floated in front of me, smiling. I felt optimistic for the first time in weeks. Maybe we could get past this summer and have a stronger relationship be-cause of it. Maybe all of this—his being high and dropping out of school—was in my head. And even if it wasn't, and both things were true, why did it have to affect us? Why couldn't I accept that our former closeness was born out of circumstance and that as we got older our connection would require more work? He swam up to the surface, the white and green of his sneakers scissoring eerily through its silent depths.

I followed. As I broke through, the noise reverberated in my eardrums. Screams and laughter were punctuated by splash after splash as everyone joyously hurled themselves into the pool with us. I closed my eyes and tread water for a second, before the inevitable barrage of flailing hands and feet pulled me under again.

22

Cynthia!" I stopped midstride to greet her. She was gardening in her front yard.

"Ruth! I thought I was the only one up this early." She rose to her feet and smiled at me from beneath the brim of her straw hat.

"It's the only time of day I can even think about running." I panted. "It's too damn hot otherwise."

"Indeed, it is. Here, let me run inside and get you some water."

"No, that's oka—"

"Not another word. Follow me." She led the way down her driveway, which was flanked on both sides by lush, green bushes.

"Your yard is gorgeous," I said, regaining my breath.

"Oh, aren't you sweet. Thanks. Gardenin' is my passion. Used to be men, but those days are long gone." She opened her back door and went inside. "Well, c'mon now, don't be shy," she said a moment later, sticking her head out of the door with a look of impatience. I joined her in the kitchen, embarrassed by my own awkwardness.

Cynthia's sun-drenched kitchen was refreshingly devoid of sports paraphernalia, porcelain cows, or wooden ducks. It was large and airy with a giant, birch island in the middle. Copper pots hung from the ceiling. A green apple sat on a cutting board, sliced down the middle.

"Here you go." She handed me the water. "Thank you so much," I said after I had finished it in one gulp.

"Here, let me get you one more." She walked to the faucet. "So, I'm sure you heard the good news about Mary," she said with her back to me.

"Yes! It is such good news. I'm so happy she's not gonna sue. I was so worried."

"You and me both, darlin'." She handed me my refill and took a seat at the glass-topped white wicker table. "Come," she offered, pulling a chair out. "Just for a minute."

I sat down, gratefully. "Cynthia?"

"What's that?"

"I had an idea. Tell me if you think I'm nuts."

"With pleasure."

"I was thinking about offering Tanisha swim lessons. So she wouldn't be scared of the water." I had been tossing the thought around in my head for a week, and it felt good to say it aloud.

"Ruth, that's a lovely idea." She looked me in the eye. "I'm not sure her mama is gonna be up for it, but I certainly think you should talk to her about it."

"You do? You don't think I'd be overstepping my bounds? Or swirling the pot again?"

"You might get a gentle swirl goin' for a minute, but nothin' good ever came out of still waters."

"Is that true?"

Cynthia laughed. "I don't know! I swear, some of the things that come out of my mouth these days are ridiculous."

I laughed too. "But it sounded good!"

"Didn't it, though?" She clapped her hands. "You need her mama's number, don't you?"

"I do."

"Well, it's your lucky day, Ruth. I have it in my office. I'll go get it for you. Worst-case scenario, she tells you to take a flyin' leap, but somethin' tells me she won't."

"You workin' today?" I looked up from stretching on the family room floor to find David looming over me.

"Naw," I said "I have the day off, actually."

"Lucky." He stretched to the ceiling. "It's so nice not to have to coach this morning. I'm glad we gave those little fuckers the morning off."

"I still can't believe we actually won a meet," I replied, extending my hand for help up. He pulled me to my feet and proceeded to the kitchen. Should I tell him about my decision to call Mary?

"I know, right? It's a miracle." He peered into the refrigerator and pulled out a carton of orange juice. No, I wanted to keep it to myself. Why should he get to keep all the secrets?

"You working this morning?" I asked.

"Yeah." He poured juice into his glass. "Hey, remember when Dad would pour us juice when we were little? He would hold it way up high but still manage to hit the cup?" He smiled broadly at me.

"Never spilled a drop. I used to think that was the coolest thing."

"I know, like a superpower or something." He took a large gulp. "Must be cool to be a dad. When your kids are little, at least."

"Yeah, then they grow up to be assholes." I sat down next to him at the table.

"Hey, Ruth?"

"Yeah?" My pulse quickened. Would he tell me now? About school?

"You've got a giant eye booger in the corner of your left eye."

"Great, thanks." I got up.

"What? I thought I was helping you out!" I walked out of the kitchen. "What?" he called after me. I peeled my running clothes off and got into the shower. Why couldn't I just ask him outright about dropping out? I wasn't sure what I was afraid of exactly. If it was a rumor, would he be upset that I had been gullible enough to buy it? And if it wasn't a rumor, how was me knowing going to change anything? The water cascaded down my face. Chris was picking me up in an hour. Today was our beach date. With my eyes closed, I smoothed my stomach down with both hands, as if willing it to be perfectly flat could make it so.

Later, in my room, I angled my mirrored closet doors so that I could get the 360-degree view. The red straps of my swimsuit cut into my back, causing my flesh to swell over them. I began to panic. *Breathe, Ruth*, I said to myself, as my body temperature rose.

Lightheaded and dizzy, I crossed to my bed, sat on it, and put my head between my hands. The rational Ruth said that those were not flesh swells at all, but rather what happened when any human being pressed something tightly against their skin. The crazy Ruth barely could see the straps—her skin puffed like a hot dog bun around each one. I wore this dumb swimsuit every day in front of an entire pool of people, and yet today felt like the first day I had put it on somehow. Yeah, right, I'd be going bikini shopping with M.K. and Jill. That would be the day. I eyed my midsection as I slumped over. A roll of fat puffed out defeatedly beneath my breasts. I sat up straight, and it all but disappeared. With a few careful readjustments of the suit's fabric, it did disappear. Even the crazy Ruth saw that. I exhaled deeply. Was I blow-drying my hair and putting makeup on now? For a day at the beach? The asshole quotient on that decision was huge, but then again—this was a date. And the idea was to distract from the body in the bathing suit, not make it the center of attention. Maddie padded in and eyed the hair dryer in my hand warily.

"You're right, this is stupid." I placed it back on my vanity table and slicked my wet hair back into a bun. I needed to relax. I also needed to eat something. My plan had been to try to skip breakfast altogether, but seeing stars every time I turned my head was a recipe for disaster in the hot sun. Crazy Ruth and rational Ruth actually agreed on that.

I pulled a tank top and some cutoffs on over my suit and slipped my feet into my flip-flops. Wait, earrings! Hoop earrings. My Beyonce at the beach look. I inserted them into my ears, stuffed a towel and a change of underwear and bra into my bag, and looked at my clock. I had twenty minutes. I had to eat.

Tossing my bag onto the couch, I made a beeline for the refrigerator. I grabbed my cereal and the milk and set the bowl clattering down on the counter.

The back door opened, and my mom entered the kitchen, her wet hair clinging to her scalp like Saran wrap.

"It has to be 110 degrees out there," she huffed. She grabbed a glass and filled it under the faucet. "Sweet Jesus, it is so hot." She took off her glasses and placed them gingerly on the counter. "You headed to work, Ruthie?"

"No, I have the day off. I'm headed to the beach."

"Oh, nice. Bring water, for goodness' sake. With the girls?"

"No, with Chris," I mumbled.

"Ooh!" My mom put her glasses back on with delight. "Well, have fun." She took a giant sip. "And lose the earrings, honey. They look ridiculous."

"So, how've you been? Saved any more lives since I last saw you?" yelled Chris, over the air hurtling by us. We had the top down on his Jeep. Although the wind kept the scorch of the sun at bay, and it was invigorating to ride shotgun in this open advertisement for coolness, my hair was a different story. *Freedom!* it cried as it curled and swirled. Plus, having a conversation was hopeless. We could barely hear the radio, and it was cranked to an obscene decibel.

I made a thumbs-up sign. "It's impossible to talk in this wind!" I yelled.

"What?" he yelled back.

"*Too loud!*" He nodded and took a hand off of the wheel to make a circle over his head with his hand.

"You wanna put the top up?" he screamed.

"No way!" I smiled as convincingly as I could as my hair blinded me. I was not going to be the girly girl who couldn't take an hour or two of gale-force winds. Nossir. I was footloose and fancy-free. One of those girls from rom-coms who watches football and eats chicken wings for breakfast, but still has a soft, sensitive side—maybe plays gin rummy with her grandmother in a nursing home three times a week, or runs a foster care program for abused dogs out of her basement. Yep, that was me. A contradiction in terms.

"*There's a hat in the back!*" he yelled.

"*A cat in the what?*"

"*A hat! A hat!*" He pointed to his own, which advertised a fishing rodeo.

"*Oh, a hat!*" I smiled gratefully, although he wouldn't have known it through the curtain of frizz that now covered my entire face. I reached into the back and retrieved a beat-up Atlanta

Braves cap that was wedged beneath one of the seats. I knew this hat. Chris and David had both returned from their seventh-grade trip to Six Flags with them, refusing to actually wear them in public until they were properly broken in. For months you could find the two of them in David's room playing video games and training the rigid brims to round themselves just so, running their hands around the perimeter of the caps like deranged potters. I jammed it onto my head now, marveling at the memory. Would I ever in a million years, as I snuck glances at Chris on the sly, have imagined that I would one day be wearing that hat on my way to the beach with him? Without David? Never.

What was going to come of this, whatever it was that we were doing? I was going back to Michigan in less than two months, and he was staying here. I snuck a glance at him in his Wayfarers and cap, his dark hair curling around his brown neck, and I decided that I would try my best just to relish what was happening now. It was best for everyone not to think beyond the summer. Then again, I was the girl whose lunch on Monday affected her dinner on Thursday, so it was easy to doubt my conviction to stay rooted in the present.

We whipped our way toward the water, and I enjoyed the easy silence, the salty air, and the happy sun bouncing on the horizon. Seagulls cawed and pelicans swooped lazily over-head. Church signs offering cringe-worthy reasons to read the Bible whizzed by us. *Jesus will save you!* they cried. *Salvation is within! And don't forget the bake sale!* You'd never see a sign like that in front of a synagogue. Or would you? *Did you call your mother today?* one might ask. *Enough with this rain!* would cry another.

Finally, the Gulf greeted us; its warm, grayish waters gently lapping at the white shore in the heat. The sand shone like sea salt. We drove away from the main thoroughfare and parked.

Chris put his hand on my leg, and I blushed underneath the brim of my hat.

"You okay?" he asked, with a grin.

"Perfect." I smiled back. "That was a great ride." He leaned in to kiss me.

"Been wantin' to do that since I picked you up." He pushed my brim up gently to see my face. "You look pretty cute in that hat." *Don't be a smart-ass, Ruth. Take the compliment.*

"Thanks. You too."

"All right, let's get on the beach. I brought a little cooler—just some drinks and snacks and stuff." He jumped out of the Jeep and reached into the back.

"Look at you! A regular Martha Stewart." I got out and stretched.

"That's me. Got some crustless sandwiches and homemade potato chips. Them tiny lemon cookies too."

"You do not!"

He laughed. "Nah, I'm playin'. Just some beers and chips. Hope that's okay."

"It's perfect." We began our walk to the water. "You had me going there for a minute, though." Our flip-flops slapped the bleached wood of the boardwalk until we reached sand. I took them off and submerged my feet into its infinite warmth.

"Nothing like a lil' sand between the toes," I said, smiling.

"Yeah, until it starts to burn your feet to a crisp around noon." We smiled and made small talk as we set up our camp. I reached for the towel in my bag.

"I brought a sheet," he offered shyly, pulling it out of his backpack.

"You thought of everything!" My heartbeat quickened as I imagined lying next to him, practically naked with nothing separating us.

"Well, it's a date. You gotta do things right if you want to impress the ladies." He gave me a wink. Underneath his bravado, I could sense his nervousness as well. Maybe I would drink a beer. I touched my stomach.

"Why do you always do that?" he asked, setting the sheet in place by sitting the cooler on one corner and his bag on the other. I put my bag and towel on the remaining two. A perfect square of baby blue looked up at us.

"Do what?" I stood there awkwardly, nervous about disrobing.

"You brush your stomach like you're pushing it off of you. Like this." He demonstrated by placing his hand underneath his chest and pushing it down across his flat abdomen.

"I do?"

"You didn't know that?" He took off his hat, and his hair gripped his skull like a yarmulke with wings. "It's cute."

"No, I didn't." I was embarrassed.

"Your hair looks really sexy, by the way," I snarked, hoping to change the subject. Now I really didn't want to take my shirt off. I sat down heavily.

"Hey, I didn't mean to make you uncomfortable." He sat down beside me. "I really think it's a cute tick."

"Like Tourette's, right?"

"No, like cute." He put his arm around me and pulled me to him. I was keenly aware of his bare chest pressing against my tank top. There was only so much longer that I could keep my shirt on without feeling like a Mormon.

"That sun feels amazing," he said, lying back on the blanket. *Okay, one, two, three, take it off.* I lay down quickly before I could obsess. The sand cupped my back like a heated foam mattress underneath the blanket.

"It really does." I agreed, stretching out my legs. "For some reason so much different here than at the pool." I stretched my arms out too.

He rolled over onto his arm and peered down at me. "What?" I asked.

"I feel like I'm on a date with Pamela Anderson." He touched my red rib cage.

"Very funny. This happens to be the only bathing suit I own." He put his arm around me and lowered his curly head onto my chest.

"I'm serious, Ruth! You look hot. Red is your color."

"What are you, my gay stylist?" I laughed. "Red is my color?"

"Gay! I'll show you gay!" He rolled on top of me and pinned me to the ground, hovering just inches from my face. His hands made my forearms feel like chopsticks. Inside, I turned to jelly. He leaned down to kiss me, and the exquisite weight of his chest on top of mine made me catch my breath.

"Okay, you're not gay," I whispered as we lay on our sides facing each other.

He smiled and touched my face.

"Want a beer?" He sat up and rummaged through the cooler.

"It's not even 11:00 AM!"

"What are you, a nun? It's a summer day at the beach." He pulled a can out and popped it open. "You want?" Cold beads of water glistened invitingly on its aluminum surface.

"Yeah, sure. Why not?" *The calories! Shut up, Ruth. You'll skip lunch.*

"Nice." He handed it to me and opened his own. I sat up as straight as I could, careful to arrange my suit over my stomach as I moved, and gazed out at the water. Our blanket smelled like coconut.

"How's David?" he asked.

"Oh, he's good, I guess."

"You guess? Don't you see each other every day at swim practice and stuff?"

"Yeah, but that doesn't mean we talk." He nodded and took another sip.

"I get that. But y'all used to be pretty close, right?"

"Depends on what you mean by close, you know? I mean, we would hang out and stuff, but we never really broke it down or anything."

"You were always hangin' out with us." He smiled. *Jesus, he was cute.*

"Yeah, volunteering for slaughter."

He laughed. "Whaddya mean? We played fair with you."

"Ruth, grab our rebounds! Ruth, watch for cars! Ruth, bring us some popcorn." I smirked. "Yeah, super fair."

"You were so cute, Ruthie. And fun too."

"I dunno about cute or fun, but I did love being around you guys. It was great to be the token chick. I didn't really have any guy friends growing up, you know. I'm a girl's girl."

"The best kind to be, if you ask me. Who the hell would want to hang out with dudes all day if they had the choice?" The beer zipped quickly down my internal highway to my brain.

"But I feel like you and David were close, even without me around."

"I guess we were when we were little," I said. "Things got more complicated around middle school. He became *David Wasserman*, you know? And I was just the same."

"Huh?"

"Yeah, with his soccer and how good-looking he was and stuff. And his good grades." I screwed my empty can deep into the sand. "He's like a celebrity."

"He's always just been David to me."

"That's because you're a celebrity too, silly."

"Oh yeah?" He smiled sadly. "That's rich. Me, a celebrity." He took his cap off and raked his hands through his hair. "Maybe I used to have a fair amount of clout in high school, but that's not the way it is now."

"What do you mean?" I asked, even though I knew the answer.

"Come on, I go to Tech, and I live at home with my mama." He smiled, but his eyes were sad. "Not that I miss that bullshit, I truly don't, but I'm just sayin' that status like that can flip on a dime. That's one of the reasons I miss talkin' to your brother. We used to really talk about shit, you know? Not just surface stuff. I wonder how he's doin' in Oxford."

"You guys really used to *talk* talk?"

"Ruth, please start sayin' 'y-all' again, at least when you're with me. That Yankee 'you guys' mess is like nails across a chalkboard."

"Oh well, excuse me. First Martha Stewart, now you're Paula Dean!" He threw his head back and laughed.

"Point for Ruth." He sighed. "But yeah, of course we used to talk. You think we just sat around from first grade to senior year playing video games and passin' gas? C'mon now."

"What would you talk about?"

"Oh you know, this and that. He may have seemed really confident on the outside, but he wasn't so much on the inside. I think he felt sort of trapped by, what did you call it, his celebrity?"

"How?"

"I mean, when you're that perfect, it's hard to fuck up, you know? Especially if you're a good guy like he is. You don't want to disappoint anybody."

"I didn't realize that it was a struggle for him."

"Well, struggle is sort of a dramatic word, but yeah, I'd say it bothered him. And then the whole art major thing. He really wanted to study that at school, but knew that it wasn't exactly a smart plan for the future."

"He knew, or my parents convinced him?"

"Probably a little of both. But listen, I don't wanna really get into this. It's stuff between me and him."

"Oh, bro code?"

"Yeah." We sat in silence for a moment, watching the waves lap at the shore.

"I'm sorry he's been so distant." I put my hand on his back, which was damp with sweat. "I know how it feels. I miss him too." I wondered if Chris had heard the rumor. Should I ask?

"Wanna get in the water?" I nodded, and he pulled me to my feet.

Another day, I would ask. Today was about us and whatever this was. Because whatever this was felt pretty great.

23

"Hello?"

"Hi, Ruth?"

"This is her. I mean, she. This is she."

"Ruth, this is Miss Mary, Tanisha's mom. You called?"

"Oh, hi." My palms immediately began to sweat, and I put the dish sponge face down on the aluminum sink. I glanced nervously at the kitchen table, where my dad was reading the paper and spooning cereal out of a giant orange bowl. Maddie's tail swished against my feet. She looked up at me expectantly.

"How are you?" I asked awkwardly.

"I'm fine. Happy Fourth of July. Y'all got somethin' goin' at the pool today?"

"Oh yes, ma'am. A big day of relays and pizza and stuff. What are you guys gonna do?"

"Our family has a big party every year down at the park. We'll be barbecuin' while the kids run around all day."

"Oh, nice."

"Listen, I wanted to talk to you about that message you left for me the other day. About swim lessons for Tanisha?"

"Sure." I walked out of the kitchen and through the family room.

"Can I ask you somethin'?"

"Please."

"Why you doin' this? Tanisha could get swim lessons from someplace else, you know, we don't need a handout."

"Oh, I—"

"Not to mention the fact that you're askin' my baby to come back to the scene of the crime—the place where she almost drowned. That could be pretty traumatic for a five-year-old."

"I understand that, Ma—, Miss Mary. I thought it might be good for her, though, to go back to the pool and see it as a safe place instead of a scary one. You know, confronting her fears and all that."

Mary laughed. "Look at you, gettin' all Dr. Phil on us! She's *five*, girl."

"Yes, ma'am, I know. Maybe that was naive of me."

"You feel guilty about what happened? Is that what this is about?"

"I don't know if 'guilty' is the right word. I just don't want her to be scared of the water. And I like Tanisha a lot—she's a sweet girl. I coach swim team anyway, so I'm up in the morning early. An extra half-hour of coaching time isn't a big deal to me."

"How come your brother ain't offerin' his services? He's the one who let her go under, isn't he? He doesn't feel guilty?"

"All due respect, Miss Mary, he didn't let her do anything. She was in his blind spot. That's why you have two lifeguards on duty at a time, in case one of you misses something. He doesn't even know I'm offering these lessons up."

"Oh, y'all don't talk?"

"Yes, we talk." She was annoying me. Were we sorority sisters shooting the shit or were we going to agree to something here? "Listen, do you want to do this? I have to get to work."

"Okay, Miss Attitude! Hold on a second." She covered the

receiver with her hand, but I could hear muffled voices. Moments later, she peeled her hand off and returned. "You know what, I think we should give the lessons a try. If it's not workin' out, we quit."

"I think that's a great idea. I really do. I like Tan—"

"Yeah, we already covered that. When do we start?"

"How about Monday at nine AM?"

"Same pool? Down at the bottom of that hill?"

"That's the one."

"All right, we'll be there."

"Great, see you then."

"Ruth?"

"Yes?"

"Thank you," she said quickly and hung up. I felt good about this—like I was doing the right, unselfish thing for once. Should I tell David? I wasn't sure how he would react. He'd either tell me that I was a busybody and that I should just have left it alone, or he'd want to get in on the action and help Tanisha too. I wanted this to be my thing. So much for unselfish.

"Who was that?" asked my dad, suddenly appearing in my doorway.

"No one! Quit snooping around."

"I'm not snooping. I was just concerned. You sounded nervous."

"Dad, take it easy. I'm a big girl." I sighed heavily. "You're such a yenta."

"You headed to the pool?"

"Yeah, I have to work all day."

"Your mom and I might come down later for some pizza or something."

"Okay, cool." I got up and grabbed my backpack. As I walked out the door, he hugged me.

"I'm sorry, Ruthie. I'll try to de-yenta-ize myself."

"It's okay, Dad, I know you can't help it."

"Hey, listen, your brother's exhibition game is this weekend—on Saturday. Your mother and I are going to drive over to Atlanta and surprise him. I don't know what your plans are, but it might be fun if you came along. A Wasserman road trip, just like the old days!"

My stomach plunged to the floor. "Do what now?"

"It's their annual Mercer opening scrimmage. All of the guys come together for a practice game before they return to school for good. Remember? We went last year."

"Why are you not telling David you're coming?" My voice cracked.

"Eh, he's been such a pill all summer. We thought it would be nice to surprise him and maybe take him out for a big meal afterward. Make him feel special. Why, what's the big deal?"

"No big deal, just asking." This was going to be a disaster of epic proportions. I wasn't sure who I wanted to protect more, them or David.

"So think about it. It would be nice if you came along." He patted me on the back and left the room.

Outside, I retrieved my bike in a haze of anxious fog. This was serious. I had no idea what to do. I couldn't warn David because he didn't know I knew. And besides, how could this be fixed? Was he going to pretend to be on the team? Suit up and then kind of linger off to the side like some kind of creepy fan? And wait—this meant that he was actually planning to pretend to go to Atlanta, so as not to tip off my parents. What was with him? Why go to all of this trouble? Unless, of course, the rumor was completely untrue and I was the gullible jerk who believed it—and wanted to believe it. Was I really a sister so desperate for her brother to screw up that she mistook hearsay for truth and gave herself an ulcer in the process?

I pedaled slowly. The road shimmered ahead of me. Should I

just confront David and get it over with? That way, if it was true, he had time to try to forge some sort of game plan, and if it wasn't true, I was just casually mentioning a rumor that I had heard. Yeah, that was the way to face it—as casually as possible. I made a left and soon was sailing down the hill that led to the pool. I closed my eyes and tried to appreciate the wind on my face.

"Ruthie!" yelled Jason from inside the snack bar as I parked. "You ready to pull double duty today?"

"Whaddya mean?" I asked as I walked in.

"Your jackass brother took off for a soccer game in Atlanta and left us high and dry. On the biggest day of the summer no less."

"What?"

"He took off for a soccer game."

"But it's not until Saturday! Today is Thursday." Never mind the fact that he doesn't even play for the team—that he doesn't even go to the damn school. *Ruth, quit jumping to conclusions. Stay calm.*

"All I know is, he said he wanted to leave today, so he left."

I threw my backpack behind the snack bar and collapsed into the white plastic chair while Jason opened the fridge and did a quick corndog tally. "We should be okay on food today. I did a huge shop this morning. Hey, who died? You're lookin' a little sour."

"Just a shitty morning." I sighed. "I'm not in the mood for this today. And how come I have to pull a double? It's bullshit."

"Join the freakin' club, princess. You think I'm in the mood to deal with a hundred screaming kids and their parents?" He pointed to his truck, which was parked in the back. "That oughta cheer you up. You know what's fillin' up that bed?"

"What?"

"Watermelons! We're gonna grease 'em up and do that relay race we did last year."

"Great, I can't wait."

"Buck up, Wasserman, I mean it. You're gonna look back on these summers when you're old and creaky and realize that this was the good life."

"Don't we need to hang some dumb American flags or something?" I rifled through my bag for a cigarette.

"Hey there, watch yer mouth. Ain't nothin' dumb about that flag. Man, I love that song—how does it go? *I'm proud to be an American—*"

"*Where at least I know I'm free,*" I chimed in flatly.

"*And I won't forget the men who dieddddddddddd—*"

I lit my cigarette and blew smoke in his face.

"Real nice, Ruth. You're just way too cool for school, ain'tcha?" He took it out of my hand and crushed it beneath his sneaker. "This is a no smoking area. Let's go check the chlorine." I sulked as I flip-flopped along behind him, straightening the plastic lounge chairs as I went. He knelt down to fill the plastic vial with water.

"It's hot as hell already," he said. "Damn."

"Hey, do you think David's been a little weird this summer?" I asked.

"Weird how?"

"I dunno, weird as in not his usual self. Sorta quiet."

"Yeah, I guess so, now that you mention it." He held the vial up to check the level. "Perfect."

"Has he said anything to you at all?"

"Has he said anything to me about bein' quiet? Ain't that an oxymoron, Ruthie?" I rolled my eyes. "Why, you worried about him?"

"No! Not worried. Just curious." It was obvious Jason knew nothing.

"Hey!" called Dana from the parking lot, interrupting the conversation.

"Dana!" he yelled back. "Get yer ass down here and lube up some watermelons!"

I blew my whistle. "No running!"

The kids were like feral cats today—screaming like banshees, jumping off every raised surface, shoving food in their faces at every opportunity, peeing in the pool. It was off the charts.

All the while I couldn't get my mind off the whole exhibition game mishigas. Not only was David lying to my parents about school, but he was lying to everyone else as well. Me, Jason, and who knows who else. Leaving early to play for an imaginary soccer team at an imaginary college where he was imaginary enrolled? I was so confused. Where was he?

"Yo, Ruth, I'm here to relieve you."

I jumped, startled by Kevin's voice below me. "Oh, sorry. This heat has melted my brain." I scooted over and kept my eyes on the pool as he climbed up.

"Hey, are we okay?" he asked. I looked up as my feet hit the pavement.

"Huh?"

"I just feel like you've been pretty frigid to me since our argument." His eyes were obscured by his mirrored sunglasses. My own face stared back at me.

"Yeah, well, you know. I don't agree with what you said." I scratched a mosquito bite on the top of my left foot with my right.

"I get that. I'm sorry I said it." He raised the umbrella slightly. "That's not how I feel all the time."

"Yeah. I guess the way I see it is that if that word is even in your vocabulary, it's the way you feel most of the time."

"Can we just agree to disagree and go back to the way things were?"

"Could you at least try to open your mind, Kevin? Just a little?"

"Deal."

"Okay, deal." I smiled at him. I knew that our conversation would most likely have no effect on him, but just to be speaking about it seemed hopeful enough.

"When's the pizza comin'?" I asked Dana back at the concession stand. I filled up my water bottle and eyed the card tables decorated with American flag paper tablecloths, napkins, and plastic utensils.

"In about a half-hour," she answered, yawning. "I am starvin'."

I was too, but I didn't know what I was going to eat. I could scrape all the toppings off the pizza and just eat the bread. That would kill two birds with one stone—hunger and the prying eyes of the pool's concerned citizen brigade. Strategizing every meal was exhausting. It was like a culinary game of "Survivor," only I was the solitary contestant.

"Ruth?" I turned to find Khaki holding up a plastic water bottle. "Could I get a refill, please?"

"Of course." I took her bottle from her. "Hey, Khaki, you look great." She had lost weight, but I hadn't been able to see it until now. The bones in her face had started to emerge. No longer round, her face was more like a small, freckled heart.

"I ran this morning," she whispered, glancing nervously at Dana, who was texting furiously on her BlackBerry.

"You did?" I came out from behind the desk and hugged her. "That's amazing! How did it feel?"

"Awful." She sighed. "Well, just at first it was awful. It got a little bit better after a couple minutes or so."

"Seriously? I am so proud of you. Running on your own? That is badass."

Her eyes widened at my curse. "Thanks, Ruth." She glanced over at the food table. "I'm gonna have some pizza later. Just a slice or two. Because I ran and stuff." She looked up at me. "I can, right? That's the moderation thing you were talking about?"

"It is. And of course you can. You've earned it."

"Ruth!" We looked up, startled. It was Laney. "Ruth, did you see Miss Khaki today? Doesn't she look wonderful?" She kneeled down and gave her daughter a peck on the cheek. "I mean, we are on our way to bein' a supermodel, aren't we, Khak?" Khaki gazed at the concrete. "Ruth, we could not be more pleased. Thank you for all of the work you've been puttin' in. Khaki just adores you." She paused. "Isn't that right, sweetie? You love Miss Ruth." Khaki nodded dejectedly.

"Oh, I didn't do anything. It's all Khaki. She a strong girl. I'm really proud of her." I took her hand and squeezed.

"Khaki, now you know Mama's got some vegetable slices all crisp and ready for you in the cooler. We'll have some of that instead of that nasty pizza, mmkay?" She smoothed Khaki's hair.

"Hey, can I steal your daughter for a sec? Just to talk?"

"Sure you can. Y'all have fun. Khaki, when you're finished, I'll be at our table settin' up lunch." Khaki nodded dejectedly.

We sat on the grass a few feet away from the entrance. "So," I said.

"So," she replied, picking at her purple toenail polish.

"Veggie slices, huh?" I asked.

"Yeah."

"Did you tell your mom that you ran today?"

"Yeah, she doesn't care."

"Are you sure?"

"Trust me."

"Well, she should. You can't deny yourself all of the time. If you do, you'll break and eat your way through ten pizzas."

"Ten?"

"Okay, ten is an exaggeration."

"Do you eat pizza?" she asked accusingly.

"Well, I—"

"Mmm hmmm. I thought so."

"Khaki, I want to tell you something. You think I'm skinny and I've got it all figured out, right?"

"You just said you did. *Moderation*, you said."

I nodded thoughtfully. "The moderation thing is true, but I—I've kind of lost my way a little, I think." I'd barely admitted this to myself, and here I was talking to a nine-year-old like she was my shrink.

"What do you mean?"

"Well, I just sort of wish that someone had been honest with me about the healthy way to lose or maintain weight when I was your age. I mean, I've told you that I've basically been on a diet myself since kindergarten."

"Like me."

"Yes, exactly like you. Except you're smarter than I was." She smiled.

"No one ever really taught me to be smart about food. I think in a lot of ways my mom was just as unhelpful as yours is with you. It's not their fault really—it comes from a place of love and concern, I think—but it's bad news to teach you an all-or-nothing attitude. It's not a fun way to live, and in the long run it does more damage than good."

"But how? You look great. You're skinny, and everyone thinks you're pretty. That doesn't sound too bad to me."

"Khaki, you know when you're scared of, say, dogs or thunder?"

"Or snakes?"

"Yeah, or snakes. Well, that's how I feel about food most of the time."

"It is?"

"Yeah. I'm scared of food. I can save a drowning kid, but I can't eat a bite of mashed potatoes because I'm scared that I'll gain weight. It's sad, and it's not a healthy way to live. I know that, rationally, but once you form a habit, it's hard to break."

"Like my mom. She smokes cigarettes, but she thinks no one knows. She hides behind the shed in the backyard."

"Exactly like that." I swallowed my tears. "I don't want you to live like that. I want you to have a piece of pizza when you feel like it. Does that make sense?"

"How come you're tellin' me to listen to this, but you won't listen yourself?"

"Your mom tells you not to smoke, right?"

"Yeah."

"But she still does, right?" Khaki nodded.

"I guess it's sort of like that. But I'm gonna try to be better, to moderate. Maybe we could both try it together."

"But you're leaving soon, to go back to Michigan. How can we do it together if you're not here?"

"Email, duh."

"Promise?"

"I promise." I stood and reached down to help her up. "And I'll talk to your mom too, okay?"

"She's not gonna like it," she replied as I pulled her to her feet.

"Yeah, I know. But we're in this together now."

Was I going to face this problem? Finally, I'd admitted out loud that it was a problem. Yes, it had been to a nine-year-old, but still. It was a start.

I sat on the deck watching Jason and Dana preside over the watermelon relay. The goal was to swim a length of the pool with a
slippery watermelon in tow. Shrieks of laughter and whistle blows
filled the air as the glistening fruit refused to cooperate. Should I
call David? I could keep my mouth shut and hope for the best—
the best being David playing in the game and no one the wiser
about the rumor and my subsequent awfulness. Or I could take a
risk and warn him ahead of time. My phone weighed heavily in
the pocket of my shorts. Could I pull it off in a text?

I pulled it out and flipped it open and shut, and open again,
debating. I had to do it. The trick was how. *Just do it, Ruth. He
probably won't even respond.* My heart raced.

Where ru?

I typed. I laid the phone on my lap and took a deep breath.
The watermelon relay continued. Khaki and her mother swam
beside each other, laughing, trying to contain the fruit between
them. I smiled, surprised.

Msspi. Why?

I felt like I was going to puke. What now?

U sure?

My sticky palms smeared the phone's keypad.

What?

Are you sure ur in Msspi?

Ruth, what the hell?

That was when I knew that he wasn't. My stomach dropped.

Pls call me.

I stood up, my heart pounding in my ears.

"Ruth, where you goin'?" yelled Jason from the other side of the pool. "We're about to play Sharks 'n' Minnows!"

"I'll be right back," I replied. I made my way to the pump room behind the pool. Inside the tiny concrete room, the pump chugged and whirled. My phone vibrated again. David was calling. I closed the door behind me.

"Hi."

"Ruth, what's happening?"

"David. Did you drop out of school?" Silence. "David?"

"Why are you asking me this?" he asked softly. I had expected him to be angry and defensive, but instead he just sounded sad and tired.

"I heard a rumor."

He sighed. "Yeah."

"Yeah, what?"

"I stopped going last semester."

"But I don't understand. Why?"

"A lotta reasons, I guess."

"But why didn't you tell Mom and Dad? Why are you still pretending to go there? Why are you still pretending to play soccer?" I was crying.

"I just—I just didn't know what else to do. I knew they would kill me, you know? I figured I'd stay in Atlanta until I figured out a plan." I heard the flick of a lighter and then a sharp inhale. "But then I really wanted to come home for the summer and work at the pool. I love that dumb place. I thought not doing that would be more suspicious, I guess. They would've wanted to come visit me here. Jesus, Ruth, are you crying?"

"No," I sniffled. "David, where did you live last semester? How did you make everything up? Your report card and stuff?"

"Ruth, I know it's fucked up. I'm fucked up right now, okay?"

"I mean, you're pretending to be in Atlanta right now, playing soccer. You're not even on the team. And they're coming down there to surprise you—"

"Wait, what?"

"That's why I texted you. Mom and Dad are coming! They want to surprise you at the game."

"Shit. Shitfuckshit."

"What are you gonna do? Where are you anyway?"

"When were they gonna leave? Saturday morning?"

"Yeah." We sat in silence. The pump heaved beside me.

"Well, I'm gonna have to tell 'em." He sighed. "Had to come out sometime, I guess."

"Where are you?"

"I'm at the beach." I sighed deeply. "Listen, I'm gonna come home tomorrow afternoon and tell them. I need you to not say anything before then, okay?"

"Great, another secret to keep for you."

"Ruth, please. I'm begging you here."

"Okay," I mumbled. "But you will come home, right? You will tell them?"

"I will. I swear."

"Okay."

"Ruth?"

"Yeah?"

"Thanks. I—I owe you."

"Yeah, I know you do." *Again.*

I hung up.

24

ooks like she's on safe and sound," said Dr. Cooper. He fidgeted with the temporary crown that was now adhered to my
throbbing gum. My entire mouth was numb, and my head
felt like a balloon. I'd had three cavities filled and a root canal
in less than two hours. I would never pass a road construction
crew again without wincing in pain.

"You okay, Ruth?"

I nodded.

"Now, you're gonna have some pain when the novocaine
wears off, no question about it. You make sure your mama has
some ibuprofen handy." *Great, no fun drugs.*

"How you gettin' home?"

"I drove," I answered. My voice bore an uncanny resemblance to Charlie Brown's teacher.

"Honey, you're not drivin' anywhere. Why don't you call
somebody to come get you?"

"But what about my car?"

"It'll be fine here till mornin', when you or your folks can
come retrieve it." He patted my hand. "You take as long as you

like arrangin' your ride home. I'll see you in a week for the rest of the work."

He left the room, and I closed my eyes in frustration. For all I knew, David was home confessing to my parents right now, and I knew M.K. and Jill were at the beach. *Shit.* I eyed my phone. Should I call Chris? I was sure I looked like a beast, which wouldn't be good for anybody involved. I hauled myself out of the chair and went to the bathroom to check out the damage. I expected to see the guy from *The Mask* staring back at me but was surprised by the reflection of the same old me. I filled a Dixie cup with water and attempted to drink it. Water spilled down my chin and neck. Sexy.

I had no choice. It was either call Chris or sit around and wait while Charlene the receptionist bored holes of hatred into my skull. I wiped my face off with a paper towel and made the call.

"To what do I owe this pleasure?"

"Hey, Chris."

"I'm sorry, what?"

"Hi," I said again, trying my best to enunciate. "I'm at the dentist."

"You're at the what?"

"*The dentist.*"

"Oh, the dentist. No wonder you sound like you're chewin' on cotton balls. You have some work done?"

"Oh yeah. Major work."

"Major Tom? What?"

"Are you busy right now?" I watched my exaggerated mouth movements in the mirror. I looked like one of those ventriloquist dummies.

"Naw, actually. I just got off work. You need me to pick you up?"

"Could you?"

"Sure, Ruth. You at Dr. Cooper's office?"

"Yeah, how'd you know?"

"Where else would you be?" Every time I forgot how small this town was, it reminded me. "No problem, I'll be there in ten."

"Thank you, Chris. I appreciate it."

"You ate what?"

"Nothing. Thanks. See you soon."

"Yep." He hung up. So this was what having a good boyfriend was like. You needed their help, and they delivered. I thought about Tony for the first time in weeks. He wouldn't even walk me home, and my dorm had been a block away.

I waited outside on the sun-drenched curb, burning the backs of my thighs in the process. I felt woozy and out of sorts, but also strangely aroused. Maybe it was because a man was on his way to rescue me. It wasn't exactly a Disney plotline, but it was enough. Chris's truck pulled into the parking lot, and he honked hello. I stood up and waved.

"Hey there," he said. He reached over to unlock my door. "Hop on in."

"Hi!"

"You okay?" He gave me a concerned look. "Is your mouth all jacked up?"

"Yeah, I got a bunch of stuff done. It's a mess."

"It doesn't look like a mess to me." He grinned and began to drive.

"How was your day?" I asked.

"Oh, it was fine. I was workin' a construction job, so I apologize for the smell." He sniffed his armpit. "I'm pretty rank."

"You smell like roses."

"Yeah, roses dipped in shit." I stole a glance at myself in his rearview mirror. Was I drooling on myself? I touched my chin. It was wet. I tried to wipe it away as subtly as possible. "So, where can I take you, m'lady? You want to go home and rest?"

"No, don't take me home." The novocaine was wearing off, but my mouth still sounded a bit like it was filled with marbles. "Let's go to the playground at Jacob Ray."

"The elementary school? Really?"

"It'll be fun. We can swing on the swings."

"What did they give you at that doctor's office?"

"C'mon, it'll be fun."

"You sure? Aren't you in pain?"

"It's not so bad anymore."

"All right. As you wish." He put his hand on my knee. "So, how was your Fourth?"

"I've had better ones."

"Why? Cuz you were workin'?" I wanted to tell him about David, but I had promised to keep my mouth shut.

"Yeah, I guess. And some family stuff."

"What kind of stuff? Is everyone okay?"

"Oh yeah, we're fine. It's nothing." We drove in silence for a bit.

"You know, you can tell me anything, Ruth. Whatever is bothering you, I'd like to know about it. I like you." He glanced at me with a hopeful smile.

"I like you too. It's nothing. Really. My mouth just hurts, that's all."

"You sure? Sometimes I feel like you keep everything inside of you, locked up."

"Whaddya mean? You haven't even really known me long enough to say that."

"Girl, I've known you since you were in kindergarten. C'mon now."

"Yeah, technically. But you don't really *know me*, know me yet." We turned into my neighborhood. "We haven't been doing this that long."

"What do you mean by 'this'?"

"You know, *this*. Us."

"That is true. What do you think about *this*, by the way?"

I blushed. "I like it. I mean, I'm going back to school soon, so there's that."

"Yeah, that's true. But that doesn't mean we can't make the most of right now, right?"

"Yeah. I guess I'm a little bit worried, though, to be honest." Maybe the ibuprofen doubled as a truth serum.

"Worried about what?" He pulled into the school parking lot.

"I mean, what is this leading to? We can't expect a long-distance thing. That just seems silly to me."

"Well, maybe. But who knows? I like you. You just said that you like me." He turned off the ignition, and I nodded. "We'll just see what happens." We got out of the car.

"See, that's hard for me—to just see what happens." He took my hand, and we walked toward the playground.

"I just have a hard time letting go, I guess. I like to be in control."

"Isn't that kind of boring?"

"Yeah, it is. But also comforting. I like seeing point A and B and C in my mind."

"So what happens when you're thrown off course? Life does that all the time, ya know."

"I freak out," I answered. "I obsess." It occurred to me that that must be a part of the reason why David's behavior was so upsetting. His character had already been formed and determined in my mind, and now his behavior was eradicating all that I expected him to be. I couldn't even fathom what his point C looked like right now.

"That doesn't sound like much fun," said Chris. "Sometimes the unexpected stuff is the best stuff." He laughed. "I sound like a Hallmark card."

"You don't. And you're right, anyway. I want to let go, but it's just really hard for me."

"What's the worst that could happen?" We stopped in front of my old third-grade classroom. I peered through the window to marvel at the tiny desks. When I stood up, he kissed me.

"Can you feel that?" he asked, cupping my jaw. "Or are you all numb still?"

"Not really," I answered, laughing. "Let's try it some more." As we kissed, I felt a wave of aggression wash over me. It was as though all of the nerves in the rest of my body were making up for those that were off-duty in my mouth. I wanted to jump up and wrap my legs around him like they did in the movies, but my fear of paralyzing him with my weight in the process stopped me. You never saw that onscreen.

"Let's see if one of the portables is open," I said. *Do it, Ruth. Just go with it.*

"You serious?"

"Do I look like I'm serious?"

"Okay, I'll start down at the other end, and you start here. If one is open, just shout," I strategized. I needed to act fast before I lost my nerve. Not only had Dr. Cooper fed me truth serum, he had apparently dissolved an ecstasy tab in that little blue cup of mouthwash as well.

I ran down the line of white boxes, feeling silly and exhilarated. Up the first set of stairs I went. *No dice*, I whispered, trying the lock. Onto the next. *Nothing.* Third time's the charm? *Nope.*

"Hey, Ruth, we've got a winner!" called Chris. He stood two portables away with the door open in front of him. Was I really doing this? For a moment, fright seized me. I hadn't shaved, my mouth was still sort of numb, and I was bloated. *Please, Ruth, stop overanalyzing everything. Just do this.* I willed my feet to run over. He took my hand as I bounded up the last step, and we looked at each other shyly.

"You sure you wanna do this? We don't—"

"I'm sure, Chris."

We began to kiss again, this time fiercely. I ripped off his baseball cap and threw it across the room.

"Hey, careful," he purred. He pulled my tank top over my head, and out of habit I sucked in my stomach nervously. "Relax, Ruth. You're beautiful." He unclasped my bra and stroked the sides of my torso before cupping my breasts gently.

I ripped off his T-shirt and pushed him back onto the desk before unbuttoning his jeans and pulling them off roughly. I straddled him and began grinding against him, as the pressure built inside of me. The pressure of not eating . . . the pressure of my parents . . . the pressure of David and his secrets . . . the pressure of not knowing what I would open the door to when I went home after this. A million vibrations coursed through me like fireworks as the dam burst, and I threw my head back in blissful surrender.

I collapsed against his chest. "Oh my God," I panted.

He picked me up and sat me back down on the desk, removing my underwear with focused concentration. He took his off and put the condom on before pulling me toward him. My whole body moved with him until he gasped and fell into me. I lay back on the desk, and he lay on top of me—his heart beating like a hummingbird's wings.

He moaned, rolling off of me. He sat on the desk's ledge. "Well, that was about as unexpected as it gets." He turned to smile at me. I sat up. We were both completely naked except for his shoes and socks.

"That's a good look for you."

He laughed. "Thanks. I got it off one of them fashion shows on the teevee," he replied in an exaggerated southern accent. He stood up and pulled on his underwear and shorts as I scrambled for mine.

"I don't know what got into me," I confessed, pulling my shirt on over my head.

"That was somethin'." He buttoned his shorts. "Let's sit here for a minute. Where are we rushin' to?" He took my hand, and we leaned against the desk.

"You seduced me," he whispered.

"I guess I did."

"How's your mouth? You wanna go get somethin' to eat?"

"I can't. I need to get home."

"Heartbreaker." He pulled me into a hug, and I closed my eyes against his heartbeat.

25

I opened the back door, and the tension suffocated me immediately. There they all were—Mom, Dad, and David—hunched around the kitchen table like zombies. Mom's eyes were red and swollen, and Dad frowned stoically into the gleaming surface of the wood. David's head was in his hands. On the floor beneath them, Maddie lifted her head limply.

"What's going on?" I asked meekly.

"Sit," Dad instructed. I obeyed, sliding into my usual spot with a thud.

"Did you know about this?" he asked. His eyes blazed with anger.

"Know about what?"

"Oh Jesus, Ruth, don't play dumb!" yelled Mom.

"I heard a rumor a few weeks back."

"And did you confront David then?" I looked at my brother, his head still in his hands.

"No. I waited."

"And during any of that time, did you even consider sharing this rumor with us?"

"No, I thought it was just a dumb rumor. There wasn't any reason to share it with anybody."

"What about when I told you that I was worried about David?" asked Dad. "Was that not a good enough reason to speak up?"

"I don't think I had heard the rumor at that point," I mumbled.

"But you knew that we were concerned, and still you said nothing." Mom slapped her hand on the table. "Nothing!"

"Why is this about me?" I cried. "David's the one with the problem." I stared her down.

"No, this is all of our problem," said Dad. "This is a family problem. We are a family, goddammit!"

"Listen, I don't know any more about this than you do. I heard a rumor, and then I told David what I had heard. That's it. That's all I know."

"She's telling the truth," said David, lifting up his head. "We only spoke about it yesterday, for God's sake."

"Fine." Dad sighed heavily. "Ruth, David's been sitting here telling us about the wonderful semester he had pretending to be in school. About all of the wonderful things he did, including forging his report card with his tech geek friend and intercepting letters about his rescinded scholarship. David, do tell us more. Please?" Dad was snarling. His tone reminded me of Mary's when we had met her in Tanisha's hospital room. This was what a threatened parent sounded like—a wounded bear caught in a steel trap.

"David, please, what we just don't understand is why?" asked Mom.

"I told you why. College is not for me right now."

"Oh, really?" asked Dad. "College is not for you. And I suppose a career is not for you? Or a family that you can support?

Or soccer? That's not for you either? Twenty-one years of playing and it's suddenly not for you?"

"Dad, I couldn't even get out of bed in the morning to go
to class."

"What? This is your excuse? You think I wake up every
morning dying to get to work?" He laughed maniacally. "That's
rich, David. It really is."

"Sam, please. Calm down for a minute," interjected Mom.
"David, go on. Please." She covered my dad's hand with her
own. "Explain this to us."

His eyes teared, as did my own. He continued softly.

"It started around October, I guess. I was tired all of the
time, and I couldn't understand why. I didn't care about my
friends, or going out, or anything. When the alarm went off in
the morning, I couldn't get out of bed. I wanted to, but I just
couldn't will myself to do it most of the time. And when I did,
and forced myself to go to class, I sat there completely uninter-
ested. It was like I was suspended in Jell-O or something."

"Were you still going to soccer practice?" asked Mom.

"I was, but I was terrible. I couldn't pass the ball. I couldn't
take shots on goal—nothing. Coach noticed, of course, but he
chalked it up to me just being lazy. Pretty soon I was riding the
bench every game, watching the games pass by from the side-
lines, feeling listless."

"Were you angry that the coach benched you?" I asked.

"Not really. Like I said, I was suspended in Jell-O. It was like
nothing mattered to me. I couldn't even find the energy to get mad."

"Didn't you have anybody to talk to?" asked Mom.

"I tried to talk about it, but it all seemed so pointless. And
I was scared a little, you know? I didn't recognize myself in the
mirror. Nothing was the same."

"Did you think about going to speak to someone? A psy-
chologist on campus?"

"I thought about it, sure. But I was embarrassed. People who go to shrinks are crazy." Mom's mouth opened to argue. "I know, I know, that's not true. But that's how I thought about it. I mean, can you imagine Dad going to a shrink? Or any of my friends? It just seemed like a waste of time to me."

"So what did you do?"

"Well, to be perfectly blunt, I smoked a lot of weed." My parents' eyes widened to comical proportions. *Here we go.*

"You did what?" asked Dad, removing his hand from underneath Mom's and balling it into a fist.

"Shit, I mean, do you want me to be honest here or what? You asked for the story, and I'm telling it to you. Okay?" Dad shook his head. "So that's what I did. And it made me feel better—less alone. And for the record, I have not dropped out, like you all keep saying. I've taken a leave of absence. I spoke to the dean and took care of the shit I needed to take care of."

"You did?" asked Mom.

"Yeah, I did."

"Didn't they advise you to see a counselor when you made the request? Or to tell us?"

"They did, and I did go once, but I just couldn't connect with him. I felt like he was condescending and sort of a jerk."

"So you can re-enroll at any time?" asked Dad.

"Yeah, I can."

"Did you happen to think about the fact that you'd certainly lose your scholarship, or did that not occur to you?"

"Of course I thought about it, Dad! I thought about it, and then I thought about how fucking miserable I was, and I went ahead with the leave of absence anyway. It's nice to know that money trumps my happiness from your perspective. Real nice. Thanks."

"You ungrateful little jerk!" Dad yelled. "All those years of driving you to soccer game after soccer game and why? Because you loved it. You told us you loved it. And then, when that kind of passion pays off with a free ride to a reputable college, you throw it down the drain because you're feeling a little low. Perfect."

"You're an asshole," replied David.

"Oh really, I'm the asshole! Great. You're forging report cards like Bernie Fucking Madoff and I'm the asshole."

"Sam, please! Try to calm down," said Mom. "Really, just take a deep breath, okay? Anger is not going to fix anything here." She turned back to David. "Which is not to say that I'm not angry as hell too, David. More about your lying than anything else. You still haven't told us why you went to all of this trouble to cover it up. Why not just come clean to us? Why not just call and tell us you needed help?"

"You're asking me that as Dad goes apeshit right here at this table? This is why. You both are why." Her face crumpled.

"Listen, I know I've screwed up. Obviously, I didn't handle this right. I get that. And that's part of the reason for the lies, I guess. Rather than face you, I thought it would be easier to play it off until I had a better plan. I just couldn't deal with anything. I'm still having a hard time."

"So why even come home at all this summer?" asked Mom.

"I love coaching. I really do. It was the only thing that I had looked forward to in a long time. Who knows why? At any rate, my plan was to come home and regroup and tell you as soon as I got a better handle on things." He glanced at me. "But then I saw Ruth, and how she was doing, and I put it off."

"What does that mean?" I asked.

"Ruth, you're a skeleton. Mom and Dad are crazy worried about you. I just figured my situation on top of yours was too much for them."

"Oh, so now it's my fault! Fuck you, David. Don't pin this on me."

"What? It's true."

I looked at my parents. They stared back sadly.

"What your mother and I can or can't handle is not your problem," said my dad slowly. "And by the way, we can handle a lot more than you think we can. We're our own people outside of just being your parents. Our own histories, our own screw-ups, our own reserves of strength."

"He's right," agreed Mom. "You've both underestimated us. Of course we worry, that's what parents do, but we also are fully aware that you two are very close to being adults now. Or so we thought, at least." She sighed. "It's been very hard for us to relinquish control, but we really tried this year. And look what happens—David is a college dropout, and Ruth eats lettuce for breakfast. I mean, Jesus."

"I didn't drop out!" yelled David. "There's a difference." We sat in silence as shadows darkened the room.

"I think it's really unfair that you are dragging me into this, David," I said finally.

"Ruth, I love how you seem to think that your issues are invisible. If anything, mine are the ones that are easily concealed."

"Yeah, literally," I said.

"Yours are on display for everyone to see, and still, if anyone brings it up, you act as though you're being persecuted. That's what I don't get about eating disorders. It's like, what the hell do you expect? Your appearance alone begs for help, but God forbid somebody offers it. You freak out, like anyone trying to help is the one who's nuts."

"So let me get this straight—you're gonna tell me how to deal with the world when you've been hiding in a bong chamber for months?"

"All right, let's just get it all out there," said Dad. "Ruth, do you know that you have a problem? Do you know that what you seem to see in the mirror is not what everybody else sees?" I was crying now.

"You don't understand," I sobbed.

"What? What don't we understand?" asked Mom gently.

"I don't want to live like this either, but I also don't know how to stop. I like looking like this."

David moved his chair closer to mine and put his arm around me. "I'm scared too, Ruth."

"We love you both so much." Mom was crying too. She and Dad held hands.

"Dad, how come you sleep in your office?" I asked abruptly.

"What?" he asked, confused by the change of topic.

"You sleep in your office." I wiped my cheeks. "Are you guys okay?"

"Oh, honey, of course we're okay," answered Mom. "We've been married almost thirty years is all. Sometimes you want to sleep alone. It's not a big deal."

"Marjorie, that's not true. If we expect these kids to be honest with us, we have to be honest as well," said Dad.

"What?" David and I asked together.

"Are you getting a divorce?" I warbled.

"No, no. Not a divorce. But this year has been difficult for us, with both of you out of the house. We're working on it."

"How?" asked David.

"We just are. Don't worry yourself with how," said Dad.

"Maybe you guys should look into therapy your own selves," I offered.

"You're probably right. And we're thinking about it," said Mom. "We love each other, but we're in a rut."

"We're all our own people, but we're also a family," said Dad. "And don't forget that your mom and I have two very distinct and integral roles to play within this family: parent and spouse. You handle it a certain way for eighteen years, and then your kids leave. Suddenly the old system is obsolete. It's not easy." Mom nodded as she squeezed his hand.

"I guess I never thought about it like that," I said.

"Of course you didn't, Ruthala. You're nineteen." She gave me a small smile. "We try not to hold it against you. Honey, I feel like I've been enabling you, and I'm sorry for that. I was afraid that if I yelled at you about your eating, you would retreat completely. And then I'd feel distance from both of my kids," she explained through her tears. "And I need you. I love you both so much."

I stood up and walked around to hug her. She was so warm and compact in my arms. "I love you too, Mom."

"Sit," she said, pointing to her lap.

"I don't want to crush you." She looked at me with disbelief. I sat.

"David, do you have any sort of a plan for the future?" asked Dad.

"I'm not really sure what's next for me," said David. "I know I'm not ready to go back to school yet. I'd like to stay here for the fall, get a job, maybe take a few art classes at Tech. I'll pay for everything."

"Where do you plan on living?" asked Dad.

"Well, here—if I could. I'd pay rent and stuff."

"You don't have to pay rent, David. But you do need to start speaking to someone about your depression. Deal?"

"But I've really made some progress this summer on my own. I'm not sure I need to—"

"Is it a deal or not?" Dad interrupted.

"Only if you guys promise to go too. All of you."

"We promise," said Mom, glancing at Dad. He nodded.

"Ruth, what about you?" asked Mom.

"I dunno," I answered. "I only have like, a month and a half left here. Wouldn't it be silly to start seeing someone now?"

"No, not at all, honey. A month and a half is a month and a half. We'll make some calls this week, okay? And we'll find someone for you to talk to in Ann Arbor." I locked eyes with David, and he gave me a small smile.

"Okay," I mumbled.

Dad got up with a sigh. "I need a glass of something. Anyone want anything?" He made his way to the kitchen, walking around my now-empty chair. David looked up at him, and suddenly, he was in Dad's arms.

"Hey, hey," said Dad softly. "We're gonna be okay. We are."

There they were—the two men in my life who had always been and would always be part of it. The Tonys and even the Chrises of the world seemed very small in comparison. Mom and I stood up and entered their hug together.

26

"Coach Ruth, do you need help putting the kickboards away?" asked a sopping wet Ali. Swim practice had just ended, and I was gathering their discarded props.

"No thanks, dolly. I can handle it."

"Okay, see ya later." She ran off, and I picked up a stack of the blue foam boards. As I walked to the storage closet, I glanced at the tarp billowing around David's mural. I considered it idly. I had promised not to look—not until he was ready.

"Ruth?" I wedged the last board into the shelf and looked up to find him looming in the doorway.

"Hey, David."

"That girl is here," he whispered.

"What girl?"

"Tanisha."

"Oh good. I'm going to need the first lane. I hope that's okay." I walked by him, and he grabbed my arm.

"What are you talking about? What's she doing here?"

"I'm giving her swim lessons," I answered matter-of-factly.

"You're what? Why?"

"Because I want to. Is there a problem?"

"Does Jason know about this? Or the board?"

"Cynthia knows." I looked him in the eye.

"And you didn't ask me about it? Didn't you think I would mind?"

"Why do you mind? What's the big deal? She needs to learn how to swim, and I thought it would be nice to teach her, all things considered." I looked down at his hand, which was still grasping my forearm. "You can let go of me now."

"Ruth, I thought this was behind us."

"Yeah, it's behind us, but it's not behind her. I didn't want her to be scared of the water for the rest of her life. I don't see what the problem is."

"I just thought this whole thing was over, I guess."

"Well, it's not." I left him by the doorway and strode toward Tanisha, who was holding Mary's hand by the snack bar.

"Hi," I greeted them, as warmly as I could. "Thanks for coming." Mary's eyes darted around nervously.

"You sure this is okay?" she asked.

"Positive." I knelt down to Tanisha's eye level. Her brown eyes regarded me coolly. "If it's okay with you, that is." She looked up at Mary.

"It's okay, baby girl. Sorry, Mama's just nervous. That's a whole lot of water." She let go of her hand. "I'ma be right here watchin' you."

"And I'm going to be holding you the whole time, Tanisha. My name is Ruth."

"I know," she replied. "I remember."

"Come on, let's go swim," I said, standing up. She looked up at Mary one last time for reassurance and took my hand.

"Do you remember this place?" I asked as we walked by David's group. Derrick whispered something to Julie, and she punched him in the arm.

"Yeah," she whispered. David still lurked in the doorway to the storage room. I chose to ignore him.

"Okay, let's get in the pool together." I put my feet on the first step of the shallow end, but Tanisha's hand pulled me back. She was shivering.

"Hey, you okay?" She shook her head, and the barrettes on the ends of her braids click-clacked together. "We don't have to do this if you don't wanna. I just thought it would be fun. Here, sit with me on the edge." I took a seat, and she followed reluctantly.

"What are they doin'?" she asked. David's kids were in the water, freestyling down their lanes.

"That's the swim team. They come here every morning to practice." She watched for a minute.

"Are you on the swim team?" she asked.

"No, I used to be. Now I coach kids your age."

"You do?"

"Yep." Her brown toes flitted through the water like minnows, leaving bubbles in their wake.

"You know how to kick?" I asked.

"Yeah." She demonstrated for me, and the water splashed onto our knees.

"That's so good! I bet you'll be a great swimmer."

"I almost drownded," she said solemnly.

"I know."

"You saved me."

"Well, I got you out of the water and onto dry land," I answered, feeling slightly embarrassed for some reason. "Was—was it scary?"

"Well, at first I didn't know what was happenin'. And then, when I tried to breathe, I got scairt. Water filled up my nose."

"You know, I can teach you how to breathe in the water. It's not hard."

"You can?"

"Yes, ma'am. And how to kick and move your arms. Like them." She followed my gaze back to the swim team. "You won't have to be scared of falling in anymore."

"Okay," she said.

"You ready? I promise not to let go." I took the steps down and held my arms out for her. She looked one last time at Mary, who made a *go on!* gesture with her hand. Tanisha reached out, and I pulled her through the water to me. She weighed as much as a feather. "You've got me," I said gently. "I'm not going anywhere." She relaxed her grip. "What does the water feel like?"

"Good," she answered.

"It does, right?" She nodded. "Let's just float around for a bit together and get a feel for it. Is that okay with you?" I pulled her around the shallow end as she slowly relaxed her grip on my forearms.

"You ready to try to put your face in the water?" I asked. She shook her head fiercely.

"No, ma'am."

"Okay, maybe we can try hanging onto the wall and kicking. Does that sound good?" She nodded.

"This is fun!" she exclaimed in excitement, as we kicked with abandon.

"It is fun!" I agreed. We smiled at each other as our heads bobbed back and forth with the rhythm of our legs. "You want to try the kickboard?"

"What's that?"

"It's the same as this, except I'll hold on to one end and you'll hold the other. You'll kick your legs just like this, but instead we'll be moving down the lane."

"Together?" she asked cautiously.

"Absolutely."

"You won't let go?"

"Nope."

"Okay," she agreed. I reached for the kickboard I had left out, only to find it gone. Crap.

"Here." I looked up to find David handing me one.

"Hey, thanks. How'd you kno—"

"What, it's a small pool? I have eyes." Tanisha eyed him quizzically.

"Hello. I'm David."

"I'm Tanisha. I remember you." He cringed a little, as did I. How did she remember him? As the guy who let her drown?

"You were at the hospital," she explained.

"Yes, I was." He shuffled his feet anxiously. "Well, nice to see you again. I'm glad you're here." She giggled, and I gave him a half-smile.

When we were finished with the lesson, I walked her back to Mary, who hugged her tightly. "Did you have fun, Miss T?" she asked.

"I did! It was fun! I was kicking."

"I saw that, girl. You were kickin' like nobody's business!" Tanisha laughed.

"Miss Ruth, can we do this again?"

"What do we say, Tanisha?"

"Please?"

"Sure we can. How about tomorrow?" I looked to Mary for the verdict.

"Same place, same time?"

"Yes, ma'am."

"Sounds good. We'll see you tomorrow, Miss Ruth. Tanisha, you got somethin' else to say?"

"Thank you, Miss Ruth!" She hugged me.

"You're very welcome, Tanisha. See you tomorrow." As

they left, I heard the distinct honk of M.K.'s car. It was my day off, and we were headed to the beach. I ran out from under the snack bar area to wave to her and gathered my things.

"You look happy," said David, appearing suddenly.

"I really am. I think this was a good idea."

"Yeah, me too. Sorry I was a dick earlier. It just kind of threw me off."

"S'okay." I grabbed my bag and shoved my feet into my flip-flops. "See ya later." I ran up the hill.

"Hey, girl," greeted M.K. as I hopped in. "You ready for the beach?"

"So ready."

We backed out of the parking lot. "Oh man, it has been a helluva week," I announced.

"Really? Do tell. Everything with me is super boring. Except me and Dwight got back together." She took her hands off the wheel and did a little raise the roof dance.

"Oh man. How long before the next breakup?"

"Just till we get bored again. Prolly like two months or somethin'."

"You guys are so weird."

"'You guys,'" she mocked.

"Where's Jill?"

"We're fixin' to pick 'er up! Hold your damn horses. Tell me about your week."

"If I tell you now, I'll just have to repeat it once she's here."

"True." She offered me a cigarette as we pulled into Jill's driveway.

"Yo," greeted Jill as she flopped into the car.

"Wow, Jill, lotion much?" asked M.K.

"What? Malik loves the way I smell." She flicked M.K. on the back of her head with neon pink nails.

"You smell like one of those paper air fresheners that people hang from their rearview mirrors."

"Very funny," replied Jill. She stretched out lazily, propping her gleaming legs onto the seat beside her.

"How ya been, Jilly?" I asked.

"Same ole. Malik is leaving me next week." She made an exaggerated pout.

"Football?" asked M.K.

"Yeah. Hey, how's Chris?"

"He's really good."

"Really good, ay? Spill it."

"Spill what?"

"Wass, quit playin' coy!" yelled M.K.

"Fine." I laughed. "I like him, okay? We have fun hanging out together."

"Is he better than you thought he would be? Like, as a person?"

"I guess. I only really knew him as David's friend before."

"Yeah."

"He's smarter than I thought. And sweeter." I pressed my thighs together, remembering the last time I'd seen him.

"Well, that's good. What are y'all gonna do about school?" asked Jill.

"Oh, we don't know."

"Whaddya mean, ya don't know?" asked M.K.

"We both decided to just try to see how it all unfolds. I mean, the chances of this enduring anything long distance are pretty slim, but we like hanging out now, so—"

"Excuse me, where is Ruth Wasserman, and what have you done with my friend?" interrupted Jill. "The Ruth I know used to plan her school outfits for the week on Sunday afternoon. Suddenly you're happy with just sitting back and letting things unfold?"

"What? What's the big deal?" I asked.

"Wass, come on, you have to admit that this is unlike you," said M.K. "I mean, it's not a bad way to be at all, but it's definitely a different frame of mind for you, right?"

"Yeah, it is. You're right. I don't know if it's the fact that it's summer and I know I'm only here for a limited time or what, but it doesn't feel so strange for some reason."

"Maybe it's because he treats you well," said Jill. "You don't have to sweat it because you're both equally into it."

"That sounds about right, I guess. And it's casual, you know? You and Malik and M.K. and Dwight have these histories to deal with. We're brand-new."

"I'd like to be brand-new," said M.K. wistfully.

"Um, you can be," said Jill. "Break up with his dumb ass, for the love of God, please!" M.K. sighed beside me and turned up the radio. The smell of beach air filtered in through the open windows, and we rode on in the kind of comfortable silence that only twelve years of friendship could afford. I thought about my family, and about David's predicament. The confrontation had been exhausting, but my parents had surprised me with their eventual empathy. Couples therapy. Wow. I never would have thought they'd be open to that, and yet they were. And then of course, there was my own predicament to think about. Would therapy work for me? I thought of Khaki. I had to try.

"Oh man, this is the life," purred Jill as we lay on the beach, our towels perfectly positioned for maximum sun exposure. "Will you think about this when it's zero degrees in Michigan?"

"Definitely." I flipped onto my stomach. "It gets so cold there. You wouldn't believe it."

"How do you stand it?" asked M.K. "Do you have one of those crazy Michelin Man jackets?"

"Yeah. My mom bought it for me. It's pretty solid."

"You'd think you would have gained weight up there instead of losing so much, just to keep warm," said Jill.

"Yeah," I mumbled. "Not so much."

"How come you decided to be so skinny, anyway? I'm just curious, I swear."

"Whaddya mean? Who doesn't want to be skinny?"

"I don't so much," she answered.

"That's cuz you just are. You've never been on a diet in your life."

"Yeah, I guess so."

"I'm gonna start seeing someone," I said quietly.

"Huh?" asked M.K. She shielded her eyes with her hand and turned her head toward me.

"I said, I'm gonna start talking to someone," I repeated, this time a little louder.

"Who's someone?" asked Jill, sitting up.

"A shrink, I guess. Someone to help me with my food stuff."

"Ruth, that's the best news I've heard since—well shit, maybe ever." M.K. inched over to me and hugged me with a sweaty arm.

"It really is, Ruth," agreed Jill. She collapsed on top of M.K., and we lay there—a tangled mass of tanned legs and arms.

"Get off of me!" I yelled, laughing. "It's like nine hundred degrees down here at the bottom of this estro-well." They peeled themselves off.

"Sorry, we're just so psyched to hear this," said Jill.

"Yeah, we've been talking shit about you all summer," confessed M.K.

"Oh great, thanks a lot, guys." I sat up too.

"I mean, not talking shit. That's the wrong way to phrase it. We've just both been so worried, you know?"

"It's true, Wass," said Jill. "Beyond the skinny stuff, you're just kind of like a different person."

"But I'm not! I'm the same Wass. Why would you think that?"

"You are, but you're not, you know?" said M.K. "You're still funny and a smart-ass and stuff, but you're also a lot quieter than you used to be. You never call us. We always have to track you down."

"I have a job! Four of them, actually. And a lot of stuff has gone down this summer."

"Four?" asked Jill.

"Yeah, besides lifeguarding and swim team, I work out with this sweet chubby girl from the neighborhood, and I started giving swim lessons to Tanisha."

"The little black girl you saved?" asked M.K.

"Yeah."

"Wow, that's a lot."

"Yeah, I know."

"Okay, we're getting a little off track here," interrupted Jill. "M.K., please? Let's focus." M.K. nodded. "Anyway, Ruth, we don't know what it is—if it's your eating thing or the fact that you go to school so far away, or what, but we both feel like you're private now to the point of being absent."

"Really?" I watched the water, thinking about all of the things I hadn't shared with them since I'd been home. There were too many to count. They were right.

"What are you thinkin' about?" asked Jill.

"Yeah, see this is exactly what you do. You retreat to some other planet all the time now. It's sort of eerie," said M.K. "Where are you?"

"I'm right here," I answered. "I guess I didn't realize that

I was pushin' y'all away. I'm really sorry." I reached over and grabbed their hands. "I mean, to be honest, I have changed. I go to school a million miles away from here. The South is its own microcosm, you know?"

"So how come you can't tell us about how Michigan is different?" asked Jill.

"I guess because I didn't think you'd care. You'd think I was being pretentious or something."

"Wass, if we thought you were being pretentious, we'd tell you," said M.K.

"And we didn't even know that you were Richard Simmonsing some chubby kid. Or about Tanisha. What's going on with that, anyway?" asked Jill.

"And the David rumor, what's happening with that?" asked M.K.

"What David rumor?" asked Jill.

I took a deep breath. There was so much to cover. "All right, you asked for it. But all talking from here on out must be done from a reclining position," I announced. "We're gonna be here a while."

27

grimaced as I poked my red chest with my finger, leaving a blinding white dot in its wake.

"Sunscreen much?" asked David, appearing in the bathroom mirror behind me.

"I'm officially an asshole," I replied. "I thought I didn't need any at the beach since I'm in the sun every day."

"Think again."

"You need to get in here?" I asked.

"No, just seein' what you were up to."

"I was at the beach with the girls all day. You worked tonight?"

"Yeah, got off a little while ago. You were with M.K. and Jill?"

"Yeah." I walked to my bedroom, and he followed. I flopped on the bed. "Ow, that hurt."

"How are they doing?"

"The same as always, I guess."

"M.K. still going out with that meathead?"

"Yeah."

He sat down on the bed, and I scooted back against the wall, diagonal from him. "Listen," he said, "I wanted to say I was sorry about how I reacted to the Tanisha thing this morning. That was pretty stupid of me."

"Why did you react that way?"

"I guess seeing her reminded me of what happened, you know? And I've been trying to forget it. Move on from it."

"Yeah, I guess I can understand that." I flexed my fingers. I could either push for his confession yet again and ruin this moment or let the conversation unfold organically. I decided to shoot for the latter.

"I think about it all the time." He bit his lip. "I really fucked up." I stayed as still as possible, as though the slightest movement would throw our whole conversation off course.

"I want to tell you something."

"Okay," I answered.

"I was high. You were right." I sat perfectly still. "I wasn't, like, out of my mind or anything, but I definitely wasn't 100 percent up there." I nodded. "But she was in my blind spot," he added. "She really was."

"I know. I'm glad you told me." I sighed deeply. "What made you want to come clean?"

"Wow, 'come clean,' Ruth? Really? We're on *Law and Order* now?"

"Sorry! How else would you say it?"

"No, I guess that's not such a bad way to phrase it, considering I had been lying about it. Our conversation the other day, around the table?"

"You're really asking me if I remember it? How could I forget?"

"Right. Well, that conversation just sort of cracked me open. You admit to one lie, and suddenly all of them fall."

"Like dominoes. One lie leads to another lie, leads to another lie, leads to—"

"Yeah, exactly like that. I really was watching the pool that day, I swear, but there was a small part of my brain that was sort of numb. And maybe that numbness affected my reflex time."

"David, it was your blind spot. That part isn't a lie. You being sober wouldn't have changed that."

"No, I know. But maybe I would have seen her wander toward the deep end or something if I'd been all there." He sighed. "I mean, who knows. If it hadn't rained, if I hadn't smoked, if the Kiddy Kare hadn't come that day. All these ifs."

"Right." I nodded. "I'm not sure I think the situation would have unfolded any differently if you were sober. For me, the issue was more about the fact that you were lying. I just found it so out of character for you. Of course, now, knowing what I know about school and all of that, it makes sense. You'd become so used to lying that it must have been second nature, right?"

"Yeah."

"Well, I'm not exactly innocent either."

"How so? You were shooting heroin in the snack bar?"

"Very funny. All of this has been pretty complicated for me."

"With your eating stuff?"

"No, not at all. More with us as brother and sister stuff. There was definitely part of me that was relishing my new role."

"What do you mean?"

"Well, you know, you've always been the golden child. I haven't. And rescuing Tanisha kind of catapulted me into a position that I wasn't even sure was available to be filled, ya know? Something was off with you, but I wasn't sure what. And instead of pressing you to come clean—sorry, I said it again—I was more than happy to push the throne out from under you."

"Yeah, but you can't really blame yourself for that, Ruth. You did an amazing thing, saving Tanisha. If that's not throne-worthy, I don't know what is. And shit, I don't want that throne anymore. I really don't." He lay back on the bed. "That's part of the reason for my depression, I think. This pressure to be some sort of king. It's like you can't change if you're already locked into people's perception of you. Good grades, check. Soccer star, check. Finance major, check."

"But what if all you care about is people's perception of you?" I asked. "That's what my weight is about, really. Being obsessed with how other people see me."

"I guess we lock ourselves in without really knowing it. I mean, we could easily blame Mom and Dad for these detours, right? Oh, Dad pissed all over my art dreams, so it's his fault. Or Mom told you not to have that second piece of pizza when you were eleven, so this is all her fault. I don't want to do that, though. It seems so lazy to me."

"Yeah, these are our decisions to own, I guess. I'm sure they probably blame themselves enough as it is, anyway."

"Can you believe that they're looking into couples therapy?" he asked. "That's pretty crazy, right?"

"It is. I'm proud of them, though. It can't be easy."

"No, I'm sure it's not. Hey," he added, "I'm sorry I've been giving you such a hard time about Chris."

"It's okay. I can understand why it's weird for you. It's certainly weird for me. He misses you, you know."

"I'm gonna give him a call soon." He rubbed his eyes.

"David, can I ask you something?"

"Sure."

"Did you really mean what you said that time about Jews having it as hard as blacks here?"

"Nah. Once it was out of my mouth, I realized I was out of line. On the other hand, it's not like our situation is so different in terms of the ignorance of other people."

"Yeah, but we can hide. The color of our skin doesn't dictate how we're treated. If we move into a neighborhood, all of the Christians don't want to move out immediately."

"How do you know?" He sat up. "You don't. That's all I'm

saying, really." He yawned. "Has Kevin said anything stupid lately?"

"No, he gave me a half-ass apology."

"Shouldn't be you he's apologizing to, huh?"

I shrugged my shoulders, yawning now too.

"Hey, you wanna go see something?" he whispered.

My eyes widened. "Is it a body?"

"No, it's the mural."

"It's done? This early?"

"Not done, but close. You wanna see?"

"Yeah, definitely."

"Okay, I'll drive. Let's go." He jumped off the bed excitedly. "You gotta get rid of these closet doors, man," he said, glancing at his reflection. "No one needs to see this many angles of themselves." He stopped to flex. "On second thought—"

"Get out of here!" I yelled, laughing. I stood up and slipped my feet into my flops. He waited for me in the doorway like an anxious puppy. "Geez, you're, like, out the door already."

"C'mon!" He led the way down the hall and through the family room—past Mom and Dad on the couch.

"Where are you two going?" asked Dad, muting the television.

"Just to the pool. David wants to show me something real quick." Dad raised his eyebrows. Mom lay propped up on the other end of the couch, her feet in his lap. "All right, be careful."

We continued out the door and climbed into his car in a heated rush of anticipation. "It's almost like you've never seen it either!" I said. "You're acting more excited than I am."

He smiled. "Painting is really the first thing that's felt good to me in a long time. Well, that's not entirely true. Coaching feels good too."

"Yeah, I'm gonna miss it." I stuck my hand out the window

as we descended the hill to the pool. "I think this is probably my last summer here."

"Really?"

"Mm hmm." It felt so final, but I knew that it was true. I couldn't imagine summer anywhere else, but that seemed to be the point.

"I don't want to think that far ahead," said David.

"We don't have to." We crunched through the gravel and came to a stop. The pool sat below us, still and serene. "It's so quiet," I whispered.

"I know. It's soothing to be up here when no one else is around." We got out, and David opened the locked gate. "You ever been here alone at night?"

"No." We ran down the hill, giddy. "So how do you paint here? The light is so bad."

"Jason has a floodlight he's letting me borrow."

"Who has a floodlight just lying around?"

"Jason."

I laughed. "Right. Of course."

He positioned the light in front of the wall and stood up, exhaling sharply. "I'm sort of nervous," he confessed.

"Don't be. You're really talented."

"How do you know? You haven't seen my stuff in years."

"Well, that is true. But still, I have faith."

"Now, it's not done or anything, you know. I'm definitely still thinking stuff through—"

"David, shhhhh. Just show me." I was nervous too now. What if it was terrible? This was my brother. He would know if I was faking.

"All right, here we go." He switched on the floodlight, turning night into day. Corner by corner, he untaped the tarp. I stepped closer to get a better look.

He had turned the wall into a hybrid of water and sky. Blue, green, gray, and white swirled together to capture the mirror that nature created. Bubbles floated lazily around the outlines of a boy and a girl, who were reaching up to touch the surface.

"Wow, David. I thought you were just going to do some sort of cartoony mascot thing or something." I reached out to touch it, but drew my hand back, remembering that the paint could be wet.

"You really thought I would do something that lame?" He sounded hurt. I looked over at him.

"No. I don't know why I said that. I knew you'd be working on something special, but this—this is beautiful."

"It's not even halfway done. I need to fill in the bodies, obviously, and add a lot of shading to the water."

"It looks so real," I said. "I love that feeling—when you're underwater looking up, and you can't tell where it ends and the sky begins." I stepped back to take it all in. "The sense of peace you feel from that level—it's so unique."

"Yeah. Like you're safe."

"How'd you capture it on a wall? You must have been out here for hours."

"Well, I pretty much have been. I mean, think about it. Whenever I claimed to be at soccer practice, I was here. I took a lot of shots with this underwater camera I bought." He was standing right beside me. "I did a lot of floating around under-water in goggles too. That peace you were talking about—I love it too."

"Well, it's here somehow, on this wall. You've really done a great job."

"Really? You think?"

"David, of course. It's fantastic."

"Thanks, Ruth." We stood in silence for a minute. "You know the girl and boy?" he asked.

"Yeah?"

"That's us. When we were little."

"What do you mean, that's us?"

"Look!" I moved closer to the outlines. Without paint, they looked like floating ghosts. "See, there's that watch you always wore."

"Oh wow, I had forgotten about that. I got that for my ninth birthday. It was purple. I never took it off."

"Yep. And if you look at the boy, you can sort of see that his bathing suit is that striped one I used to always wear."

"Yes! I see it. You wore it every single day." I laughed, remembering. "And you refused to let Mom wash it." I moved closer to the wall. "And there's that silly friendship bracelet I used to wear around my ankle!" I looked at him. "You remember that?"

"Of course. That's all you, M.K., and Jill did—braid those things morning, noon, and night. Your room was like a Bolivian clothing factory or something."

"It was! I remember."

"I mean, they're not going to have our faces or anything." He reached out to brush a fluttering moth off of the boy's leg.

"Well, no, that would be weird."

"Can you imagine?" he laughed. "And now, I'd like to unveil my mural—"

"Of myself," I finished.

"But we'll know it's us."

"We will." I stepped back and took his hand shyly. "Thanks, David. For making me a part of this. It's a beautiful mural."

"You're welcome." He squeezed my hand. "You're always a part of this." He pointed to himself with his other hand. "Of me."

"You too," I whispered, squeezing back.

Acknowledgments

Thank you to my brother, Brenner, for his support and trust. Thank you to my parents, Ethan and Sue, for believing in me.

A big thanks to Mollie Glick—a fantastic agent as well as a quality hang. I'm so glad I found you. Thank you to my wonderful editor, Jeanette Perez, whose insight and wisdom made this a much better novel, and also to Brittany Hamblin who jumped in so graciously and offered such excellent advice.

Thanks to the Shacham family—Nurit, Ronen, Yaniv, and Karen. Moti was such a life force, and your journey since his passing inspires me every day. I am very grateful for all of you. Ronen, I couldn't ask for a better partner. Thanks for loving me, even when I am a pain in the ass.

And a final shout-out to my fellow swim clubbers circa 1984–1996. Writing this novel brought so many happy memories back—the intoxicating odor of grass clippings, chlorine, and corn dogs; the unrivaled refreshment of the Otter Pop; and the victory of finally mastering the elusive front flip, just to name a few. Thank you.

About the author

About the book

Read on

Insights,
Interviews
& More . . .

My Writing Journey

I ALWAYS KNEW that I wanted to be a writer. Or actually, I should rephrase that a bit. I always felt most comfortable when I was involved in the process of writing. I can vividly remember walking home from kindergarten, drunk with power as I imagined the stage I would set for that afternoon's Barbie drama.

Or another time in first grade, when we were supposed to be drawing and/or glittering quietly, sitting with paper and pencil next to my classmate and instead transcribing the various ways by which he should spend quality time with his girlfriend. One of these activities involved taking a bubble bath together. Not soon after declaring this a must-do, my teacher took the paper up. I don't remember what happened next, but I do remember making him and myself happy by expressing the things he could not. Or most likely, forcing him to express the things he could not for my own entertainment. I was a bossy kid.

I started keeping a journal in the third grade (a Ramona Quimby journal, to be exact) and continued through my late twenties—sometimes religiously, sometimes sporadically, but always happily. My worries were considerably less threatening on paper. Nine times out of ten, they had to do with boys. Boys, boys, boys. Reading them now, which I sometimes do when I'm procrastinating, is both remarkably hilarious and painful at the same time. *Oh, Zoe*, I whisper, shaking my head and cringing incessantly. *Oof*.

But it was these journals that always made me feel like a writer, even if I was writing nothing else. In my twenties, working in book publishing, I would marvel at the discipline required to bring books to life. These were writers who made it happen. And someday, I would too, as soon as I watched this last marathon of *Laguna Beach* or pressed snooze one last time on the alarm clock.

At a certain point, I got tired of hearing myself complain about my lack of drive. It was time for some discipline. In my mind, I had two choices—join the army, which I was pretty sure was out of the question given my advanced age, or enter the New York Marathon lottery. I went with option two, and to my great surprise and initial despair, was picked.

That summer, I became a training machine. Drinking, having sex, and smoking were out. Running was in. And when I somehow managed to cross that finish line, I was a new person. If I could drag these Jewish breasts across five boroughs without dropping dead, I could certainly commit to writing a damn novel. And eventually, I did.

With this, my second novel, I'm still a bit nervous to call myself a writer. Am I? Really? Am I that lucky? Well, yeah, ▶

Marvi Lacar

ZOE FISHMAN is the author of *Balancing Acts*. She lives in Atlanta, Georgia, with her husband. ᵔ

My Writing Journey *(continued)*

I am. I'm eternally grateful and humbled by that fact. I'm pretty sure my marathon days are behind me, but I hope that my writing ones have just begun. ∾

A Life in Books

First book you remember reading?

Best Friends for Frances by Russell
and Lillian Hoban

Favorite little known novel?

The Slaves of Solitude by Patrick
Hamilton (This may not be little known
at all as it was originally published in
1947, but I recently read it thanks to
my pal Damian, and was blown away.
So witty and sharp.)

Favorite bookshop?

Book Court in Brooklyn

Best film based on a novel?

The House of Sand and Fog by
Andre Dubus III

Best short story you've ever read?

Anything by Aimee Bender

*Any authors you'd like to have dinner
with?*

Anne Lamott, Jhumpa Lahiri, Elizabeth
Strout, Ann Patchett, David Sedaris . . .

Books on your nightstand?

Swamplandia by Karen Russell, *The
Marriage Plot* by Jeffrey Eugenides, ▶

A Life in Books *(continued)*

and *Your Pregnancy Week By Week*
by Dr. Glade B. Curtis, OB/GYN,
and Judith Schuler, M.S.

All-time favorite literary character?

Olive Kittredge from *Olive Kittredge*
by Elizabeth Strout ∾

Q&A with Zoe Fishman

Who are some of your biggest literary influences? Was there a book that changed your life or inspired you to "pick up a pen"?

I am inspired by the writing of so many authors, but if I had to pick a select few, I would say that Ann Patchett, Anne Lamott, Jhumpa Lahiri, Zadie Smith, David Sedaris, and Elizabeth Strout are at the front of the pack. I'm not quite sure I can say that a book inspired me to pick up a pen, since really it was my parents' encouragement of reading and writing from a very young age that lit the fire, but I do remember entering a short story contest in high school. My work was eventually published in the school's literary magazine and my art teacher at the time, whom I really admired, pulled me aside to tell me that my writing reminded her of Alice Hoffman's. As I had just finished *Turtle Moon* and loved it, it was the ultimate compliment. I think that was the first moment I sincerely thought about writing a novel of my own some day.

Do you have any writing rituals? Or perhaps vices that help get you through the process of writing a novel?

I write best in the early morning. It's a combination about the lack of distraction—no one else is awake to ▶

Q&A with Zoe Fishman *(continued)*

bother me and online gossip reading and/or shopping just isn't as interesting at 5:30 in the morning—and the fact that I'm not alert enough to question every sentence I write that works for me. I don't really have any vices at this point (God, how boring) but if I'm up against a wall, I have been known to treat myself to a little something from my virtual mall in order to restart my engine. Also, tweezing is good. There's something about the immediate gratification of errant hair extraction that soothes me. That said, there's a fine line between casual plucking and outright brow removal. Most of the time, shopping is safer.

In your first book, Balancing Acts, *you focused on four women in New York City. But in* Saving Ruth *you have a much different setting. What was it like to write about your hometown? Was it hard to write about a place you were so close to?*

It wasn't hard so much as tricky. Ruth is nineteen, as I was the last time I lived in my hometown for an extended period of time. That's sixteen years ago for goodness sake. As my circumstances have changed, so have my perceptions over the years. I wanted to stay true to that frame of mind however, as that's key to her story.

Race and religion come to the forefront in this story. These are two hot topics

*that many find it hard to talk about.
Was it difficult to include them in your
story? Why did you want Ruth to face
these questions of identity?*

It was difficult to include them, because
I think that whenever you do, you
run the risk of misinterpretation or
offending someone indirectly. They
came up organically as the plot took
shape, largely because, like Ruth and
David, I grew up Jewish in the south.
I think it was very important for Ruth
to face these questions of identity, since
she's so obviously at the start of her own
journey to figuring out who she really
is. She's moving outside of her self-
indulgent bubble for what's really the
first time and developing a genuine
interest in the wherefores and whys
of other people's behavior.

Saving Ruth *could be seen as a family
novel, a coming-of-age novel, or a look
into a small town. Did you set out to
write one of these? Does one of these
labels feel more correct than the
others?*

I really wanted to write about a
brother and a sister at a crossroads,
as I had yet to encounter a novel
that specifically dealt with that
unique relationship. Through that
desire came the coming-of-age, familial,
and small town themes, which really
appealed to me as both a writer and a
reader.

Q&A with Zoe Fishman *(continued)*

What advice would you give to aspiring writers?

Practice, practice, practice. Try your very best to carve out a little writing time each day. Discipline has been the key to my confidence. There's nothing like a breakthrough after several pages of blah. One of my top five feelings, for sure. ∾

The Birth of Ruth

LIKE RUTH, I WAS A SWIM COACH and lifeguard during the summers of my teens. I always wanted to write about those summers—the private jokes between the lifeguards, the quirks of the patrons, and the very specific beauty of southern twilight time. Sitting on the electric blue wooden stand, watching the pool lazily while classic rock wafted over the loudspeakers and kids splashed beneath me in that rose-tinted light— that was the perfect encapsulation of my youth.

The pool at which I worked inspired *Saving Ruth*. I changed some things of course (I never had to rescue anyone, and weed was never smoked on the job), but tried my best to stay true to its vibe. So many times while writing this novel I could feel the relentless heat radiating through the concrete deck beneath my feet or my wet hair dripping down my back; taste the sugary Skittles from the snack bar and see the way my red bathing suit contrasted against my brown thigh. All I had to do was close my eyes at my makeshift desk in Brooklyn. Time travel is easy when the memories are that close to the surface.

Some of my favorite times as a lifeguard were spent during the inevitable thunderstorms that crept up almost every afternoon. The sky would darken, the air would grow heavy, and in the distance a bolt of lightning would extend its tentacles menacingly. ▶

The Birth of Ruth *(continued)*

Immediately, I would count backward from fifteen—fifteen, fourteen, thirteen, twelve—and if thunder rumbled before I got to one, it was everybody out or else. The kids would fly out of the pool in terror, fleeing the premises entirely. Whoever I shared the shift with and I would sit inside the snack bar, feet up, wrapped in our damp towels, smoking cigarettes and sipping cans of ice cold soda until it passed over.

Although short in length, that hour or so almost always provided the perfect backdrop for a confession of some kind. I think the relief that the rain provided—from the heat and the kids—encouraged it. I knew I wanted Ruth and David to share that time together, and in writing about that I became interested in the juxtaposition of something as serious as a drowning or near drowning happening immediately after. I wanted to take their vulnerable relationship from that rare moment of good natured stillness to utter chaos.

I really enjoyed writing about Ruth and David's relationship. What brothers and sisters mean to each other changes so much as they get older, especially as they're searching for their own identity outside of the family they were both raised in. That thread of communication is so easily lost; I think more so between sisters and brothers than between sisters because of the fact that they're so incredibly unrecognizable to each other at certain points—first through puberty and later as a result of the different interests they invariably develop.

The race and religion issues came up organically as the plot took shape, largely because, like Ruth and David, I grew up Jewish in the south. To be clear, I know that racists are everywhere, and that Judaism is misunderstood all over the world. I'm just writing about what I experienced, good and bad. Racism and ignorance is not the rule in the South by any means.

Further to this, I worried as I was writing that readers would assume that the book was autobiographical. Yes, I have a wonderful brother and parents that I love very much, but they are not David, Marjorie, and Sam. Sure, there are small pieces of them here, just as there were pieces of myself and my friends in *Balancing Acts*. I think that this kind of transferrence is inevitable for a writer.

Ruth, on the other hand, is very much like the nineteen-year-old me of yesteryear. College was the first time I had ever really been away from home, and boy did it blow me wide open. I developed an eating disorder and was seduced by its power very quickly. People treated me differently when I was rail thin. Most important, boys treated me differently. Suddenly I wasn't just the funny smart ass. I was pretty and it was intoxicating. ▶

The Birth of Ruth *(continued)*

I became terrified of food and of relinquishing my newfound power. However, even as I was in the throes of my disorder, in the back of my mind I knew that I couldn't live that way forever. That internal battle between the irrational me and the sane me was something I always wanted to write about. With Ruth, I got that chance.

࿆

Balancing Acts

BALANCING ACTS: A NOVEL

With beauty, brains, and a high-paying Wall Street job, Charlie seemed to have it all—until she turned thirty and took stock of her life, or lack thereof. She left it all to pursue yoga, and now, two years later, she's looking to drum up business for her fledgling studio in Brooklyn. Attending her college's alumni night with flyers in tow, she reconnects with three former classmates whose post-graduation lives, like hers, haven't turned out like they'd hoped.

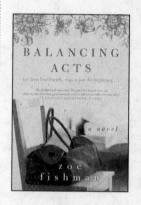

"An ebullient and wise novel. The pages flew by and I was sad when my time with these great characters ended—but not too sad to try some yoga."

—Valerie Frankel,
author of *This Is the New Happy*

Romance book editor Sabine still longs to write the novel that's bottled up inside her. Once an up-and-coming photographer and Upper East Side social darling, Naomi is now a single mom who hasn't picked up her camera in years. And Bess, who dreamed of being a serious investigative journalist a la Christiane Amanpour, is stuck in a rut, writing snarky captions for a ▶

gossip mag. But at their weekly yoga class, the four friends, reunited ten years after college, will forge new bonds and take new chances—as they start over, fall in love, and try to change their lives. ∾